Giles Ashby Needs A Nanny

K. Sterling

Copyright © 2023 by K. Sterling

Illustrations by Jayla, Sabastian Broome, and @epsilynn

All rights reserved.

No part of this book may be reproduced in any form or by any electronic or mechanical means, including information storage and retrieval systems, without written permission from the author, except for the use of brief quotations in a book review.

A Note About Anxiety Disorders & Giles Ashby

Like most authors, I can't help but leave little bits of me in every character I write, but Giles Ashby is different. His anxiety and panic disorder are *my* anxiety and panic disorder. Much of his treatment and routines are based on my own experiences with mental illness, therapy, and drugs.

Anxiety disorders such as panic disorders, phobias, or post-traumatic stress disorder (PTSD) are considered disabilities by the Social Security Administration (SSA). An anxiety disorder is a condition characterized by persistent feelings of apprehension, tension, or uneasiness. For those who are truly disabled on the basis of such a disorder, these feelings are not simply nerves or nervousness, but rather are overwhelming feelings of alarm and even terror that can be provoked by ordinary events or situations occurring in everyday life.

According to the American Psychiatric Association (APA), anxiety disorders are the most common of mental disorders and affect nearly 30% of adults at some point in their lives. There are several types of anxiety disorders, including generalized anxiety disorder, panic disorder, specific phobias, agoraphobia, social anxiety disorder, and separation anxiety disorder.

The core symptom of panic disorder is recurrent panic attacks, an overwhelming combination of physical and psychological distress. Because the symptoms are so severe, many people who experience a panic attack may believe they are having a heart attack or other life-threatening illness. The mean age for onset of panic disorder is 20-24. Panic attacks may occur with other mental disorders such as depression or PTSD.

The causes of anxiety disorders are currently unknown but likely involve a combination of factors including genetic, environmental, psychological and developmental. Anxiety disorders can run in families, suggesting that a combination of genes and environmental stresses can produce the disorders.

This is ultimately a work of fiction and should be taken as such. If you'd like to learn more about anxiety disorders and disabilities you can find more information by visiting the APA at www.psychiatry.org.

Content Warnings

Please be mindful that in addition to anxiety and mental illness, other sensitive topics are mentioned. There is on-page marijuana use and homophobia is discussed in relation to past events. Abortion is mentioned and respected as a choice.

Giles Ashby Needs a *Nanny*

by K. STERLING

Cover Illustration by Jayla

Interior and back cover illustrations by
Sebastian Broome and @epsilynn

Giles Ashby Needs a Nanny Playlist

Trick Of The Moon	Eloise
The Most Beautiful Thing	Bruno Major
No Surprises	Radiohead
1234	Feist
My Stupid Mouth	John Mayer
Everybody's Changing	Keane
Cherry Wine	grentperez
Take On Me- 2017 Acoustic	a-ha
Hysteric	Yeah Yeah Yeahs
Fake Plastic Trees	Radiohead
Sweet Disposition	The Temper Trap
Magic	Coldplay
Such Great Heights	The Postal Service
Oh, What A World	Kacey Musgraves

*This one is for the beta heroes and heroines.
It takes a lot of strength to be gentle in a hard world.*

To Roshni and Melissa for their amazing friendship and support.

And for Reese Ryan. She's been a source of inspiration and my loudest cheerleader and I couldn't have done this without her.

Finally, I am deeply grateful and it has been an honor to work with the brilliant and incredibly patient Charles Griemsman. He's everything I've ever dreamed of in an editor.

Chapter One

All it took was a glance at the bar and Riley Fitzgerald knew he was about to get dumped. *Again.* For the thirty-fourth time. That's why it was only a matter of seconds before Riley sized up the situation and concluded that Taylor was preparing to make a quick getaway. He waited at the bar texting feverishly, then guiltily jammed his phone into his pocket when he spotted Riley. Taylor's cheeks and nose were still pink because he'd just ducked in, but he hadn't taken off his coat, scarf, or gloves because he wasn't planning on staying.

Riley sighed, looking down at the freshly ironed shirt under his tweed coat. He'd even shaved *everything* and was wearing his best boxers. They were pink silk and had little peaches on them. He'd planned to do his "shakin' my peach" dance for Taylor and Riley was going to make him French toast with spiced peaches for breakfast. It was his perfect morning after fantasy and Riley really thought he had a chance this time, but it looked like the curse was about to strike again.

Riley was too optimistic to accept defeat, though, and told

himself to give Taylor the benefit of the doubt. Maybe he wasn't planning on staying because they were going straight to Riley's. It was a long shot, but Riley smiled bravely and waved as he weaved through the bodies and tables on his way to the bar.

"Missed you!" Riley said, stretching to give Taylor a kiss when he reached him.

"Thanks." It was a mumble as Taylor offered his cheek and waved at the bartender. "Today's been nonstop, you know?" He held up two fingers, then nodded at the bartender before flashing Riley a wide, too-bright smile. Riley's lips pulled tight and he braced himself as Taylor pushed out something that was half grunt and half groan. "Please don't hate me. I wasn't sure if it was worth coming all the way out here, but I didn't want to do this in a text."

"Text. It's so much more humane and less humiliating," Riley said brightly, but he couldn't help that his eyes watered and his nose was starting to tingle and run. Damn it all, he *really* liked Taylor, and thought he'd get a second sleepover and his morning after this time. They'd had sex a little over a week ago after their third date, but Riley couldn't stay the night. He'd had to take two trains and a bus home at 2:00 A.M. on a Friday morning because he had to be at work at seven. It was a hair-raising trip but Riley hadn't minded. He was still basking in the post-coital glow and looking forward to sharing every magical moment in detail later.

"Listen, Riley..."

"But you said that I was perfect and that you could have spent the whole night worshiping my lips," Riley said, earning a pained look from Taylor.

"You are! And I meant it. *Then,*" he added apologetically. "But with my schedule... I get that you work a lot, but so do I and my work is a little more...important. And it kind of sucks when I get a day off and you're not free because you've got kids to take to the park."

"More important?" Riley couldn't think of anything more important than being trusted with someone's *children* and keeping them safe and happy.

"Don't get me wrong! You were *amazing,* but half the fun of a new relationship is all the sex and that's not really happening for us, is it?" Taylor asked, his tone rising patronizingly as his head tilted.

"I invited you to my place."

"In Brooklyn?" Taylor laughed and thanked the bartender when two neat bourbons were placed in front of them. "I'm a surgeon, Riley. I'm not going to waste the few precious free hours I get slogging back and forth to Brooklyn in the rain for a maybe who dresses like my gramps."

"A maybe? Your gramps?" Riley asked weakly, but Taylor just gave him another pitying look.

"I think it's great that you're so dedicated to your job and you care about the environment but..." His voice trailed off before he tipped back his drink, finishing half of it. Riley slid his glass next to Taylor's on the bar. Dark liquors made Riley weepy and he always threw up.

"But?"

Taylor waved it off. "There's this oncologist I've been into for a while. He just got out of this two-year thing with this guy I used to hook up with when I was a resident. I knew it wasn't going to last and decided to go for it since we're both single. Turns out we're practically neighbors. And let's be honest, Riley, I have a lot more in common with someone like him."

Ouch.

"Well." Riley offered Taylor his sunniest smile. "Thanks for..." His bravery almost buckled when Taylor glanced at the clock over the bar, radiating impatience. "The drink," Riley finished. "Take care of yourself," he said, quickly backing away.

"Riley..."

"No! It's cool! I need to get going." Riley wished he hadn't said it was cool because it wasn't. But he didn't want Taylor to know that he was upset. Or that Riley was probably going to cry as soon as he was sure Taylor couldn't see him.

"I'm sorry," Taylor called, but Riley shook his head quickly.

Then, he fled. Riley always ran when he got dumped and usually cried, but this time stung a little more. He'd believed Taylor and thought that it was *finally* happening. Riley fell for it every time because he was so optimistic and hopelessly romantic, but he'd been convinced the curse had finally been broken. They'd met at a wedding after Riley accidentally caught the bouquet. Riley was there as his lesbian cousin's plus one and had tripped, trying to catch the best man's eye.

Turns out, the best man was straight, but Taylor had asked Riley to dance. They went on three rather romantic dates despite the absurd amount of phone tag and the sex had been phenomenal. *It was mostly me if we're being honest.* Riley smiled wryly at the sidewalk, keeping his head down as he rushed to the closest station. If he hurried he could be home and drinking in his boxers in under an hour.

Riley treated every first time like a job interview, doing his best to highlight his strongest talents and his flexibility. He'd made Taylor scream and swear, and for a moment, he'd looked like he might propose. They'd kissed and whispered for hours before Riley had to leave and Taylor's messages remained upbeat and flirty until a few days ago.

"I hope you're miserable with your oncologist," Riley grumbled, knowing he didn't mean it.

He was such a sap because deep down, he hoped his loss hadn't been in vain and that Taylor lived happily ever after.

Riley told himself there *had to be* a man out there who appreciated cozy, colorful sweaters and wanted a soft guy who loved to cook and bake. He knew that men could be shallow and selfish, but there were also decent men who dated guys under six-feet and didn't care about salaries and clothing labels. *He* dated men of all types and didn't care about how tall a man was or his occupation. And Riley had several guy friends who were good, decent people.

Unfortunately, the men Riley attracted treated him like a thrift shop sweater, discarding him after a few dates or one night. But Riley refused to give up, reasoning that like his sweaters and cardigans, someone would see him for the prize that he was and take him home. He'd recently witnessed his best friend, Finley Marshall, fall in love and live happily ever after. Fin's dating history had been almost as tragic as Riley's before meeting Walker Cameron III.

Fin had been Riley's loudest cheerleader and security blanket for so long, he'd left a bit of a void when he married a billionaire widower and moved to The Killian House on Manhattan's Upper West Side. Riley wouldn't change a thing and couldn't have been happier for his best friend, but it was lonely going back to their basement apartment in Bed-Stuy knowing that Fin wouldn't be there and was never coming back.

"When's it gonna be my turn?" Riley wondered and decided he'd soothe his battered heart by getting a pizza to eat on the train.

Chapter Two

The next morning was even grimmer than Riley had expected. His emotional support pizza hadn't cheered him up as much as he'd hoped and he'd cried in the bathtub. He'd woken up feeling extra pathetic. Taylor's remarks about his job being more important and his gramps rolled around in Riley's psyche like marbles. It was his first day off in weeks and he'd planned to spend the morning having sex with his new boyfriend.

Instead, he had a mild hangover and was profoundly worried that no one was ever going to want him. Normally, he would have accepted that it wasn't meant to be with Taylor and that *next time* would be different.

He told himself not to give up hope as he poured himself a cup of coffee and stared longingly at the door to Fin's old room. They'd been inseparable since middle school, with the exception of the years Fin had spent in Europe. And even then, they hadn't gone a day without talking, and Riley had spent every spare penny he had on plane tickets so he could visit Fin whenever he had the chance.

Giles Ashby Needs A Nanny

Fin had his own family now, and for Riley, the morning after a breakup felt a little colder and crueler without his best friend to commiserate with. Apparently, he wasn't shaking this one off as easily. He made his way around the apartment, watering, plucking dead leaves, and whispering words of affirmation to his babies, but his plants failed to cheer him up.

He still had Reid and Gavin so Riley pulled on his coziest striped cardigan, corduroys, and a pair of Converse and put on a brave smile as he set out for Manhattan. It helped, knowing they were waiting to offer their unwavering support.

Despite having zero actual siblings, Riley had the best brothers in the world because he had Fin and his older brother, Reid Marshall. Through Reid, Riley had also gained Gavin and Penn. Gavin had been Reid's childhood sidekick and Penn had been Reid's roommate in college. The three of them were only older than Riley by about six years, but he looked up to them and often sought out their counsel.

He stopped into his favorite bodega on the way to Lenox Hill. When pizza, crying in the tub, and his plants failed, an everything bagel with bacon, egg, and cheese *and* a chopped cheese could usually cure whatever ailed him. Riley didn't know where he got his hollow legs or his metabolism but was grateful as he inhaled the New York delicacies, tossing the empty wrappers in the trash along the way. He ran his mitten across his face to make sure it was clean when the elegant facade of 42 Briarwood Terrace came into view.

The stately mansion had been built during the height of the Gilded Age but had later been converted into six luxury units. Reid and Gavin occupied the larger downstairs unit and Riley considered it his home away from home. It was closer than his parents' place in Park Slope, who were rarely home during the day due to their busy schedules anyway.

He rang the buzzer and heard a clarinet playing when the intercom came on.

"Riley?" Reid asked.

"It's me."

"How was last night?" Reid's voice rose hopefully through the speaker.

The bagel and the chopped cheese hadn't worked their magic and Riley was still feeling pretty low, but he didn't want to bring everyone else down. "The curse has struck again but I'm fine."

A heavy sigh came from the intercom. "You're not cursed and I was really hoping you'd be in a good mood this morning. Get in here."

There was a click from the lock, but Riley's nose wrinkled as he considered the knob. He was still smarting over Taylor, and Reid sounded worried. But there was no way Riley would ever let Reid down so he steeled himself as he pushed open the door.

Despite his bruised feelings, Riley trusted Reid implicitly. And the steady income had been nice since Reid started his new nanny agency. All of Riley's jobs had been temporary until after the holidays and Reid could find the right long-term position. But Riley was having fun, filling in for nannies while they were on much-needed vacations or taking care of families on vacation. He'd spent several weeks caring for a lovely family while Penn was taking care of his ailing dad. And Riley got to meet some interesting celebrities while they were visiting the city with their families.

"Hey, Norman!" Riley waved at the elderly doorman nodding off on his stool in the corner of the elegant lobby. As always, Riley admired the massive antique chandelier as he headed past the stairs and took a left to the old, converted conservatory. Reid was waiting, wincing as he hugged his chest and leaned against the doorjamb.

"I guess Taylor's on my shit list," Reid said, making Riley smile as he pulled him into a warm embrace and patted him on the back. It didn't matter who the guy was or if it was his fault or not, anyone who broke Riley's heart went on Reid's list.

It might take years, but Reid would find a way to deliver that man a well-deserved comeuppance, be it at a party, on a train, or in a bookstore. Once, Reid ran into one of Riley's exes in a restaurant bathroom and "accidentally" bumped into him at the sink, causing said ex to return to a business lunch with the front of his trousers soaked and sudsy.

"Did you at least tell him he's an idiot and blew the best thing that's ever happened to him?"

"No. I ran away before he could see me cry. What do you think I am, an adult?" Riley made a dismissive *pffft!* sound.

"You're an adult, Riley."

Reid mussed his hair affectionately, making Riley feel like he was thirteen. He was almost twenty-eight, but people often laughed when Riley told them he was old enough to buy alcohol. He'd tried growing a mustache once and the heckling on the train had been brutal and unrelenting. A woman had offered Riley a napkin to wipe the chocolate milk off his top lip and a gang of high schoolers jumped in to correct her. They all had scruffy faces and a few even had respectable beards, but they all hooted and jeered when it was discovered that Riley was closer to thirty than eighteen.

"Just give me the bad news. I can tell you're worried," Riley said, disengaging so he could prepare himself another cup of coffee. The first cup at home was enough to get Riley to Briarwood Terrace, but Reid's coffee was so much better and the French press was gloriously full and still steaming. "I can handle whatever it is as long as I've got this," he said as he filled a mug. Riley saw Reid grimace and whisper a prayer. "You run a nanny agency, not the National Guard. How bad can it be?" Riley wondered out loud as he added raw sugar and stirred. He took a sip and hummed contentedly at the chocolaty richness.

"Giles Ashby needs a nanny," Reid announced.

"Ack!" Riley coughed into his cup and there was a bitter taste in his mouth as he set it down. "God, why? And why me?" He asked warily. "You know he's been my nemesis since..." Riley squinted at the murky leaded windows and thought back, but couldn't remember a time in his life when he didn't detest Giles Ashby. "Since the planetarium, at least. Possibly since the beginning of time. I bet he was someone really miserable in a past life and I bet we were neighbors or rival shop owners and I hated him then, too," he mused.

"I see he's taking the news well," Gavin murmured as he strolled into the kitchen with his paper under his arm.

"He is not," Reid said, waving at Riley on the way to his seat across from Gavin's at the little round table. Reid sat with a weary groan, then slid Riley a pleading look. "You know how he can be. *He* knows how he can be. That's why he called and asked me to send my most patient nanny."

"Then send Penny or one of the new guys," Riley suggested. "Did you tell him you were sending me? Because I promise he won't be happy."

"He sounded...surprised at first. Then, he seemed relieved. I think he'd rather have someone he knows there instead of a stranger."

"Penny's really patient. She's an angel!" Riley argued, but Reid shook his head.

"She's covering that family from Norway while they're here for the holidays. Penn and his sister are both tied up and won't be free for another two weeks, but Giles needs someone *now*.

His ex-wife took a job in Japan and he says he's in over his head."

"I'd move to Japan too if I was married to Giles Ashby," Riley muttered under his breath before taking another sip of his coffee.

"*Riley.*" Reid shot him a scolding look. "This isn't middle school anymore. He's worried about his family and he's asked for help. He's thinking about what's best for his son, not your feud."

"You're right." Riley ducked his head apologetically. "How old is his son?" He asked, trying to recall the last time he'd seen the eccentric software mogul. They'd run into each other a few times after high school, despite having taken very different education and career paths. Giles's grandmother had passed away a few years ago, but she had lived a few doors down from Riley's parents. And Giles had purchased an apartment in the Olympia, across the street from Central Park and just around the corner from The Killian House. Giles was rumored to be a shut-in, but Riley recalled spotting his childhood nemesis around Manhattan with his family on a few occasions. People with kids tended to gravitate to the same parks and bookstores, especially if they had money like the Ashbys and Riley's clients.

"Milo is nine..." Reid said slowly, setting off warning bells.

"Nine? Why would a nine-year-old need a nanny? Shouldn't he be in school most of the day?"

It wasn't good, the way Reid's lips pulled tight as he scrubbed his jaw. He was about to deliver some really bad news. "I told you, *Giles Ashby* needs a nanny. He said that Milo's the greatest; it's his dad who needs supervision."

Riley's face pinched. "What are you talking about? I'm not babysitting Giles."

"He's never been on his own like this as a parent and he

sounded overwhelmed. There was an incident at school, apparently," Reid explained with a mystified shrug. "He said he can't do all the 'dad things' and needs someone Milo's teachers and peers will approve of," he added with a pointed look.

"At least he's self-aware," Riley said as he went to join them. He took his usual seat next to Reid's. "Why did he have to choose *this* agency? I didn't even know he was queer. Then again, I can't recall him dating *anyone* when we were in school," he mused.

Reid's nose wrinkled. "I wasn't going to question him or ask for his 'credentials.' It isn't any of my business as long as the client understands that my nannies *are* and will be treated with respect. But I did point out that other people might make assumptions about his sexuality because he chose our agency."

"And what did he say about that?" Riley asked suspiciously but Reid shrugged.

"He said he's more afraid of bringing a perfect stranger into his home than people finding out that he's bisexual. It's a little easier to trust us with his child because Giles remembers us from the old neighborhood," he explained.

Riley hummed thoughtfully. "Self-aware *and* rational."

"He's not that bad," Gavin replied from behind his paper, and Riley stuck his tongue out at him.

"You're only saying that because you don't know him like I do and because he has a lot of money. You're an accountant so you always think rich people are cool."

The paper flipped down. "Rich people are rarely cool. I know that as an accountant and a rich person, unfortunately," he said, then snapped out his paper and gave it a brisk refold.

Reid and Riley traded discreet smirks. Gavin came from "old money" and rarely had anything kind to say about his family. For good reason. He'd been disowned for refusing to marry the young heiress his grandfather had chosen for him.

Giles Ashby Needs A Nanny

Fortunately, Gavin had inherited Briarwood Terrace from his maternal uncle and was a well-respected accountant and financial analyst.

"Regardless," Reid said loudly. "Giles can be a little..."

"Bit of a dick?" Riley guessed, then grunted when Reid elbowed him.

"He's always been a little aloof and arrogant. But I don't think he could help it. Everyone knew he was the smartest kid in school and look at what his parents were like."

A shudder passed around the table because Giles's dad ran a hedge fund and his mother had run off with his partner. The divorce had been messy and very public with both of Giles's parents behaving poorly. Giles had moved to Park Slope with his paternal grandmother when he was eight and immediately established himself as the neighborhood grouch.

"Smartest and the richest," Riley confirmed. "Everyone went on and on about how much money Giles's dad had, and he acted like he was too cool to hang out with any of us. And he was really mean to me. I don't know why they didn't put him in boarding school."

"Maybe he didn't want to go," Reid suggested. "But that's why I'm sending you. You already know him and I think you're the best person for the job. *If* you can let go of the past and be the rockstar nanny I know you can be."

"Of course, I can," Riley said, giving them a decisive nod.

"This is an unusual situation and it might not be temporary. He's looking for a backup parent for a busy kid from the sound of things and Milo's just going to get busier." It was a gentle warning, laced with concern. Reid put a hand on Riley's shoulder and gave it a firm squeeze. "Everyone's still on vacation or booked because of the holidays. I'll have to shuffle Giles around until Penn's available if you don't want to take this. I can do it, but I'm worried about Milo."

"No, I'll do it. He needs help now," Riley agreed, his conscience getting the better of him. Reid was right. They weren't children anymore and Riley had an opportunity to show Giles just how wrong he'd been. Giles had thought he was a scrawny pest in school, but Riley was going to prove that he'd grown into a competent and capable adult. Giles would soon learn how lucky he was to have a rockstar like Riley working for him.

"It sounds like Giles has changed a lot and I've heard that Milo's a really sweet kid," Reid offered.

"That is encouraging," Riley conceded, rubbing his lips together thoughtfully. "And nine can be a really fun age."

"It can be," Reid agreed, raising his mug at Riley as he sat back.

"I'll find a way to make this work."

"I knew you would."

Chapter Three

Why did it have to be Riley Fitzgerald?

There were *many* things that could trigger a panic attack, but nothing made Giles dizzy, hot, and nauseous like the mention of Riley Fitzgerald. Not that it had happened often because they had always moved in very different circles, but Giles felt like his own secrets were being exposed whenever someone said Riley's name.

Now, Giles had to explain one of the more confusing aspects of his past during what would already be a fraught journey to the school and back. He glanced at his son nervously and Giles's hand was shaking as he reached for the button to call the elevator. "You know how we're meeting our new nanny later?" Giles asked. Milo nodded and they stepped into the elevator when the door opened.

Giles waited until the doors closed and he had Milo's attention again to give his nose a boop. Milo's giant brown eyes stared up at Giles raptly and he looked like a toddler again for a moment. He still had soft curls and the ends peeked from beneath his beanie, but Milo's cheeks had lost most of their soft, full roundness. If Giles's grandmother were still alive, she'd swear that Milo was a carbon copy of his father. The thought made Giles sad because he knew Milo would start stretching and putting on muscle in a few years and all traces of his little boy would be gone. Giles took a mental snapshot and mustered his courage. He'd need every bit of inspiration and luck this morning.

"His name is Riley and some of the kids at school and people around the building might say something because he's gay and the agency he works for supports nannies and parents that are LGBTQ+ like me. They might say some mean things about us, but I want you to let me and your teachers know and try not to engage, okay?"

Milo nodded quickly. "People can love whoever they want. You were married to Mom, but you like boys too," he summarized in his matter-of-fact way.

"That's right..." Giles agreed hesitantly. He was still uncomfortable talking about his sexuality with *anyone* other than his ex-wife, Claire, but Giles was proud of his son. His support had been instant and unwavering when Giles came out to Milo during the divorce. While Giles wasn't optimistic about his prospects as a single man, it was important that he finally came out in his own quiet way. Choosing the Marshall Agency allowed Giles to quietly signal that he might not be straight while supporting a queer-owned business. It was subtle and less likely to excite the gossips, but Giles wanted to live as "openly" and authentically as he could.

The "open" part scared the hell out of Giles in that he *never* wanted to leave 8B or the Olympia, but he no longer wanted to hide *who* he was when he did go out. He'd told Claire that he was bisexual "in theory" when they first met because he'd never been with *anyone*. But he'd had feelings—of the romantic and pants variety—for a boy first. And Giles wanted his son to understand that families came in different shapes and sizes. Their family was extremely unorthodox, after all, and Giles was grateful to have found such a supportive agency.

It had seemed like a miracle when Giles heard that Reid Marshall had started his own agency and had recruited some of the best nannies in the city. They had grown up within a few blocks of each other in Park Slope and Giles was relieved to learn that Marshall remembered him as well until...

"You're in luck, Ashby. My best nanny happens to be available," Marshall had said, but Giles sensed danger.

"What's the catch?"

"It's Riley. Riley Fitzgerald," Marshall said, sending Giles right back to the sixth grade.

Giles's left eye twitched and he felt too hot. "Ri... Ri...ley Fitzgerald?" His voice had gone unusually high and cracked.

"You remember Riley, right?"

"Riley...?" Giles stalled. He was no longer thirty or six-foot-four. He shrank until he was a gangly twelve-year-old and his tongue tied right into a knot. "Sure," he managed.

"I've kept Riley and Penny as floaters for the season because they're my angels. A lot of celebrities and dignitaries like to visit the city with their families for the holidays. They always need emergency childcare for a few days or a week and those can be pretty stressful gigs for an inexperienced nanny. But you know Riley, he's Mr. Sunshine and everybody loves him. And he's a *really* competent, caring nanny who knows this city like the back of his hand. He's been handling all those tricky temp jobs, but the season's winding down. I'd be happy to send him over if you think you can work with him."

Everybody loves him.

Everyone had always loved Riley Fitzgerald because he was a walking ray of sunshine and showered all he met with unconditional kindness. It didn't surprise Giles that Riley was Reid Marshall's best nanny. And the screaming inferno that was his brain went silent for just a moment and a calm, rational voice said that this was exactly what he and Milo needed.

"I can work with him."

Giles braced himself when the elevator doors opened. The lobby was almost clear but the doorman, Carl, hurried around his desk to greet Giles. "Morning, Ashbys! You ready to have a great day at school, young man?" He asked Milo as he walked with them.

"Yup," Milo replied and accepted a high-five from Carl. "We're getting a new nanny today."

"That's exciting!" Carl said and looked to Giles for confirmation.

"Yes. His name is Riley Fitzgerald and he should be stopping by sometime this morning."

"I'll keep an eye out and let the front know."

"Thanks," Giles murmured, ducking his head as Carl got the door for them.

Carl could be chatty if you gave him an opening, but he was a gentle breeze compared to what awaited Giles outside the Olympia. They hurried through the courtyard and passed the doormen in the building's front lobby on 72nd Street. Giles kept his head down and held on tight to Milo's hand as they headed toward the school. Both knew their way and were accustomed to the morning traffic around Central Park West, yet it was still jarring for Giles when he was bumped and jostled and surrounded by bodies rushing in different directions.

It was quieter on 70th Street and Giles was able to catch his breath. "About Riley..." He started and gave Milo's hand a reassuring squeeze. "I know that new people can be scary and it might seem strange having someone new in 8B, but I know

Riley. He's pretty cool and he's really nice. I think you'll like him."

"Is he your friend?"

"Sort of..." Giles said, stalling again. How could he explain all that Riley had meant to Giles during his most formative years? Or that Giles didn't really have any friends. "You remember my grandma Ida?"

"She played the piano and she let me have as many cookies as I wanted."

Grandma Ida had been a saint and had taken Giles after his parents' divorce. Neither of his parents wanted the responsibility and the inconvenience of raising a young child so Giles was sent to live in Park Slope. Giles's father was ashamed of his middle-class roots and liked to brag about his connection to British royalty on Grandma Ida's side of the family tree. But Nigel Ashby, Jr., was the spoiled son of a simple shopkeeper and a piano teacher.

Nigel Sr. had sold the shop and passed away before Giles was born, leaving Grandma Ida with the house and a small fortune. And plenty of time to dote on Giles, bless her soul. She had been the only person who had loved Giles as a child, and he hadn't made that easy.

"She was great," Giles said with a smile. "Riley and his friends lived on the same street as Grandma Ida and they were all really nice kids."

"They were nice kids?" Milo asked and his eyes grew wider when Giles nodded. "Nice kids" was shorthand for kids who weren't bullies and tended to look out for others. Giles wanted Milo to develop his own radar and to trust his instincts, but it was good to remind him that there were kind, caring people like Riley and the Marshalls. They had all been popular for their winning personalities *and* for being genuinely good people.

And Riley Fitzgerald was the brightest and the best of their little "gang" from Park Slope.

"They were nice and I think you're really going to like Riley," he said, then gave Milo a moment to process everything. Giles had decided it was time to call Reid Marshall for help and had explained his plan to Milo over dinner the night before. While he understood why Giles needed help, Milo didn't always handle new people and big changes to his routine well. And the last few months had seen some dramatic changes and near catastrophic failures on Giles's part.

Witnesses of Giles's most recent catastrophe were glaring at him as they crossed the street and approached the mayhem in front of Milo's school. Kids shrieked, shouted, and shoved while parents and teachers did their best to maintain order by yelling and whistling.

"Thought he would have given it at least a week before showing his face around here," someone said with a disgusted humph. There were snorts and loud hums of agreement, but Giles kept his eyes on the pavement and let Milo lead.

Milo hugged Giles around the middle when the first bell rang and it was time for them to part ways. "It's okay, Dad. You didn't mean to call Mr. Collins a washed-up clown and he started it."

"I shouldn't have engaged. He's a bully and I should have taken it up with the principal," Giles said quietly, then hugged Milo and said goodbye before retreating across the street and heading home.

The overbearing gym teacher was a washed-up clown in that he had been a tight end who lost his shot to play football in college because he'd partied too hard. He didn't seem to enjoy teaching either, based on his demeanor and the backhanded nicknames he assigned his students. Giles had simply asked that Collins not call Milo a runt or "Mild Ashby."

Giles Ashby Needs A Nanny

Collins didn't appreciate being criticized in front of all the other teachers and parents in the drop-off area. But Giles didn't think it was right, embarrassing kids for being small or quiet. Giles didn't like confrontation and he hadn't wanted to make a scene so he tried to de-escalate the situation. Collins began shouting and calling Giles an entitled brat and said that Milo was "soft" because he was spoiled.

"We should probably discuss this privately," Giles suggested.

"We're already outside, pretty boy. You wanna go?" Collins asked, then stepped up to Giles until they were practically kissing.

His breath was a hot, stale melange of cigarettes and coffee but it was his aftershave that made Giles recoil. It was cheap and loud like Collins and he had obviously doused himself in it instead of bathing because the man didn't appear to own a razor. His jaw was covered in salt-and-pepper bristles that grazed Giles's chin as the gym teacher shouted childish taunts.

"Back off," Giles had warned tightly.

"What're ya gonna do about it?" Collins asked and went to slap Giles on the side of the head or flick him.

Giles swatted his hand away. "Don't touch me."

"Or what?"

Collins laughed and tried again, but Giles ducked and swung at him.

And that's how Coach Collins ended up unconscious on the sidewalk in front of the school. Somehow, that was Giles's fault and *he* was booed and hissed at for being a jerk and overreacting. The police weren't called, but the principal made an appearance. After reviewing recordings from several different phones, it was determined that Mr. Collins had "started it." The principal apologized profusely, but suggested that it would be better if someone else accompanied Milo to school for a while.

Giles was mortified because while he couldn't take all the credit for his confrontation with Collins, a pattern was evolving. And Giles was the common denominator. That's why Giles *had to* make it work with Riley. He wasn't an "outside" person like Claire was and she'd taken all their friends and connections with her when she left for Japan. Not literally, because most of their neighbors and Milo's teachers were still in the city, but they weren't big fans of Giles.

Especially given his behavior over the holidays. Giles hadn't set out to be the building's biggest grinch or ruin the school Christmas play by nearly starting a fistfight, but the entire season had been one bungle after another.

The truth was, Giles desperately *needed* someone with more charisma and...sunshine to make up for the mess that he'd made. Milo was already too much like his father and at risk of becoming an awkward outcast as well if Giles didn't clean up his act.

Claire was the one who went to all the meetings and was good at talking to the other parents. Giles hated talking to *anyone* unless it was about software testing or writing code, but he didn't have a choice anymore. They had agreed that it was time for them to go after the lives they truly wanted.

The outside world imagined that it was a far more dramatic split and expected a big tech bust-up from two minor software moguls. In reality, their divorce was a harmonious separation.

Giles and Claire had bonded as scared freshmen at Princeton and formed what proved to be an unbreakable friendship *and* a highly-profitable partnership. They sold their first app-based game before graduating at the top of their class. Claire had been valedictorian and was the brains behind their success. Giles was just a super nerd with a father who was ready to finance anything he could put his name on.

But Giles had never really cared about the company or the money. He was in it to prove they could do it, because it was fun, and because he loved Claire. And she loved him so much, she gave Giles the only thing he'd ever wanted: a real family.

Their relationship had been more best friends-and-business-partners-with-benefits until Claire got pregnant. She had big dreams and marriage and motherhood were not part of Claire's plan so Giles left the decision to her. But secretly, he *yearned* for that little life and the family he'd build for them. Claire somehow sensed that Giles's true destiny was to be Milo's father and decided to continue the pregnancy.

And that was how it had always been with the three of them, in Giles's mind. His best friend had given birth to his other best friend. Giles defied his father's firmest wishes and married Claire without a prenup so she'd have the protection of his name for as long as she wanted it. But very little changed within their relationship. They remained best friends and business partners—with very enjoyable benefits—while co-parenting their son.

Then, as Claire turned the corner on her twenty-ninth year, she realized there were still bigger prizes for her to win. She wasn't ready to settle down or slow down and Giles wanted her to follow her passion and fulfill her potential. And Giles hoped that one day someone would figure out how to sweep his ultra-practical and hyper-organized best friend off her feet.

Once the decision had been made and everything was explained to Milo, the rest of the divorce proceeded rather simply and swiftly. The only real downside was that Claire's dreams would lead her to Japan, but Giles and Milo were still excited for her.

That did leave Giles without his buffer and the holiday season had been a rude awakening for him and the outside world. For no one realized just how much Giles had hidden behind Claire—including Giles—until she got in a car and left for her flight out of JFK. He'd been able to hide his anxiety and agoraphobic tendencies until an ill-fated choir performance at the middle school.

"For the love of God! I do not want your face this close to mine!"

Giles hadn't meant to yell, but "Kelsey's dad" kept whispering in his ear about his daughter and his idea for a dating app for conservative divorcees. No amount of throat-clearing or side-stepping had gotten the point across and Giles was recording the performance for Claire. He was envisioning cute captions and cheesy Christmas emojis in post-production, but the irritating man wouldn't shut up about an app that actually favored guys with dad bods.

But now that Riley's arrival was imminent, Giles's confidence and resolve were crumbling.

How is this going to work?

Everyone had moments from their past that haunted them when they were tossing and turning. Giles had *many* and he owed most of them to Riley Fitzgerald. Not that Riley knew or was to blame. It was always Giles who panicked and said the worst possible thing or fled before he could put his foot in his mouth.

How could Riley ever know?

Claire was the only one Giles had ever told, but the first time he felt a tingle "down there" was because of one of Riley's smiles. And it just got worse every time Riley smiled, which was *all the time*. Giles couldn't help but look and feel that tingle and he couldn't help but wish that Riley would smile at him.

Giles Ashby Needs A Nanny

Of course, Riley never did. Giles did manage to elicit several frowns and grimaces over the years. There was even a pained grunt when Giles accidentally stomped on Riley's foot in the lunch line. And then there was the time Giles tried to cut the line at the planetarium so he could sit next to Riley. Lovestruck and distracted, Giles had tripped into Riley and caused a dramatic scene.

Instead of apologizing like a gentleman, he blamed it on Riley and ran. It was a little unfair, living in such close proximity to your first crush and humiliating yourself over and over again. And it had stung, seeing Riley smile at everyone else but him.

Now, Riley would be right under Giles's roof. Damn near every day if Giles didn't scare him away. Giles knew better than to hope that he'd outgrown his crush or that Riley had outgrown his bright, magnetic charm. Manhattan was crowded, but it was small and it was easy to trip over the same people if you had children so Giles often caught sight of Riley and could tell he hadn't changed a bit.

In the end, it was that alluring warmth and radiant kindness that Giles lacked so he'd do his best to prove he'd changed. Even though he hadn't, and didn't know if he'd ever get over Riley Fitzgerald.

Chapter Four

Why did it have to be Giles Ashby?

Everyone had someone they wished they could go back in time and tell off. There was *always* that person whose memory stuck out like a sore thumb when you needed someone to be mad at. Whenever Riley thought of a good zinger he'd wish he had said *that* the day Giles Ashby called him a clumsy little jerk.

Anything would have been better than *"You're the jerk, Giles! You've always been a jerk and that's why no one likes you!*

Granted, it had been middle school and they had barely made eye contact in the years that had followed. But the die had been cast that day at the planetarium and Giles's aloof temperament only seemed to get worse in high school.

Giles generally kept to himself but they often walked the same route to school and occasionally crossed paths in the halls. They rarely acknowledged each other and Riley preferred to keep his distance from surly, but incredibly hot Giles Ashby.

But if Riley was being honest, he had resented Giles for being tall, rich, and handsome and not appreciating his

Giles Ashby Needs A Nanny

Superman good looks. Giles morphed into an Adonis right before high school, then went on to graduate early and got accepted into Princeton on some kind of rowing scholarship. He kept on glowing up and society continued to favor Giles despite his prickly demeanor. And whenever Riley felt scrawny and inadequate, he heard Giles Ashby calling him a clumsy little jerk and it rankled just a little bit more.

Few were surprised when news spread that Giles Ashby had married right after college and bought a place in the Olympia. The historic apartment building had been one of the most coveted addresses in the city since it opened in the late 1800s. Madonna and Cher had been turned down by the co-op's board, but Giles had purchased four palatial bedrooms and six bathrooms just before his son was born.

Riley felt a giddy thrill when the security guard at the porte-cochère waved him through the ornate iron gates at the 72nd Street entrance. He got chills as another guard wearing white gloves directed him to the lobby in the northeast corner of the I-shaped courtyard. The twin fountains were silent and frosted from the previous night's ice storm, but Riley was enchanted by the building's famed German Gothic and French Renaissance architecture. The elegant finials and classic gables reminded him of a fairytale castle as he hurried through the breezeway.

"Where are you headed?" A doorman asked, his eyes narrowing curiously beneath bushy silver brows.

"8B. I'm Riley, the new nanny!" Riley said, then coughed suggestively. "If all goes well," he added.

"That's right! And God bless ya. My name's Carl. Follow me," the doorman said and waved at the elevators on the other side of the elegant lobby. Riley took a moment to admire the original marble, mahogany, and cherry inlaid floors and moldings. And the tremendous Gilded Age crystal chandelier stopped Riley in his tracks. He gave his head a shake and jogged to catch up with Carl. Riley was also keen to get a little…background on his employer without being too obvious.

"Do you know the Ashbys well?" He asked, earning a snort from Carl.

"Not much to know. Most boring people in the building if you ask me. Which is a good thing in my book," he said, holding up a finger so Riley knew he was serious. "They keep to themselves and they don't cause any trouble, unlike some people," he said loudly and glared around them. Riley noticed a pair of elderly women eavesdropping from a bank of mailboxes and a middle-aged couple in matching sweaters by the bulletin board. It was tempting to ask for details because Riley couldn't imagine what kind of trouble they could cause, but he bit down on his lips and gestured for Carl to continue. "She was good people and that kid of theirs is an angel. Him?" Carl's mustache tilted into a grimace. "He might be the most miserable man in the city as far as I can tell, but she seemed to like him enough. Even after they split. Strangest divorce I've ever seen."

"Good for them, though."

"I guess. And Milo seems to be doing okay, but he's always been a sweet, easygoing kid."

"It's a shame things didn't work out," Riley said with a heavy sigh.

Carl gestured dismissively as he reached for the elevator's call button. "I get the feeling things worked out just the way they should. I heard that she's a genius. And that he was the one who wanted to sell the company and that he told her to take the job in Japan."

"Really? I guess it could have gone a lot worse," Riley said, flashing Carl a wide smile. He didn't want to say anything unprofessional or that might be considered encouraging, but Carl was a wealth of information.

"Yeah. We could have had fireworks and drama. But instead, we got a snooze fest and now we're stuck with *him*." Carl said, then laughed as he clapped Riley on the back, making him slip so his Converse squeaked on the glossy marble. "I'm kidding."

"Have you been at the Olympia for long?" Riley asked. It was always smart to be on good terms with the doorman.

"Me? Since I was a young man. So only a few years," Carl said with an exaggerated wink. Riley laughed and gave him a playful nudge.

"Just a few!"

"You're gonna take a left when you get to the eighth floor and it's on your right. Real nice place."

"Thanks!" Riley gave him a jaunty salute as he stepped inside and pressed the button for the eighth floor. He waited until the doors were closed to let out a surprised grunt. "And here I thought he'd scared her off by being cruel and unbearable."

The doors opened a few moments later, revealing a charming hallway with black and cream marble tile and another opulent chandelier. He went left and braced himself as he approached 8B.

He already knew that Giles Ashby was obscenely handsome. There was no need to drown in Giles's deep, dark eyes or feel weak at the sight of his chiseled jaw and the cleft in his chin. It was pointless to resent Giles for being so brooding and taciturn. So what if Riley had secretly cast Giles as the Mr. Darcy to his Elizabeth when he was fifteen?

None of that had any bearing whatsoever on the present, and Riley had been hired to help *a family*. That was far more important than a grudge that started at the Hayden Planetarium when they were in middle school. They were different people now. Surely.

Riley raised his fist to knock, then swore at the sight of his brightly colored, striped mitten. He quickly yanked both off and stuffed them in the pockets of his coat. His hand was sweaty and shaking as he tapped a knuckle. He stepped back and had just enough time to wipe his palms on the sides of his corduroys before the door was thrown open.

"You're here," Giles declared, then stepped aside with an impatient wave.

"Good to see you again..." Riley said as he leaned over the threshold and cautiously scanned the apartment. The grand foyer was bright and modern and the furniture and decor that he could see were cheerful and inviting. A living room with an oversized leather sectional and a stunning view of the park drew Riley's attention before he was momentarily distracted by what looked like a library/den to his left. "It's been a while," he murmured.

Whatever you do, do not stare directly into the smolder.

It figured that Giles would be even more handsome and brooding than the last time his picture had been in the paper. It was a little unsettling for Riley, being this close to Giles, though. They hadn't been within speaking range since high school and that had been a formative moment for Riley as well. Few people could hear their crush compare them to a Dickensian urchin and survive such a direct blow, but Riley carried that badge of honor with pride.

"Has it?" Giles checked his watch. "Milo won't be home for a few hours," he added abruptly.

"No..." Riley squinted as he tried to recall what time the elementary schools got out and how far the closest school was. "Does he walk home by himself?"

Giles shook his head quickly. "No. I've been walking with

him, but my sister-in-law checked him out early for a dentist appointment."

"Oh. Does she usually handle Milo's medical and dental appointments?"

"No. My wife—Claire—usually took care of those, but Julie's got a son Milo's age and she's been scheduling all their appointments together. Milo and Jack are like brothers," Giles explained, his gaze bouncing around as if he was afraid to look directly at the urchin in his foyer.

"That's cool. I was an only child, but I didn't have any cousins I could run amuck with. Thank God I had Fin and Reid," he added and caught what might have been a flinch as Giles tugged at the collar of his dark gray V-neck sweater.

"Right. The Marshalls. I heard Fin married Walker Cameron. How's that going?"

"Really good," Riley said, and Giles might have flinched again. He recalled that Giles was an only child as well and didn't have any cousins as far as Riley knew. Riley thought back and wondered whom Giles had relied upon. Who had been his Fin? Did he have a Reid to run to? Riley was drawing a blank and felt a little sorry for past Giles. "Fin lives just around the corner now," Riley added, then mentally rolled his eyes. Giles would know that Walker lived at The Killian House and that it was just a few blocks away from the Olympia.

"You've been walking Milo to school and walking him home?" Riley recapped to fill the lull, hoping to keep the conversation moving.

"Yes!" Giles gasped as if he'd been holding his breath and nodded. "I've been taking Milo since Claire left, but it's...not going well," he confided and if Riley didn't know better, he'd say Giles was squirming. And possibly blushing.

"I did hear that the...transition has been a little challenging," Riley offered.

Giles nodded again, then did something that Riley was not expecting. He cleared his throat and slid Riley the most pathetic look he'd ever witnessed. Giles's gloomy, glowering eyes turned to big brown puppy dog eyes and trembled back at Riley. "Could you do...all of that from now on? I know it makes me sound ridiculous and possibly childish, but I don't deal well with...people," Giles admitted, the slight waver and huskiness in his voice making Riley's knees wobble just a little.

"Sure. Of course," Riley replied, attempting a breezy tone. "That's what I'm here for."

"Thanks," Giles rasped. He coughed and pulled in a reinforcing breath. "I'm a mess. I've never been good with people. My therapist says I used Claire as a crutch and a shield and that it's good for me to get out. But the thing is, I wouldn't care if it weren't for Milo. I'd live back there, in my office," he said, waving at the hall off the left of the foyer. "I don't really like leaving this apartment, but I only did that for Claire and Milo. Now, I have to go out all the time and *I hate it!*"

This was stunning. In the truest sense for Riley. He'd never heard Giles say so many words all at once and he was incredibly self-aware. And he had a therapist?

"You're a mess?"

"Yeah. Always have been."

"Huh." Riley scratched his jaw, then tugged off his beanie as he considered the domestic perfection of Giles's haven. The Ashbys had purchased almost 4,000 square feet of prime Manhattan real estate, but someone had turned it into an elegant yet cozy home. "I can't really blame you for never wanting to leave. It's wild out there."

"It is. And I don't really like people, but I don't want everyone to hate Milo because I'm an asshole. It's a relief to know that you'll handle all the...peopling for us from now on. I'm so *bad* at it," Giles said, flashing what appeared to be an apologetic almost-smile. While Riley wasn't exactly shocked to learn that Giles didn't like talking to people, it was a shock to hear him admit that he needed help. Riley had been far off when he assumed Giles didn't give a damn about other people or what anyone thought about him. Giles had what appeared to be a severe anxiety disorder.

"I think I can manage most of that, but you can't cut yourself off from the world completely," Riley said, earning a glum nod from Giles.

"I know. I've tried. We're also— Can you cook?" He asked in a rush, confusing Riley and making him a touch dizzy with the sudden shift. It didn't help that Giles was slowly retreating and kept throwing longing glances over his shoulder at the shelf-lined hallway behind him.

Riley cleared his throat, causing Giles to jump. "Yes. I love to cook. And bake."

"Excellent. Doris's husband had a stroke. He's expected to make a full recovery, but she wants to spend more time with him and I haven't found anyone else yet. I will, obviously, but it was just last week and—" Giles continued rapidly but stopped when Riley held up a finger.

"And Doris is...?"

"Our cook. Doris was our cook. She was great, but she's gone now. I can pay you extra until I find someone. If it's not too much trouble." Giles bowed his head, and this time he was definitely blushing.

Oh. No wonder he kept to himself.

Riley had never seen anyone so awkward and anxious, but if he'd had any common sense and had paid closer attention, he would have seen it in high school. Because Giles had obviously masked his severe anxiety disorder by being a reclusive asshole. And this particular asshole clearly needed help.

"Don't worry about hiring a cook for now. I don't have a lot to do for Milo while he's at school and it's always a hassle figuring out where or what to eat after I get off work. We'll fend for ourselves and see if we need one after a few weeks," Riley said, but Giles's brow furrowed.

"I'm not a...kitchen person. I order food."

"Okay. We'll work on that too," Riley decided and rubbed his hands together as he looked around. "I assume you aren't a cleaning person and still have a housekeeper."

Giles gave him a flat look. "I clean up after myself and messes make Milo nervous. We have a housekeeper named Wendy. She's here from eight to two every other weekday. She's been leaving us *casseroles*," he said, his tone deepening ominously. "She is not a kitchen person either."

That made Riley laugh. "I see. Show me around and tell me more about Milo and what his day is like," he said and Giles seemed to relax.

"That, I can do. I think I could talk about Milo Ashby all day. He's my universe."

Chapter Five

Giles was not lying when he said he could talk about Milo all day. It had been a revelation watching cold, cranky Giles Ashby transform into a gushing, doting dad as he led Riley on a tour of the apartment.

The massive living area and kitchen were the heart of the home. The bright, airy dining area opened onto the terrace and was as big as Riley's whole basement apartment. So was Milo's outer space-themed suite. The bunk bed was perfect for sleepovers with Jack. But the rest of the bedroom looked more like a junior research center with a massive L-shaped desk, two rolling chairs, and whiteboard walls covered in math and space graffiti. Milo also had his own little library, a walk-in closet, a kick-ass galaxy-inspired bathroom, and a game room any teenager would kill for.

"Is Milo a big gamer?" Riley asked.

Giles shook his head. "Not really, aside from *Animal Crossing*. I still play a bit. It was my only contribution to all of this," he said, gesturing around them. "Claire and her sister did most of it. Julie's an interior designer, but they put me in charge of my office and Milo's game room."

"It seems like you and your ex-wife are on good terms," Riley observed as they made their way back to the kitchen. "No one ever wins when a divorce turns ugly. And the children suffer the most."

A thoughtful frown furrowed Giles's brow. Riley was quickly establishing a furrow scale in order to gauge Giles's mood and he was calling this one a 3. "I remember what it was like and I'd never put Milo through that. But there was no reason for it to get ugly. Our marriage was a success. We put ten years into it and created a beautiful life together. We have this home and an amazing son, but that doesn't mean we both have to stop here and want this forever. Milo's enough for me and I'm happy with my quiet inside life. That's not enough for Claire and I want more for her."

"You've come a long way, Giles Ashby," Riley admitted begrudgingly while cutting his eyes at Giles. He was teasing Giles but Riley meant it. For one, Giles was *talking*. Riley was impressed by how open and vulnerable Giles was and it was touching to learn that he pushed himself so hard in therapy for his family. Riley felt a little bad for Giles in hindsight. The poor man had clearly been hiding his severe anxiety since he was a young child. But being rude and impatient never made anything better.

"I hope so. My therapist is a pain in my backside, but I pay Dr. Vargas a fortune to fix this," Giles said, pointing at himself. He didn't seem to like his therapist all that much, but at least he was listening and trying.

The tour also included a brief glimpse of Giles's office. Much of the view and natural light were obscured by heavy white curtains. They'd been hung to cut the glare on the row of monitors on the long teak and glass desk, but the space was still cozy and inviting. Riley noted the stacks of books and the oversized sofa and armchairs in rich brown velvet. Giles was clearly a reader. And still an avid rower. A rather serious-looking rowing machine was sprawled in the corner of Giles's office and there was a case of medals and trophies in the hall.

The photos in the trophy case stopped Riley in his tracks. Literally. He did a double-take when he spotted a picture of Giles and the Princeton rowing team. He hadn't realized how fit rowers were or that they tended to have thick, strong thighs, but he would be paying more attention in the future. Giles didn't notice his slack-jawed expression—thank goodness—but Riley had a whole new appreciation for the sport.

And this man is in therapy and lives for nothing but his son.

Riley knew a trap when he saw one and this was just the sort of bait he couldn't resist.

You had better run straight to Reid and let him know that this isn't going to work.

It wasn't lost on Riley either that Giles was *still* everything he wished he could be—tall, strong, and *very* handsome. But that hadn't solved all of Giles's problems. Giles thought he was a mess and was practically begging Riley to save him. Someone was going to have to save Riley because hot + asshole + needs help = Doom. There was no way Riley wasn't going to fall in love—and Giles was going to walk all over him and break his heart.

There was a quick tap at the front door before it opened and a smiling, middle-aged woman swept into the apartment. She headed straight for Giles, reaching for him. She was petite and radiated energy. Riley adored her instantly. She was a knockout in a slouchy sweater dress and ankle boots. Her long brown hair had been twisted into a messy yet stylish bun and she was wearing giant round Iris Apfel eyeglasses.

"Can't stay. Jack's in the car with Ken and we're trying to

beat the rush out of the city," the woman said, stretching on her toes to kiss Giles's cheek.

"Thanks for taking care of the dentist and for dropping Milo off." Giles gave her a one-armed squeeze, then nodded at Riley. "Julie, this is Riley. Riley, this is Julie, Claire's sister."

"It's a pleasure to meet you. Giles has told me a lot about you and Jack," Riley said as they shook hands.

"Only believe the good things. I have to go but I already have your number and I'll be in touch," she said, then turned and kissed the tiny, cowering face hiding behind Giles before leaving them.

Riley had been in danger before, but he was sunk as Giles reached around and ruffled the little boy's dark waves. He had to have the biggest brown eyes Riley had ever seen. They glowed with intense curiosity, swallowing Riley as Milo stepped out from behind his father. But Milo's lower lip wobbled and he was shaking as he bravely offered Riley his hand. He was indeed a clone of his father, but Riley didn't remember Giles being this timid or utterly precious.

Giles Ashby Needs A Nanny

"Milo, this is Riley. Remember what I told you? He's really nice and he's here to help us."

"Hey, Milo!" Riley said, lowering to a knee so they were on the same level. "Your dad and I have been catching up and he's told me all kinds of awesome things about you. Did you know we used to go to school together and that I used to live a few houses down from your great grandma Ida?" He asked. Milo nodded and looked up at Giles when he laughed softly.

"He was two years behind me but we were in the same gym class three times," Giles said. Milo looked reassured, but Riley popped up and offered Giles a skeptical look.

"We were? I remember us having the same period twice in high school," he said, holding up two fingers.

"We were in the same class the first year I switched schools. I had a weird schedule because I had to go down the street to the high school for math."

"That's right! You weren't tall yet so we all thought you

were one of us," Riley recalled. He humphed and gave Milo a suspicious look. "Don't even think about getting tall or growing those shoulders out," he said, making Milo giggle. "I bet you like spaghetti."

"It's one of my favorites!" Milo confirmed.

Riley held out his hand so Milo could slap it. "We're gonna be best friends," he predicted. "Let's get to making the sauce and we can work on your homework while it's simmering," he suggested, then glanced at Giles. "I'll take a look in the fridge and the pantry and work on a menu. You can go and unwind for a bit in your office or you can hang out. You might pick up a few things," he said, winking playfully before he waved for Milo to follow him around the counter.

He had offered Giles an opportunity to retreat and decompress. But Riley was rather pleased when Giles shrugged and mumbled that he could stay and that it might not hurt to learn how spaghetti was made since it was one of his favorites as well.

Riley wasn't going to reflect on that too much, though. Then, he'd have to ask why he wanted to spend *more* time with Giles Ashby. He might even have to admit that he was enjoying their first afternoon together. And that would mean that Riley was in serious trouble.

Chapter Six

Turns out, the day hadn't been his worst nightmare. Giles had survived his first afternoon with Riley, and Milo now had a stellar nanny to take care of all their outside problems for them. There weren't words to convey the profound existential relief Giles felt that evening as he watched Milo and Riley exchange high fives and say goodbye.

They were making plans for the rest of the week and Giles was delighted, having found someone so much *better* to stand in for him. Claire had always made him look like a decent person and a more competent parent and deep down, *that* was the only thing about their divorce that had scared Giles.

Claire had become his crutch and his shield when they'd first met at freshman orientation and he became more and more dependent on her as the years passed. It was pathetic to admit it, but Giles realized immediately that having a girlfriend made *every* social interaction infinitely easier and had latched right onto Claire.

He could mumble "Go ahead and order for us," into a drink without a server batting an eye. And Giles just looked besotted or like the typical bored husband when he let Claire do all the talking at dinner parties and building meetings.

She had warned him when he proposed. Loving someone and being in love weren't the same thing and he wouldn't be able to hide behind her forever. But they went ahead and married quietly and Giles never took a moment of his blissfully sheltered life with Claire for granted.

It had crossed his mind that it might be better to learn how to cope with people, but in the end, Giles decided that hiring a nanny was easier and neater. He was doing his best to unlearn thirty years' worth of bad habits with his therapist, but Giles wasn't optimistic. He'd rather be alone with a piece of code, or a book, or meditating as he rowed than deal with humanity. But there was still hope for Milo.

Milo had always been the line.

All of Giles's priorities shifted after Milo's birth and nothing else mattered. His father had crossed the line when he mocked Giles for selling out to be nothing but a stay-at-home dad when Milo started to walk and was learning to talk. Nothing could have illuminated the difference between Giles and his father more or served as a better lesson. To Giles, it was the ultimate privilege to be able to witness all those magical firsts with Milo. A lot of dads didn't have the option to go on paternity leave, let alone retire in their twenties.

And thanks to his soulless dirtbag of a father, Giles could. Nigel Ashby had pushed his son to be the best in school and pushed Giles into Princeton for the clout. Then, his father had pushed Giles into starting his own software company before graduating. He had wanted all the flashy PR and it had been Nigel Ashby's influence that tipped the co-op's vote in their favor when Giles requested permission to buy 8B.

Giles was never going to win a popularity contest, but he drew the line and cut his father out of his life after selling the company. He wouldn't be pressured to move on and "do something serious" with his time and his money. Giles had no interest in Ponzi schemes and insider trading or the other white-collar crimes his father was probably involved in, so Giles stopped taking his calls.

Nothing would ever be more important than being Milo's dad.

It was also a relief to no longer pretend he enjoyed golf. He hadn't stepped foot on a green since Milo was two, but Giles was still traumatized. He couldn't see a set of clubs or look at argyle and not shudder at the hours of lectures about his swing and his lack of ambition. And all the shitty metaphors about the size of his balls and his drive being weak or not "straight enough."

In reality, it had been Nigel Ashby's pushing and bullying that drove Giles to be a better father. Giles vowed that he'd never be like Nigel or fail Milo the way his father had failed him. He'd stumbled off course a bit after Claire left for Japan, but everything was back on track now that Riley was on board.

"I'll be back in the morning to walk you to school," Riley told Milo while winding a scarf around his neck.

He grinned at Giles as he tugged on his gloves. The cheerful colors and patterns had been Riley's trademark since he was a child. He had been teased, but Giles admired Riley for having the confidence to wear what made him happy. And Giles thought it was generous of Riley, spreading smiles everywhere he went. Because how could you look at a boy with a beautiful smile and *not* smile back or feel warmer at the sight of his chunky cardigan and colorful mittens?

"I'll bring bagels if you can handle the coffee," Riley challenged Giles playfully.

Giles clutched his stomach when it flipped. "I'm not completely useless. I can make a pot of coffee." He hadn't meant to growl. Or, maybe he had meant to growl at himself because coffee was his *only* use in the kitchen. He was an early riser and his coffee ritual was a sacred act of meditation each morning. The thought of possibly impressing Riley with his unique expertise shouldn't have thrilled Giles the way it had and he shouldn't have gotten so excited at the prospect of seeing his new nanny in the morning. But there he was, saying the wrong thing and offending Riley again.

"I didn't say you were useless," Riley replied with a weary eye roll, then offered his mitten to Milo for a fist bump. "Later, my man."

"See you tomorrow, Riley!" Milo hopped and waved excitedly. The door shut behind Riley and Milo's arms shot into the air. "Isn't he the *coolest*, Dad?" He moonwalked across the marble, then spun. "Riley says he knows a shortcut to school. And Riley said we can take the long way through the park on the way home when it's nice. Did you know that Riley knows how to make every kind of friendship bracelet? We're going to make some and Riley said we can make one for you too. Riley's going to bring his album so I can see his plants. He says they're his babies. Did you know that Riley can ride a skateboard and he said..."

Giles hummed and nodded along as he herded Milo back to his suite. The two of them had hit it off even better than Giles had hoped. Not that Giles had any doubt in Riley; he was more concerned with how long it might take Milo to come out of his shell. It could take a while for Milo to warm up to new people and big changes to his routine could be stressful for him. But Milo already trusted Riley enough to try a shortcut to school.

I didn't know about the plants...

He did know about the skateboarding. Both Riley and Fin still traveled around the city with a board tucked under one arm when the weather was nicer. It pained Giles to admit it, but he got even more nervous when he found himself in an elevator with a man with a skateboard. Giles was in mortal peril if said man was wearing a tight T-shirt, a wristful of friendship bracelets, and a pair of Converse.

That would always be Giles's type, apparently. He wondered why he hadn't grown out of that particular weakness as he tidied Milo's closet and laid out pajamas and the next day's clothes. Milo continued to shout his observations from the shower and the closet, but had run out of steam by the time he climbed onto the top bunk of his bed. He was—as always—intently focused as Giles read a chapter from a tattered copy of *The Hitchhiker's Guide to the Galaxy*. They'd have to replace it soon and Giles's nerdy heart swelled with joy because it would be the third copy they had worn out together. He had purchased their first while Milo was still in the womb and read it to Claire's growing belly every night.

"I have to tell Riley so he knows what our favorite book is," Milo said and Giles hummed in agreement, tugging the duvet and quilt up to his chin. He hoped Riley could keep up. Once the seal was broken and Milo decided you were trustworthy, there was no stopping the sharing.

"That's probably a good thing to know."

Milo's hand slipped free and yanked at Giles's sleeve. "The field trip is in *a month*," he said solemnly. "You're still coming, right?" The sudden shift and change of topic were somewhat alarming.

"The planetarium?" Giles recalled, nodding slowly. "I'm sure Riley would be happy to go. You should ask him." There was no way Giles would. His soul curdled at the thought of even mentioning the planetarium in Riley's presence.

"You have to go!" Milo protested as he shoved the covers

down and sat up. "I have to go in case *he's* there, but I can't go if you don't go."

"But...you have Riley now. He probably knows exactly where everything is and he'll be way more fun."

"I can't go without you!" Milo's distress was mounting.

"Why? We go all the time. You don't want me there when you're with your class," Giles insisted, but Milo shook his head.

"I don't like going without you and you said you'd go. I told Mrs. Simpson you'd be a chaperone."

"I'm sure she'd rather have Riley."

"Dad!" Milo wailed. "I have to prepare for my presentation and be ready if *he's* there. I can't do it without you."

"Right. The presentation." Giles chuckled and rolled his eyes. "How could I forget? We've got to get ready for Pluto's big day." He kissed Milo's forehead. "We'll get everything figured out and you're going to crush the science fair." He offered his fist and they made exploding sounds as Milo's bumped Giles's.

There were *two* things Milo was passionate about:

1. Milo believed with his whole being that Pluto deserved to be reinstated as a planet and was determined to prove it. The big "presentation" was the speaking portion of Milo's science fair project and would be his first attempt to make a case in front of a panel of judges. He intended to carry his argument on behalf of Pluto all the way to the International Astronomical Union and the first step in his grand plan was to win his school's science fair. After that, he'd win the regional, state, and international science fair, and gain the attention and support of his idol, Neil deGrasse Tyson.

2. The Hayden Planetarium was Milo's very favorite place in the city. He knew *everything* about the Rose Center for Earth and Space and its famous director, the above-mentioned Neil deGrasse Tyson.

If the stars aligned, the field trip to the Hayden could be

Milo's golden ticket to meeting and impressing the planetarium's director.

"But you'll be there," Milo confirmed.

"As long as nothing big comes up," Giles said, easing Milo back so he could re-tuck the covers. "I'll make sure Riley knows just how important this is," he added before Milo could get upset again. "I love you very much and I can't wait to hug you in the morning."

That always worked like a charm. Milo's eyes grew heavy and his lips curved into a drowsy grin. "I love you too, Daddy."

Giles hummed "Beautiful Boy" as he turned off the lamp and passed Milo the little remote for the projector. The ceiling lit up with stars and distant galaxies, the faraway destinations of Milo's dreams. His little boy had fallen in love with space as a toddler and declared he wanted to be an astrophysicist when he was six. Giles suspected that Milo preferred space because it wasn't as scary as Earth and its inhabitants.

Computers, the internet, and coding held a similar allure for Giles and offered him the same shelter from humanity. A formula could be learned and applied with predictable, consistent results. Humans, on the other hand, had impossible and often illogical expectations. For example, Giles couldn't understand why people expected him to have a personality, let alone a charming one, just because he was rich and attractive.

To him, the math didn't add up because most of the wealthy people he knew were assholes. And they rarely had good taste or above-average intelligence. They paid smarter, more talented people to style their lives and solve their problems for them so they just looked like decent people.

That had always been so tiring for Giles and he didn't want to waste his time or limited bandwidth on people he'd never please. He saved his energy for Milo, Claire, and friends like Julie and Wendy. He relied on them so it behooved Giles to do his best for the small handful of amazing people he had in his life. Hiring Riley was the first serious adult decision Giles had made since Claire had left and it already felt like he'd nailed it as he locked up and headed back to his corner of the apartment.

"As long as I don't screw this up," he told himself. Which was incredibly likely because Giles always screwed up whenever Riley was involved.

Chapter Seven

An extra blustery day called for an extra special cardigan. Riley picked one with a cheerful snowman pattern and paired it with a bright magenta scarf and matching mittens. He received several compliments while he was in line for bagels, and the hot guy at the newsstand tossed Riley a bag of Takis and called him "cutie."

He was no longer feeling sorry for himself about getting dumped or being compared to Taylor's gramps. Riley had a new family to focus on and he had a free bag of Takis. He was unstoppable and he was a cutie.

There were other fish in the sea and New York was teeming with them, Riley told himself as he rode the train to Manhattan. He wasn't going to change his profession, his attitude, or his wardrobe just to attract more men. Someone was waiting for a kind, caring man just like Riley, and that man would get all the sex, love, and home cooking his heart could handle.

Riley was more old-fashioned than the rest of his friends and the other nannies. He wanted his own family like the ones he cared for and wasn't afraid of settling down and easing into middle age. Perhaps it was because he was an only child and a latchkey kid of two hardworking business owners, but Riley longed for the day that he could say he was someone's husband and boast about how proud he was of his own kids. He saw his work as a nanny as a way of utilizing his childcare talents while providing the warm nurturing home life he craved for himself.

He was always "practicing" for the real thing when he went on dates and fell in love with other people's kids. Riley reasoned that when his time finally did come, that man and their future family would be the recipients of his well-tested love and their happiness would be worth all the disappointment and frustration he'd endured.

"It's gonna happen and it's gonna be worth it," he reminded himself, whispering his mantra as he crossed 72nd Street. He checked in with the doorman as he headed into the Olympia for his second day with the Ashbys. Riley was even more determined to give them his best effort because there was no telling how many cosmic brownie points were up for grabs if he could make Giles Ashby happy.

Riley acknowledged that Giles had indeed grown up and wasn't the self-centered jerk he had always imagined. But he didn't delude himself into believing that Giles had changed enough to believe they were equals or that Riley mattered in the grand scheme of things. Riley was there to perform a very important job: he was assisting a father whose extreme anxiety amounted to a disability.

There was no questioning Giles's devotion to Milo or how seriously he took his responsibilities. Riley found that incredibly admirable and compelling. And that was why he smiled and waved at Carl, radiating positivity and optimism as the older man hurried to open the door for Riley.

"Morning, Carl! I love what you've done with your mustache this morning! It's very curly."

"I'm trying out this fancy wax the misses found," Carl said and the two chatted about which boroughs they were from as he escorted Riley to the elevator.

"My parents still live out in Park Slope. My dad's a pediatric dentist and my mom owns a used bookstore so I don't get to see them as much with our busy schedules."

Carl clicked his teeth at Riley. "You gotta make time while you still can. Both of my parents passed, but I still get out to Yonkers a few times a month to see my sisters."

"You're absolutely right and I'm going to do better," Riley vowed. The elevator doors opened and Riley gave Carl a thumbs-up before he hopped inside. "Wish me luck!" He said as he pushed the button for the 8th floor.

"You've got this!" Carl crossed his white-gloved fingers, then returned Riley's thumbs up as the doors shut.

"At least it's Friday."

Things had taken a disappointing turn on Wednesday night, and Riley was sure it would only get worse with the reintroduction of Giles Ashby into his life. But they had gotten off to a good start and the week was almost over.

The soft ding announced that he had arrived at the 8th floor and Riley was surprised at the tickle of anticipation he felt as he turned toward the Ashbys' door. He realized that this could be a dream job with a little extra patience. Giles wasn't as bad as he used to be. He'd clearly done a lot of work with his therapist and was finding better ways to cope with his anxiety. And Milo was probably the coolest little guy ever.

"Giles was almost nice," Riley said to himself, removing his mittens and raising a fist to knock. He paused and his nose scrunched. "Almost. He might not be an asshole and he might be unforgivably dreamy, but he's your boss now."

Riley nodded at the door resolutely before giving it a brisk *tap-tap-tap*. He barely got the last tap in; the door swung open and Giles offered him a gruff, "Coffee's ready."

Maybe still a little bit of an asshole.

Riley told himself to be patient and that Giles was dealing with some huge changes and navigating through some complicated emotions. That was why Riley was there, so he mentally rolled up his sleeves and dug in.

He might not be a morning person, but Giles was already dressed in another effortlessly dashing cashmere sweater, gray trousers, and black suede loafers. His shave was immaculate and his hair fell in beguiling waves as he tossed his chin toward the kitchen.

Riley refused to be intimidated by Giles's surly greeting and the unnecessary display of hotness. "Good morning!" He said as cheerfully as he could, stripping off his layers at the door and stopping Giles in his tracks.

Giles huffed out a soft swear as he hung his head. "Right. Sorry. Good morning, Riley."

"It's gonna be a cold one, though! I packed us a thermos of cocoa for the road," Riley said, bringing his backpack with him. It was his survival kit and contained half a dozen bagels from Riley's favorite shop.

Giles's eyelids flickered for a moment and there was just a moderate furrow to his brow. A 2 on the Ashby scale. "For the road?"

"There's a little park on the way and I thought we might grab a bench for a morning pep talk if we have some extra time," Riley explained and the furrow vanished.

"Ah." Giles gestured at the kitchen. "Milo's just about ready. He likes his bagels toasted but plain."

"Good to know," Riley said as he slid out of his backpack. He left it on the floor by the sectional and began hunting through the bag of bagels. "I got two everything, two cinnamon, two plain."

"I prefer plain and Milo likes the cinnamon bagels. Here."

Riley reared back as a cup and saucer were pushed at him. He raised a brow at Giles and handed over the bag so he could take the saucer. "Thank you... Sugar?"

"Raw or white?" Giles stepped aside, revealing two bowls on the otherwise immaculate counter. A French press was drying in the dish rack by the sink.

"Raw, please!" Riley said and went to add two spoons to his cup. He admired the heady aroma as he stirred, but was a little concerned with the way Giles chewed on a thumbnail and leaned in when Riley took his first sip. "Wow. That's perfect." Riley nodded appreciatively and took another drink, enjoying the rich, velvety smoothness.

A hard breath whooshed from Giles. "Good," he said, resting his hands on his hips. He looked around the kitchen as if his work was done. "There's a toaster in one of these cabinets," he stated before wandering around the counter and down his hallway. He disappeared, leaving Riley with his coffee and the bag of bagels.

Riley didn't have long to reflect on the curious encounter before Milo hustled into the kitchen with his backpack on. "Morning, Riley!"

"Morning, Champ! You look like you're ready to have a great day!"

"Today's a half day and I'm going to Jack's after school," Milo informed him.

"Is that so?" Riley was intrigued and delighted at the prospect of a little extra planning time. And possibly an early day for himself as well if Milo wasn't going to be around after school. They quickly ate their bagels and Giles reappeared to see Milo off.

"Have fun and learn something really cool, okay?" Giles said softly as he picked Milo up and gave him one last squeeze. Riley had to look away and pretended he had some dust in his eye. They really were the closest and the sweetest pair Riley had ever seen.

"I will. Will you talk to Riley about the field trip?" Milo whispered and squeezed Giles's neck.

"Why don't you give him all the details on the way to school? I'll work everything out with him when he gets back."

"Okay!" Milo kissed Giles's cheek loudly and then they were off. "I like your snowman sweater," Milo told Riley as they bundled up to head out.

Riley gave the front of his cardigan a tug as he inspected it. "You know, it was in a bin of free clothes that no one wanted at the thrift shop." He got the door and held up a hand so he could whisper behind it. "I *like* the sweaters that no one wants because I know I can make them look good and I never have to worry about someone wearing the same thing as me."

"That's cool! I have to wear a uniform to school, but I have four space sweatshirts. My favorite is black and it has Pluto on it and says 'Never Forget' and the years 1930-2006."

"That sounds epic. I want one," Riley said. "What's this about a field trip?" He asked as they got into the elevator.

"We're going to the Hayden Planetarium!" The elevator could have launched to the moon, Milo was so excited. He bounced and tugged on the straps of his backpack as he recited facts about the Rose Center for Earth and Space and the Hayden planetarium. *And* Pluto. Giles had mentioned that Milo loved space and it was obvious as soon as you stepped into his wing of the apartment, but Riley was not aware of the little guy's love for Pluto.

Milo Ashby's life goal was to get Pluto reinstated as a planet. He didn't think it was fair that Pluto had been demoted because of its size and believed that even the smallest planet mattered and deserved to be counted and studied along with its galactic brethren. Riley's scrawny nerd heart almost exploded and he immediately pledged his life in aid of Milo's cause.

Phase 1 of Milo's plan was to win his school's fourth-grade science fair. He had been preparing his "big presentation" for two years. It was a journey that had begun with a trip to the planetarium where he learned about Pluto's demotion and took up the dwarf planet's cause.

"Have you been?" Milo asked as they sat on a bench and sipped their cocoa.

"Me? Sure! Lots of times," Riley said, then winced sheepishly. "I'm more of an arts guy and theater is where my heart was at in school. But I think space is fascinating and the planetarium is super cool. A lot cooler now that I'm an adult and don't have to stay with the class and eat a sack lunch," he confided.

"I don't like field trips," Milo whispered up at Riley. "My dad usually takes me on quiet days and we get to look at whatever we want. But my whole class is going in a month and I have to ride the bus."

"No sweat," Riley promised, hopping to his feet and offering Milo a hand. They threw their paper cups away and turned toward the school. "My first field trip to the Hayden was *awful*, but I've become a field trip expert and I've chaperoned dozens of trips."

"Why was it awful?"

"Oh." Riley's cheeks puffed out. "Well... This mean boy tripped into me while I was looking up at the Sphere and caused *me* to trip into this girl who fell and broke her glasses. She cried and got mad at me and the mean kid called me a clumsy little jerk and said it was my fault."

"I'm really sorry that happened. Did she forgive you?" Milo asked.

Riley's shoulders bounced. "She probably doesn't even remember it. I'm not sure why I even remember it," he admitted. Probably because Giles had called him little and made Riley feel like a pest for getting in his way. "But I've been back plenty of times and I'll make sure nobody trips into us. Want to introduce me to your teacher and your friends?" He asked.

The sidewalk and steps in front of the school swarmed with little people in giant backpacks, buzzing with energy as harried parents and teachers ushered the hive into the building. Riley watched Milo closely to see how he managed crowds, but the little boy only seemed to become nervous when he was noticed. Like Giles, Milo was happiest when he was left alone and allowed to hurry along without interference.

"He's a pistol once you get him going!" Mrs. Simpson told Riley once Milo had introduced them. "Timid as a mouse, but one of the smartest little dudes I've ever met!"

That had tracked with Riley's experience as well. It had taken Milo a few moments to feel safe and accepted, but he was an adorable chatterbox once he knew he could trust Riley. "I've only known him for about twenty-four hours and I can already tell that we're going to be best friends for life," Riley predicted.

He peeked through the little window in the door and observed Milo in class for about half an hour, then headed back to the Olympia to get a better handle on his duties. Milo didn't need as much support in his day-to-day routine as far as Riley could tell. It was Giles who needed backup and to learn some skills to make socializing as a parent less stressful.

From what Riley could tell, Giles was able to manage his anxiety and juggle his business and parenting responsibilities until his wife moved to Japan. But he'd lost his emotional support person in Claire and had hired Riley to replace her. Which was not something Riley would have *ever* predicted. Or believed he'd ever want to do. But after meeting Milo and seeing how badly Giles needed a buffer, Riley was determined to help them.

How, though?

One of Giles's neighbors provided Riley with one of his first tasks: social rehabilitation.

"You're the Ashbys' new nanny?" A woman asked as they shared the elevator. She was tall and slender and reminded Riley of an ostrich with her long neck, upturned nose, and spiky brown hair. She tugged her billowy black fur coat tighter against the chill and eyed him with uncertainty, making her look even more ostrich-esque.

"Yup! I'm Riley."

"Joan Cadbury-Baines," she informed Riley haughtily. He assumed that meant she was related to someone impressive and widened his eyes appreciatively.

"I'm just a common Fitzgerald, but I have a cousin who holds the record for eating the most carrot cake."

"Really?" She asked and he nodded proudly.

"I helped her train. She ate ten pounds of cake in eight minutes. Which was two-and-a-half cakes, if you were wondering."

"I was," Joan said, looking sufficiently impressed as well. "Don't let that awful Ashby scare you off." She gave his arm an affectionate pat.

"Who? Giles?" Riley asked and snorted. "We go way back, actually, and he's not nearly as bad as he seems. All bark and no bite, that guy."

"Could have fooled me. He barked at me once for standing too close to him."

"That's not cool and I'll tell him to mind his manners. He's got serious anxiety issues. The barking is just a defense mechanism."

"I have a nephew like that." She nodded and hummed sympathetically. "But he doesn't leave his apartment. *Ever.* Makes a good living doing still life photography, though."

"Good for him!"

"This is me," she announced when the elevator stopped and the doors opened. "I'll see you around, Riley. Say hello to the Ashbys for me."

"Will do and it was nice meeting you!" He said, feeling pleased with himself. And he was confident that the rest of Giles's neighbors would be as understanding once word spread about his disability. It never hurt to be reminded that you don't always know what another person's struggles are. He was certainly learning that with Giles. If anyone *should* have had an ideal, carefree existence, it would be Giles Ashby.

So where else could Riley make a solid improvement in the Ashbys' daily lives?

The kitchen.

Food was definitely Riley's love language and how he often comforted himself—both through cooking and sharing meals with the people he felt safest with. He could do a lot better than bagels, but he had to get the lay of the land and learn more about his new clients.

Food was a facilitator of communication and a great way for Giles and Milo to form more positive core memories together. Riley would assess both Giles and Milo to get a sense of their palettes, abilities, and how adventurous they were in addition to helping them bond over meals.

Riley recalled that Giles's Grandma Ida was renowned for her pies and he thought pastry would be a great place to showcase Riley's baking talent. In addition to a killer carrot cake recipe, he had a solid repertoire of savory and sweet pies that were perfect for winter's gray days and darker, dreary evenings.

He was particularly good at decorating pies with cute pastry shapes like chickens, cows, and fish for savory pies, and fruits and berries for sweet. And fun seasonal shapes like mittens, snowflakes, *and snowmen.*

His baking plans were put on hold when Riley knocked on the door of the apartment and an older woman with a short silver bob answered. "You must be Riley!" She swept him into a hug and ushered him inside. "I'm Wendy and I am so glad to finally have someone to talk to! Milo's always at school while I'm here and Doris was as fun as a box of thumbtacks. And Mr. Ashby never knows who or what I'm talking about. My mother gets out more than he does and she died ten years ago."

"I'm in. Let's do this," Riley said as he hung up his backpack and took off his coat and cardigan. His romantic radar was completely busted, but Riley could tell when he found a kindred spirit.

"I'll give you Doris's keys. Did Ashby give you all the security codes?" She asked, then scowled in the direction of Giles's office when Riley shook his head. "As brilliant as they come, but couldn't find his ass with a map on a clear day. We'll get you squared away so you don't have to hang out on the doorstep like a stranger."

"What's that?" Giles said as he wandered into the kitchen with his nose in a book.

"How's he supposed to do his job without a key, Zuckerberg?" She asked and Giles's furrow intensified to a 4 as he looked between her and Riley, then shrugged at Wendy.

"I don't know. I assumed you'd explain how things work around here since you're in charge," he countered. He shook his head, looking irritated as he went to fill a bottle from the tap on the refrigerator door.

"There you go!" She said as if Giles had just proved her point. "And welcome aboard. I'm here until two every other day, but you can call me *any time at all* if you need anything, doll."

"Thanks, Wendy! This week was on track to be the worst, but I think things might be looking up," he said.

Hopefully, he hadn't gone and jinxed himself.

Chapter Eight

Try as he might, Giles couldn't find a book or a snippet of code to keep him occupied. He was too distracted by the delightful upheaval occurring in his kitchen. It was a touch nerve-wracking, having a "new" person in 8B and trusting them with the things that were most precious to Giles: his son and his home.

But it was easy to trust Reid Marshall and Giles didn't have a single doubt that his family was in safe hands with Riley. Which was why Giles lingered after Milo said his goodbyes and left with Julie for the weekend. He waited until Wendy was doing the bed linens to lay himself at Riley's feet and beg for mercy.

He found Riley in the kitchen on his tiptoes with his head stuck in one of the cabinets. "Could I trouble you for a moment?" Giles asked.

"Sure!" Riley closed the cabinet and held up a notepad. "I was just going through your spices and getting an inventory. What's up?"

"I'm afraid I need your help. Again." Giles grimaced apologetically, but Riley seemed unfazed.

"That is what you're paying me for. It even says so in my contract, Giles."

"Right... This might be outside of your regular duties. Not that this is anything improper!" Giles reassured Riley.

"Why don't you just tell me what it is you need help with?"

Giles scrubbed his face to smother a groan as his nerves fizzed and sparked with anxiety and frustration. He'd really gone and put his foot in it this time. "It's this field trip."

"Ah." Riley crossed his arms over his chest. There was a calculating gleam in his eyes that gave Giles second thoughts and made him want to retreat. "Milo's really looking forward to this."

"He is. The fifth graders go every year. Milo would rather go without one hundred of his closest classmates, but Neil deGrasse Tyson makes occasional appearances during field trips. Milo worships Tyson and is hoping he'll see him."

"Couldn't you...?" Riley coughed suggestively. "Introduce them and ask Tyson to do something?"

"*No.*" Giles tapped his lips and looked around to make sure Milo was still on his way to Great Neck and there were no other witnesses in the room. "You think I haven't looked into this? I'm already a mega-donor and I've pleaded with the Museum of Natural History to put Pluto back. Tyson can't actually reinstate Pluto and Milo isn't going to understand that the planetarium made a decision based on budgetary considerations and what was best for the longevity of the exhibit," he explained in a hurried, hushed whisper.

"You already looked into it?" Riley asked.

"Of course. I would have set up the meeting *months* ago and paid if it was a matter of funding the exhibit. But they can't call Pluto a planet if the International Astronomical Union has classified it as a dwarf planet."

"No... That would be a credibility issue for the museum, I suppose."

"I've been sneaking Milo around the Hayden for two years so he *won't* meet Tyson because he won't understand and it'll break his heart if he hears that from his idol," Giles said. "And I'm not sure if I want Milo to meet him, after all that's come out."

"That could be a pretty big letdown. What are you going to do?"

Giles held up his hands. "I have no idea. For now, I'll keep supporting Milo and pray he figures it out for himself without losing his love for Pluto."

"Ride it out. That's smart. And who knows, the scientific community might change its mind."

"That would be amazing and the last miracle I'd ever ask for." Giles pressed his hands together as he glanced at the ceiling.

"Oh, God. I thought this was going somewhere cold and disappointing, but this is really sweet. What can I do to help?"

"Sweet?" Giles didn't know what to do with that. No one had ever accused him of being sweet and he certainly never expected to win any points with Riley over this field trip. "I... would do anything to make Milo happy."

"I know!" Riley clutched his chest. "You keep saying you're a mess and I was really invested in believing that you didn't have a heart. But then you go and say something perfectly sweet and act like a total prince."

"I'm sorry?" Giles attempted, earning a frustrated grunt from Riley as he nodded.

"You should be," he said, then winked at Giles. "I'm kidding. How can I help?" He asked, but Giles was still glitching. Riley had called him sweet and a prince and had winked at him.

"Uh..." His gaze dropped to Riley's lips and Giles wondered if he'd ever be sweet enough to deserve a kiss from *his* prince. Maybe he was on the right track with this planetarium debacle... Perhaps Riley would rescue Giles with a kiss. And a perfectly plausible excuse that would make Milo happy. "Please get me out of this field trip," he whispered, then closed his eyes and made a wish.

"No way! You have to go!"

"What?" Giles's eyes snapped open and he frowned at Riley. "You said you would help me."

"Not with that!" Riley said, sounding as if Giles had asked him to drive a getaway car. "Milo told me that that's *your place* and that it's his favorite thing in the whole city because you've always taken him."

"Exactly... We go all the time. And I'll take him as many times as he wants, but he won't want me there with his teachers and his peers after I've embarrassed him." Giles could already see it. He would make another scene and this time, Riley would be there to witness karma in action. "It's already a minefield and the odds of Tyson making an appearance increase exponentially if a mega-donor is there. And the probability of Tyson answering *my* son's burning question and crushing his heart in front of all the other fourth graders becomes unacceptably high."

"Okay. I see your point there," Riley conceded. He scratched his chin thoughtfully, then smirked at Giles. "That's where you flex your über rich guy muscles. Make sure that the king of the astrophysicists *doesn't* show up and make a scene while you're trying to be a normal dad and enjoy a field trip with your son."

"But I don't want to go and I won't enjoy it," Giles stated.

"That doesn't matter!"

Giles's eyes flicked to the ceiling. "Are you certain because—?"

"Yes. In most situations, your comfort and happiness supersede all other considerations, but in this instance, we're going to do what's best for Milo."

"Me losing my temper and making an ass out of myself because Kelsey's dad or some other grasping loser won't leave me alone is not what's best for Milo," Giles ground out. His temper crackled at the thought. "You cannot begin to fathom the *suggestions* the mothers have made on the sidewalk in front of that school in broad daylight! And I'm not talking about the single moms." He widened his eyes at Riley to convey the horror. "I *can't* enjoy a field trip with my son like a normal father and to be honest, I really don't enjoy other people's children. Bless you for loving them as much as you do because the only child I can tolerate is Milo. Even Jack gets on my nerves and I've known that boy since he was three days old." Giles immediately knew he'd said too much and bit down on his lips. He waited as Riley visibly reeled.

Riley pushed out a long, cleansing breath, then smiled serenely at Giles. "Let's try this again." He clasped his hands together like a patron saint addressing a lamb. "This isn't about Pluto, the other parents, or the other children. This is about your son. You're his person and he's counting on you for support in a high-stress situation."

"That's not fair," Giles protested. His throat tightened and his insides clenched because Riley was right.

"Fair?" Riley's head canted. "We're talking about a field trip, Giles. I'll deal with the teachers and the other parents, but on the scale of things that aren't fair..." His lips pulled tight and he swallowed an amused chirp. "I suggest opening your eyes the next time you leave the Olympia."

That hurt like a kick in the groin. "Open my eyes?" Giles shouted. He didn't need to be reminded of how privileged he was. Giles just wanted to skip *one* tedious field trip to the planetarium. Apparently, he couldn't and he was going to fall flat on his face again. And he'd do it in front of Milo and Riley. "*What is the point of you, then?*" He howled.

"Mr. Ashby!" Wendy hurried into the kitchen from Milo's hallway. "You apologize right now!"

Giles covered his mouth, wishing he could stuff the words back down his throat. He had a feeling it was too late and he was about to choke on them. "Of course. I'm sorry, Riley."

Riley took another serene breath and his lips curved beatifically. "No worries! I have my grocery list and I'll get everything while I'm shopping this weekend." He held up his notepad, then turned to address Wendy, dismissing Giles. "I need a long walk and a slice so I'm going to take off for lunch now, but I'll see *you* on Monday!" He tapped his brow with the notepad and headed for the door, ignoring Giles as he reached for his cardigan.

Giles hung his head. He couldn't look at Wendy as Riley calmly put on his coat, scarf, and mittens, then took his backpack off the hook. The door closed quietly behind him, but Giles jumped as if it had slammed.

"What is the point of him?" Wendy wagged her duster at Giles angrily. "You go...row or sit in your sauna and think about where you'll be if he doesn't come back."

"Yes, ma'am," Giles mumbled and took himself off for a hard row and a time-out in the sauna.

Chapter Nine

Riley's walk turned out to be a lot shorter than he had initially planned. His feet carried him around the corner and he soon found himself climbing the front steps of The Killian House. He knocked on the door and his mood improved slightly when the butler, Pierce, answered. The dour older man's stiff welcome never failed to tickle Riley because he knew that deep down, Pierce was a teddy bear and completely devoted to the Camerons. Including Fin.

"Afternoon, Pierce. What's Fin up to?" He asked as he hung his scarf next to his coat. Riley noticed that there were no little coats on the hooks by the door.

"He's in the nursery."

"Thanks," Riley said, then sprinted up the stairs.

Fin was in the nursery, but he was alone and most of the furniture had been moved and drop cloths had been laid out along one of the walls. Fin had a paintbrush in one hand and Riley gasped excitedly as he hurried to see what they were painting.

"It's gonna be a carousel!" Fin informed him giddily. "It'll cheer the girls up when it's too yucky out to go to the park."

"I love it. What can I work on?"

"Pick a unicorn and go nuts," Fin said, pointing at the faint unicorns sketched on the wall. There were five—one for each of the Camerons. "I'm envisioning something like a Lisa Frank binder."

"Nice!"

The bright jars of paint didn't soothe the stinging as much as Riley would have liked. He was still feeling tender and was particularly bitter about the *What is the point of you?* remark.

"It took him less than two days to forget why he hired me," he muttered.

"I was wondering why you looked so serious. Unicorns usually cheer you up," Fin said, giving Riley's ribs a poke with the end of his brush.

"I mean, what's better than a unicorn? Nothing." Riley sighed at the pink-maned dream he was creating for Amelia.

"I can't think of anything." Fin turned and fell against an unpainted section of the wall. He tilted his head so he could see Riley's face. "Whatever he said, I have a feeling he didn't mean it. Not that it gives Giles any right to say hateful things."

The tingle in Riley's nose only added insult to injury. Why was it still so easy for Giles to make him cry? Riley felt small and insignificant again as his eyes began to water. "He *always* has to say the worst thing. He's like that with everyone and I'm already making excuses to the doorman and the neighbors for him. And the worst part is that I know he didn't *mean it* and why he snapped but it still gets to me. It's like we're in middle school again." Riley lamented.

A sly grin spread across Fin's face. "Maybe...because you still like him?"

"I can admit that he's not as much of a jerk as I thought he was and I kind of feel sorry for him, but I wouldn't say I like him."

"Why do you care if the doorman thinks Giles is rude? And Giles *is* rude. Whether he intends to be or not. His behavior was rude, therefore he was."

"Thank you, Socrates," Riley said flatly. "You're saying it's okay that Giles is rude?"

"Why does it matter?" Fin challenged and held up a finger. "He has a disability, but I don't think that's the *only* reason or that it's that serious. Some people are just rude and they don't mind the consequences, like Giles and Walker. Personally, I think cranky is really sexy. It's cruelty and selfishness you want to steer clear of, but Giles never came across as cruel or selfish. And I bet that doorman doesn't really care or sees through Giles and thinks that he's rude because he's scared and lonely."

"I'm the one who has to explain and apologize for him now," Riley argued, but Fin's nose wrinkled.

"Do you? I don't think that's part of your job description or that Giles really cares if he's popular. He just doesn't want all the kids and teachers to think that Milo's dad is an asshole and shun him." Fin threw an arm around Riley's neck. "Sounds a little familiar and like he's sitting on some childhood trauma."

"You were supposed to be on my side," Riley said. He passed Fin his paintbrush and looked longingly at the pink unicorn. "Sorry I can't stay and give you legs, pal."

"I'll make sure he gets them," Fin said and gave Riley a gentle punch in the arm. "I'm always on your side. You tell me we're fighting Giles Ashby, I'm fighting Giles Ashby."

Riley laughed. "He would destroy us!"

"Probably, but I'd still ride at dawn if you told me he hurt you."

"I know, and he didn't. Too much. Thanks for being awesome."

"That's what best friends are for," Fin said, then became serious. "You're going to feel terrible until you work this out with Giles. Give him a chance to apologize and think about why it's so easy for him to get under your skin."

"I will." Riley gave Fin a hug and went to face Giles.

He thought about putting it off until Monday, but he didn't want either of them dwelling on a silly argument about the planetarium and Neil deGrasse Tyson. There was no point ruining both of their weekends so Riley trudged back to the Olympia and went right up to the 8th floor.

Wendy had already left and the apartment appeared to be vacant when Riley leaned through the front door. He thought he was alone until he peeked down Giles's hall and heard the rowing machine and Giles huffing and puffing. Riley backtracked and decided to wait in the kitchen.

He hadn't done an inventory of the cookie cutters yet and that seemed like a good way to kill time. Riley found some in a large Ziplock bag in the pantry, but the selection was rather lacking and unimaginative. Soon about a dozen round and square cutters in various sizes were scattered on the floor between his outstretched legs.

"Not a single mitten or even a pumpkin?" He shook his head at the collection.

His notebook was open and he was making a list of shapes when he heard Giles whistling. He sat up straighter and stretched his neck to see over the counter when Giles strolled around and nearly walked into Riley.

Without a stitch of clothing on.

Giles did have a towel, but it hung from around his neck and his rather large, semi-erect penis dangled about a foot away from Riley's face.

Giles Ashby Needs A Nanny

"Um..."

"Jesus!" Giles jumped and attempted to cover himself with his water bottle. It didn't cover as much as he had hoped so Riley threw a hand up to shield his eyes. "I'm so sorry!" Giles spun around, but that wasn't any better.

Well. His backside was also *really nice* and Riley's eyes flared as he peeked between his fingers while Giles fumbled with the towel and the bottle. "I wanted to let you know that I didn't have any hard feelings about what happened earlier," Riley said. He regretted the words as soon as they came out of his mouth. "I mean, I'm not mad at you or anything."

"Fuck! Just stay right there," Giles said before he dashed from the kitchen.

"Okay. I'll stay right here," Riley agreed weakly. He didn't think his legs would work anyways. But his hands worked and he had his phone out and was texting Fin.

Riley

Holy fucking smoke show! I just saw Giles naked and I'm going to need you to send an ambulance.

I'm kidding. Do not send an ambulance and do not call me. I will call you ASAP.

"I am so, so, so, so *sorry!*" Giles said as he ran back into the kitchen wearing a pair of joggers. He was still shirtless and there was a telling bulge in the front of his pants, but Riley wasn't going to tell Giles that he'd only made his appearance slightly less graphic.

"It's cool!" Riley hid his phone behind his back but it vibrated loudly at the barrage of incoming messages. "Accidents happen and it's not like I've never seen a naked man before. I've seen lots of naked men and you're...fine," he said, his face on fire and his eyes watering with mortification. *I've seen lots of naked men and he's FINE?*

"Good. Great. I was in the sauna and I thought you weren't coming back until Monday. I thought I was alone until Sunday."

"Totally. I'd be naked too," Riley said quickly. He raised a knuckle and bit into it as the urge to scream swelled. "I wish I could stop saying weird things!" He whispered up at Giles.

Giles had turned a bright shade of red. "What if we pretended like it never happened and I've never ever been naked, not once in my life?"

"Deal!" Riley's hand swung out and Giles snatched it. He gave it a firm shake and they both pushed out loud, relieved breaths.

"And I am really sorry about what I said earlier. I need you, Riley. Desperately."

Perhaps it was because Riley had just seen every gloriously naked inch of Giles's body, but it was easy to imagine they were having a very different conversation. Riley pulled his backpack onto his lap as he started to get warm *down there.*

"You need me?"

Giles nodded. "When Reid said you were available, I knew right away that we were going to be alright because you're one of the kindest, happiest, smartest people I've ever met. You're exactly what Milo needs. There's no one I trust more in this city."

"Wow. Really?" It wasn't as hot or as thrilling as *I desper-*

ately need you to get naked with me. But Riley was incredibly flattered. "I wasn't even sure if you remembered me."

"Remembered you?" Giles shot him a hard look. Riley couldn't tell if Giles was angry, hungry, or deeply confused. The furrow was an intense 7 and a muscle in Giles's jaw twitched. "I could never forget you." With that, Giles offered Riley a terse nod and fled the kitchen.

Riley stared after Giles until his eyes grew dry and began to burn. "What's that supposed to mean?"

He gathered up all the cookie cutters and his things, careful not to rattle or slam anything in the kitchen. He wasn't sure why he tiptoed out of the apartment or why he didn't pull in a deep breath until the elevator doors closed behind him.

"What the hell does that mean?" He asked loudly. His phone vibrated in his pocket and Riley gasped Fin's name as he took it out. There were twelve messages. Riley gave them a quick scan as the doors opened and he rushed through the lobby and the breezeway to the porte-cochère. He waved at the doorman as he zipped past, then dialed Fin's number.

"You can't leave a message like that and tell me not to call!" Fin yelled as soon as Riley answered.

"I didn't have time to explain!"

"What the hell happened? I said give the guy another chance, not give him head. Not that I'd blame you if you went for it," Fin added.

"I kind of wanted to!" Riley whispered into his phone. He charged into the subway and jogged down the steps, keeping his head down. "We made a deal that we'd forget that it happened. And then he said he was sorry and that there's no one he trusts more than me. But the whole time, I was just thinking about having sex with him."

"Been there," Fin said with a snort.

"We're not going down that road because I don't *like* Giles when he isn't naked or shirtless."

"Are you sure? Because an hour ago—"

"I usually find out a guy's an asshole *after* I have sex with him. I already know Giles is an asshole and I know how this curse works, I go to bed with a prince and wake up with a frog. I go to bed with a frog and I'll wake up with a dragon. No thanks."

"What if you went to bed with a frog and woke up with a prince?"

A loud guffaw burst from Riley, but no one noticed. The platform was nearly full, but the other passengers remained unaware, minding their own business while Riley had an existential crisis.

"I told you about the time he called me a Dickensian urchin."

"You overheard Giles and another prick talking like a couple of pricks. You don't even know what the rest of the conversation was about."

Riley stubbornly pressed his lips together. He had scraped together his courage and approached Giles at the homecoming dance. Riley was a freshman and was only there because student council members were allowed to stick around after decorating and working at the concession stand. Giles looked miserable—as always—in the corner, so Riley had wandered over to say hello.

Had he secretly hoped that Giles would tell him he looked nice in the coat Riley had borrowed from Reid? Possibly. Was he discreetly sucking on an Altoid in case Giles asked him to dance? A strong possibility as well.

But he definitely heard Jared Thompson slap Giles on the back and say that Riley Fitzgerald liked boys and was looking for someone to dance with him.

"Fitzgerald? Isn't he the one who looks like a Dickensian urchin?"

There was no mistaking whom they were talking about and what Giles thought of him. Riley pretended he hadn't heard and asked a girl to dance instead. She was a junior and had taken pity on Riley because she had heard and spent the entire song reassuring him that short guys could still be hot.

Riley grew until he settled at a rather average 5'8", but he would always feel like a short, skinny fifteen-year-old when he thought about that night.

"He said he could never forget me. What do you think that means?"

"I think it means that you got under his skin too."

"I don't see how. Or, if I did, I don't think it was in a good way."

"Do you want to tap out and tell Reid to send someone else? We'll all understand," Fin said, sincere concern in his voice.

Riley's whole being screamed "No!" He couldn't wait to see Milo on Monday and was actually looking forward to the field trip. Riley had a feeling that it would be like visiting a whole new planetarium, seeing it through Milo's eyes. And he wanted to prove to Giles that the three of them could handle that outing together as a team, that it wouldn't end in embarrassment or heartache.

Then, Riley thought about Giles's sweet confession. "He tried to make them take Pluto back."

"Who?"

"The Hayden."

Fin gasped. "Why would he do that?"

"For Milo. It means everything to him and Giles tried to use his money and throw his weight around to get them to make

Pluto a planet again, but it didn't work. He's afraid Milo will find out and it'll break his heart."

"Wait. That's kind of precious."

"I know."

"What are you going to do?"

"No clue. I guess we'll just have to wait and see," Riley said and ended the call so he could board the train as it arrived.

Chapter Ten

As far as Giles could tell, everything looked...

"Fine?" He turned in front of the mirror in his closet and looked over his shoulder at his bare backside. "He was probably in shock. Anyone would be in shock."

It had certainly been a shock for Giles. He had rowed harder than he had in years, ranting and berating himself. He couldn't make it *two days* without making an ass out of himself in front of Riley. Giles punished himself until his muscles turned to jelly, then stripped off his sweaty shorts on the way to the sauna. The best part of those twenty steamy, stifling minutes was feeling the cool air on his skin after he stepped out.

Giles was an anxious introvert, but he didn't like being alone. Having time with Claire's family was important, so Milo spent every other weekend in Great Neck with Jack. But Giles got terribly lonely while he was away. The one upside was how much Giles enjoyed walking around the apartment naked when he had the place to himself. That rarely happened before

Claire left; now Giles barely wore clothes on his weekends alone.

In the beginning, he felt rebellious, strolling into the kitchen for a cup of coffee in his birthday suit. It took him weeks before he had the nerve to sit on the couch and he couldn't stop giggling the first time he vacuumed naked.

But Giles had never really considered his body. He knew that he was a very attractive man. Both of his parents were beautiful people and he was blessed to have inherited a favorable combination of their genes. It had all been wasted on Giles, unfortunately. He hadn't inherited his father's charisma or his mother's unshakable confidence. He certainly didn't have their narcissism and Giles never understood his parents' fear of aging.

He barely recognized his mother now. She looked more like a Kardashian than the woman who'd visited him on holidays as a child. And his father just looked like a wax replica of himself. He hadn't managed to make himself look younger, but like his face had been peeled out of a mold.

Giles had locked all the doors and stripped off his joggers as soon as Riley left. He watched himself in the mirror as he recreated every naked moment in the kitchen, from every angle. Giles strolled and jumped, spun, and dashed away from the mirror dozens of times in an attempt to see what Riley had seen.

He glanced down at his flaccid cock and sighed at it. Giles was also blessed in that respect. But he'd never been confident enough or felt the urge to expose himself to anyone. Now that he had, Giles was suddenly concerned that Riley's "fine" meant that something about his appearance might have been a disappointment.

Giles had fooled around with two other people in college, but Claire was the only person he'd ever had sex with. They'd had a healthy sex life and he was certain she would have told him if something wasn't right or if something could be improved. She'd always been frank and she'd taught Giles well.

"I should call her." He didn't know why he hadn't called Claire as soon as Riley left, instead of contorting himself and doing jumping jacks in front of the mirror. Giles pulled on a robe and fell into bed with his phone. She answered on the third ring.

"Hey! How's it going?"

"Great! Good morning!" He hadn't meant to yell.

"Good...early evening. What are you up to?" Her voice rose suspiciously.

"Not much. Milo's at your sister's for the weekend. He got out of school early so she took the boys to lunch and back to Great Neck. The new nanny started yesterday."

"I know! Milo says Riley's amazing. You should see all the messages and the pictures he sent me. I talked to Riley briefly, but I was waiting to hear what you thought of him before I got too excited."

"Riley's great," Giles confirmed. "I could not have found a better nanny."

"Yay! I'm so glad. And the two of you are getting along?" She asked. Because she knew better.

Giles clutched his forehead. "It's been a little bumpy and it's kind of complicated."

"Oh, dear. What did you do?"

"I don't think it could have gone worse, actually..."

"Did he quit?" She asked loudly, her tone heavy with accusation.

"No. Thank God. But Riley wouldn't. He's never been a quitter."

"Never been a quitter?"

"Milo didn't tell you that we were neighbors and went to school together?"

"He did not!"

"Yeah..." Giles was beginning to regret the decision to call Claire. "Remember the boy I told you about? The one I could *never* talk to because I'd always, always, always get too nervous and say the worst thing possible."

"Please, please, please tell me you hired him!" She let out a high-pitched squeal and Giles had to hold the phone away from his head.

"I did."

"Yessss!"

"And then I screamed at him and showed him my entire naked body."

Of course, she laughed. Giles set the phone on his chest and stared at the ceiling while Claire sobbed and wheezed.

"Are you finished?" He asked when there was a pause.

"Why?" She fell apart again so Giles got up and went to get a drink. He made it all the way to the kitchen and prepared himself a scotch on the rocks while she carried on like an air-raid siren. "I knew I should have left you a list of interview questions. You're never good when you wing it."

"I wasn't winging it. I blew up about the field trip to the Hayden and then I thought I was home alone."

"I can't decide if this makes you the worst or the best boss ever."

"Can I ask you a question?"

"You'd better get it in while you can because I have hundreds, Giles."

He took two large gulps from his glass and braced himself. "I can't figure out how embarrassed I should be about this," he admitted. "It was incredibly inappropriate and I'm so sorry that it happened. But, it did and...he said I was fine."

That unleashed another gale of laughter, giving Giles time to top off his drink and head back to his room. "You poor thing! Naked in front of your ultimate crush and no one thought to bring a scorecard."

"I don't want a score," he snapped.

"Liar."

"Alright. Maybe I do. I'd like to know how much I was offending him. Was it *Oh, God. My boss is naked, but at least I still like having eyes* or *Oh, God. My boss is naked. Get these cursed things out of my head and set them on fire?*"

"I am going to make a wild guess here and say he's keeping his eyes. Unless he really isn't into men with spectacular bodies and perfect hair."

"I do have really nice hair."

"I miss running my fingers through it. You have hair like a chinchilla and you purr like a kitten when you get your scalp scratched."

Giles missed that too. He missed intimacy, but he wanted to try it with someone he also felt a spark with. They had always been tender and affectionate with each other, but there was never any heat. "What if I wanted to ask him out?"

"This doesn't seem all that hypothetical, babe."

"It's extremely hypothetical. I'm scared and I would be in so much trouble if Riley quit. Milo would never forgive me and I doubt Reid Marshall would send another one of his nannies to the Olympia."

"Nonsense. Once they learn about your benefits package, you'll have nannies lined up for blocks."

"I bet they're loving you in Osaka."

"They don't know what to make of me yet and I'm using that to my advantage."

"They probably think you're mercurial and unconventional. They're going to be disappointed when they realize you're just super corny and have bad taste in clothes."

"But I am good at speaking nerd and I know what nerds want to buy."

"Riley isn't a nerd. Well, he's not the same kind of nerd. How do I get him to want to...buy me? Or subscribe for the trial, at least."

"This feels like a reboot so your best play is to lean into the nostalgia. How is the new Giles better than the old Giles? What's still the same and what's improving with age?"

"Nothing, if I had to guess. If anything, I'm getting worse."

"That's a lie. You use sentences now. You communicated in grumbles and nods when we first met. And you acknowledge that you have feelings other than dread and are so much better at sharing them."

"I pay a man hundreds of dollars an hour to pry them out of my psyche. I'm just getting my money's worth."

"I know and I'm so proud. You should go for it if you really like him. It's so rare for you to like anyone and we don't know when this'll happen again," she said. This time she was gentle and Giles could feel the subtle nudge.

"I do like him. The same way I like you and Milo."

"That's really huge."

The *only* people Giles had ever *liked* were Claire and Milo. He had felt disconnected from his parents and humanity until he met Claire and she became pregnant with Milo. Giles's brain was too loud around other people, too distracted by their expectations and their perceptions of him. He couldn't look someone in the eyes without wondering what they wanted from him or if they wished he had just an ounce of charm or some personality to go along with his handsome face.

It wasn't like that with Claire. She saw a fellow nerd and introvert but she took charge and saved Giles when they hid behind the same vending machine in the student union during orientation. Her smile was so big and warm and she laughed *at* Giles for all the reasons he laughed at himself. Mostly because she laughed at herself for the exact same reasons.

Claire and Julie were born fifteen months apart and were raised in Queens by a hardworking single mother. Genevieve passed away when the sisters were in high school. Claire had to bust her ass to get into Princeton and seeing her succeed brought Giles more pride than any of his own achievements.

They were awkward soulmates, but she blossomed when their silly Angry Monkeys app game blew up. The side project they started in Giles's dorm room eventually put Claire in the boardroom and it had been his greatest joy until they had Milo.

Giles felt a similar trust and connection with Riley after only a handful of hours together. He had always imagined it would be just like that. But Giles couldn't just walk up to Riley when he was ten or sixteen and say "I think you might be one of my people." without sounding like an extremely weird prick. Still, Giles could tell that they were made for each other the way he and Claire were. Giles never would have overcome the screaming in his head and the awful sinking feeling in his stomach and done something about it if it wasn't for Milo. He wouldn't have called Reid if he hadn't been so scared of scarring Milo and making him an outcast.

"I've always liked Riley. I was just too scared I'd mess up. I'd get so in my head about saying the wrong thing and him never talking to me again, that I...never talked to him."

"Never?"

Giles groaned into his scotch as one of his earliest regrets tugged at his conscience. "I called him a clumsy jerk when we were around Milo's age. We were on a field trip to the Hayden."

Claire gasped. *"You did not."*

"I did. After I bumped into him."

"Giles!"

"Who does that, right? I was staring at him and I was going to ask him if I could sit next to him and if he wanted to walk together sometimes. I used to wait so I could watch him walk to school and after school when I didn't have practice. He was under the Sphere and the sun was coming through the windows and he looked so bright and so soft." Giles laughed at himself. "I thought he was an angel. I looked up to see what he was staring at and I tripped into him. Then he bumped into this girl and she made the biggest scene and everyone was staring. I panicked and blamed it on him. And then I ran."

"I don't know what to say."

"I don't think Riley remembers, thank goodness."

There was another dramatic gasp. "Oh, I guarantee he remembers."

"No. I avoided him for weeks, and when I finally 'bumped' into him in the library, I said excuse me and he said it was totally cool and acted like nothing had ever happened."

She hissed as if she'd witnessed a crash. "I think you were dead to him."

"How do you know and why would you say that?"

"Milo sent me a video of the two of them and I know a theater nerd when I see one. I was a math nerd, which is almost like a theater nerd, just without the rhythm and coordination. Riley's gorgeous, but I bet he got stuffed in a locker at least once. And what you displayed under the Sphere was bully-like behavior. You would have been dead to me."

"Wonderful."

"Actually." She giggled. "I think you might be even now."

"What are you talking about?"

"Hear me out: that incident at the planetarium was just about as embarrassing as being naked in public for someone

Riley's age. And I can't think of anything more embarrassing for you than being naked in front of your new nanny aka life-long crush."

"Wonderful." Giles had spent the last twenty or so years of his life wishing it had never happened. It would have been worth it if the sight of Giles's bare ass had erased the memory from Riley's brain, but that didn't seem likely.

"There's your nostalgia!"

"No. Not that."

"It's perfect."

"Why would I want to remind him? It was terrible, Claire. A girl cried." Giles held the hand with the glass against his stomach as the memory made him queasy.

"This is your chance to show him that the new Giles is better than the old Giles!"

"Even though he isn't."

"Stop it." She pushed out an irritated breath, making him smile. "Think about how the new Giles is better than the old Giles and show Riley. He's already seen how much you've improved with age."

"This is a lot of abuse to put up with for a few scraps of decent advice. I can't get out of this field trip so I might as well. I'll need to make sure Tyson doesn't show up *and* I have to figure out how the new Giles is better than the old Giles."

"I believe in you!" She insisted. "When was the last time you smoked?"

Giles's lips fluttered as he forced out a hard breath. "Last night. There was no shutting it all down after yesterday."

"Might be a good call tonight, too," she said and Giles chuckled in agreement.

His brain's chemistry didn't react well to anti-anxiety drugs like Xanax. Giles turned into a Dr. Jekyll who didn't care about *anything*. Once, he bought the entire Zegna section at Bloomingdale's because there weren't enough brands with Zs in their names in his closet.

Marijuana was a great alternative for Giles, quieting his brain when it was too loud for him to rest and allowing him to focus when he wanted to work or enjoy books and movies. It helped him sleep when the voices and his nerves got particularly loud. But Giles had no time-management skills when he was high and could get lost in a book or a bit of code for hours if he wasn't careful.

"It's probably a good call," he said, wincing at the French doors. His corner of the rooftop balcony had a comfortable seating area with an outdoor heater, but he still didn't relish the thought of going out in his robe. "I better put on some pants. I've got a lot of thinking to do."

Chapter Eleven

The apologies began as soon as Riley stepped foot in 8B and Giles handed him his coffee Monday morning. Just not for the thing they agreed had never happened.

Giles was terribly sorry for switching to a different type of coffee, but had assured Riley that he was expecting a delivery of his preferred beans later and that tomorrow's coffee would be up to his standards. Riley insisted that the coffee had been superb. And Giles apologized in case it had been too invasive to ask if Riley had enjoyed his weekend. It had not been. There was also some debate as to whether it had been rude of Giles to assume that Riley didn't understand Latin. Because Riley didn't and said he'd assumed that only monks did.

"I suppose that explains why I studied it," Giles replied with a self-deprecating grin.

And it was no one else's fault but Riley's when he smashed his own thumb in the drawer because he was staring at Giles.

"My God. Are these *all* the Band-Aids we have?" Giles fretted while hunting through an alarmingly large first aid kit.

"I don't actually need one. Thumb feels fine now." Riley held it up, but Giles was still upset about not being prepared for *any* type of wound and ordered more.

All that before 9:00 AM. Riley counted sixteen apologies by the time Giles peeked around the wall and said he was sorry for how loud his last visitor had sneezed in the foyer.

"I'm just glad he sneezed into his elbow. I can teach a child to do that, but do you know how often I see grown men blasting their germs on the train?" Riley said with a dismissive wave.

"As long as you weren't disturbed." Giles's brows pulled together even more, though, as he shifted a little closer and rested his hip against the edge of the counter. "Did you...um...? What do you have planned for your day?" He asked, risking a quick glance at Riley. He retreated a bit, as if he'd crept into Riley's territory and regretted it. Which was odd, seeing as it was Giles's kitchen, but he seemed to have ceded the space to Riley for his own particular use.

"I was thinking I'd run to the Fairway Market for a few things. It looks like you're out of juice and Milo said it's been forever since you guys have had tacos so I'm getting everything for those. I'll get you two set up for a taco bar later because I've gotta get out of here about half an hour early. I'm teaching swimming lessons over by my parents'," Riley explained. "Did you want me to pick something up for you?" He offered and Giles shook his head.

"No. I was just wondering. Do you...want me to go with you?" He asked, looking a touch green and shiny. Giles squirmed and squeezed an eye shut like he was afraid Riley would say yes.

"I can go by myself," Riley laughed and waved for Giles to go on. "I know you're not a 'kitchen person' and everyone gets stressed out in grocery stores." Especially in the city because everything was tighter and prices could get scary. What might cost you a dollar or two in New Jersey could run you six to eight dollars in Manhattan. Riley wondered if that was why Giles was offering to accompany him. "Wendy already gave me the card for the household expenses and told me to go crazy and see if I could make you cry."

"No!" Giles shook his head. "I won't. Get whatever you want. I thought I might go with you...to learn," he added, holding up his hands.

"Sure... If you want to. You did hire me to handle these sorts of things and it's just taco night. No point in stressing yourself out unnecessarily," Riley said and gave Giles's shoulder a reassuring punch.

Giles's eyes followed Riley's hand and he swallowed loudly. "It's fine. I haven't been out in a few days so I probably should," he said, smiling nervously at Riley.

It was touching to know that Giles felt comfortable enough with Riley to face the Fairway Market, and it shouldn't be too busy at that hour. But there was no reason for Giles to put himself out for such a mundane chore. Especially one that Riley could easily manage on his own. Nonetheless, Giles insisted, so the two pulled on their coats and headed out together. Riley couldn't help but smile at the way Giles stuffed his hands in his pockets and sulked down 73rd.

That was how Riley truly remembered him, and for a moment, they were kids again and the tree-lined sidewalk and classic brownstones were in Brooklyn instead of Manhattan. They'd often leave for school around the same time in the morning and Riley would catch Giles out of the corner of his eye now and then. Giles only seemed to have a few acquaintances despite being athletically gifted and playing on several teams in school. He kept his head down and usually had a duffle bag slung over his shoulder for his equipment, drifting to school and back like a ghost.

Giles still carried himself like an apparition, and he haunted Riley's steps and his senses as they wordlessly strolled together to get juice and taco ingredients.

I see you now. And I'm beginning to see who you were.

In many ways, Giles was the same short-tempered and withdrawn little boy that Riley remembered. He'd always had the disgruntled frown and an aura of irritated impatience. But Giles was warier and recoiled more when other people entered his personal space. Both Claire and Julie had called Riley to discuss Giles's anxiety disorder and warned that his thresholds had only gotten lower as he got older. They agreed that it was a combination of Giles's growing notoriety as an eccentric millionaire and the horrifying awareness of reality and mortality most people faced as they turned thirty. Plus, the inevitable fear of the future that could accompany parenthood.

Claire said that she did her best to get him out of 8B whenever she could, but wasn't sure if that had helped, made Giles worse, or had even been worth it most of the time. And she wasn't a "kitchen person" either. That was why they had Doris and lived on takeout on the weekends. Which was why Riley didn't like the idea of pulling Giles even farther outside of his comfort zone for juice and tacos.

"Do you like carrot cake?" Riley asked as he steered a shopping cart into the store. Fairway was pretty roomy by New York standards, but Riley considered the narrow aisles and worried they'd still be too congested with carts and mid-morning shoppers. He hoped he could distract Giles with cake and keep him calm and talking. Riley found it hard to be upset or stressed out when he knew cake was in his future.

"Me?" Giles whipped around and ducked when the woman next to him shouted for help with the produce. His eyes were huge as he took everything in and he moved in closer, sticking to Riley's side. "Yeah. I love carrot cake. Want to buy one?"

"I was thinking of making one, actually. If you think Milo would like it."

"Milo loves carrot cake. Any kind of cake, but especially if it's got frosting on it," Giles said. His eyes managed to grow even wider when they passed the seafood and he seemed legitimately confounded by the price of things. Riley reminded himself that Grandma Ida had doted on Giles until he went away to college.

"This juice is $14?" Giles whispered to Riley. "Is that good? Should we get more? It's Milo's favorite."

"That's...what it usually costs around here," Riley said and stopped Giles from putting two more bottles in the cart. "We're carrying whatever we can't fit in my backpack."

"I don't mind carrying them. *It's Milo's favorite*," he repeated.

"Just a bottle will do us," Riley promised him, then laughed at Giles's disappointed frown. "It's not a good deal. That's why Julie brings it from Great Neck," he said out of the side of his mouth.

"Oh. Was that caviar a good deal, because...?" Giles pointed back at the seafood.

"No!" Riley whispered back.

"That's why Doris never bought it."

"Do you like caviar?" Riley asked and Giles paused.

"Sure... I like the little blinis. Do they sell those here?"

They both leaned and looked when an older man cleared his throat and waved at Giles. He appeared to be in his fifties. His name, Joe, along with a rake were embroidered on his chest pocket. Riley guessed that the man was in landscaping.

"What about an app called *Time Wasters* that lets you calculate how much your time is worth so you can bill people who waste it?" Joe said, grinning and wiggling his brows at Giles excitedly. He looked at Riley for his reaction, then looked back at Giles. "Pretty good, right?" He persisted but Riley and Giles both stared at him. "What do you think?" He demanded of Giles.

Giles's eyes narrowed and Riley braced for impact. "What's my time worth? You gonna pay me for wasting it?" Giles snapped back.

"Oh! Pardon the fuck out of me!" Joe said loudly, looking around the store for witnesses. "Didn't mean to bother his highness while he's out shopping for caviar. Not for nothin', but why don't you do something good with all that money instead of wasting it on yourself and fuckin' caviar?" Joe asked, shoving his finger in Giles's direction.

Giles's cheeks turned bright red and his nostrils flared. "Something good?" He asked with a curl of his lip. "And what would that be?"

"I don't know..." Joe rubbed his chin as if the answer was obvious. "When was the last time you had a look at the subways or got on a bus, my guy?"

"Hey!" Riley brought the cart around, putting himself between Joe and Giles. "Mr. Ashby thanks you for your vote!"

"My vote?" Joe gestured for Riley to get out of the way.

"For mayor," Riley explained and Joe laughed mockingly.

"He ain't mayor."

"That's right!" Riley gasped, then gave Joe a flat look. "Maybe you should take the state of public transportation up with him, then. We're just here because it's taco night."

"Mind your business, kid. I'm talking to the useless prick with millions of dollars," Joe said and rolled his eyes.

"I'm not a kid, but I know childish behavior when I see it," Riley countered sweetly.

"Yeah...? Kiss my ass!" Joe held up his middle finger and kicked Riley's cart.

Giles recoiled in shock, then straightened. His eyes sparked with fury and Riley threw out a hand, holding Giles back. "Easy! We don't want to make a scene," he told Giles calmly and cleared his throat suggestively at Joe. But Joe looked past him and snickered at Giles.

"Cute bodyguard. Or is he the guy you pay to touch things so you don't get your fingers dirty?"

"And what is it you get paid to do, Joe?" Giles asked loudly. He'd clearly reached his threshold. "Because *that's* what you're really pissed off about. I could fund every ridiculous pitch that gets tossed my way or hand every dime I've got to the transit authority, but you're still gonna be a sad chump with a rake on his shirt and you're still gonna think I'm a prick. So, if it's alright with you, I'm gonna pass on the financial advice," he bit out, but half the store had heard him and Joe was practically purple.

"Oh yeah? Your mother!" He shouted at Giles.

Giles leaned back and looked at Joe as if he'd uttered something ludicrous. "What of her? Wanna hear about your father?"

"Okay!" Riley hooked an arm around Giles's and pulled him and the cart away from Joe. "This is escalating so we're going to part ways now, but some of us might want to brush up on our manners," he said, glaring at Joe until they were at the other end of the aisle. "You know, it's extremely rare for me to get into a confrontation, but I kind of wanted to fight that guy," he muttered under his breath.

A horrified laugh slipped from Giles and he covered his mouth. "I shouldn't have said that!" He whispered.

"Eh." Riley looked back and Joe was berating a woman with a walker. "He had it coming and he's lucky your bodyguard was here."

Giles laughed again and it was more relaxed. "We both are," he said, then reached around Riley's hands and took hold of the cart. "Why don't you lead and I'll follow?"

"Alright," Riley said weakly. He held on for a moment, enjoying the way their sides bumped and brushed and the beguiling scent of Giles's cologne. "I'll make you a carrot cake," he murmured dazedly. *Stop it!* Riley gave himself a shake. "I'm making a carrot cake. Let's get some carrots."

They encountered a few more stares, but Giles was able to tune everyone out and marveled at Riley's ability to turn a few ingredients into a cake. Giles insisted that he and Milo would starve if he had to feed them with whatever he could find in 8B.

"You have a freezer I can fit in and there are two ducks and a turkey in there," Riley informed him as they made their way back to the Olympia with their bags.

"If I defrost one bird," Giles asked, making the question sound more like a logic problem, "will he teach me how to cook the others?"

"Oh, no! You can't make that poor bird cook his friends," Riley said and Giles shrugged.

"At least he isn't getting cooked. If anyone should be worried, it's me. The bird knows how to operate a stove and can wield a knife. I'm probably next."

Riley had to stop and set his bags between his feet, he giggled so hard. "Have you always been this funny?" He asked, wiping his eyes and picking up his bags.

"No," Giles said flatly and waited just a moment before winking at Riley.

That had Riley smirking and tittering to himself all afternoon. Who knew that Giles was *funny*? He had a dry wit and an incredible sense of humor beneath his stern, snappy exterior, Riley was learning.

He lost track of Giles and Milo while he was frosting their

cake and putting the finishing touches on their taco bar. They were in Milo's room, stretched out on the bottom bunk. Giles had an arm folded behind his head and was watching the ceiling as constellations drifted softly overhead. Milo was resting in the crook of Giles's arm and they were holding hands as they murmured softly to each other.

"I shouldn't have put that guy down for his job, though. All work is important work. And the only thing I can do with a rake is step on it and hurt myself. But that's all I had and now I feel like a jerk for picking on a guy because of his job."

"Riley was right, though. It's not your responsibility to fix the subways and you help a lot of people," Milo argued. Riley nodded in agreement and propped his shoulder against the wall so he could eavesdrop for a few more minutes.

"I know, but I still *feel* like a jerk and a lot of people are going to think I am because I lost my cool."

"I kind of did that today too. We had to read out loud and I was ready for my turn but Mrs. Simpson skipped me. I was really scared and I didn't want to read my paragraph but I was ready."

"Why did she skip you?"

"Some girls were talking and she made one of them read instead so they would pay attention."

"That makes sense, right?" Giles asked, sounding concerned.

"Yeah. But I was scared and I started to read and I felt like *I* messed up in front of everyone. And then I started to cry."

"That's why I always hated reading out loud," Giles said with a heavy sigh. Then Milo chuckled as his father squeezed and kissed him. "I think teachers make students read out loud so everyone pays attention, not to make us suffer. But the normal people don't seem to enjoy it either and I doubt they notice when we mess up," Giles mused.

"I still feel shaky like I messed up something really bad, though, and like everyone laughed at me. Even though they didn't. And only a few people saw me crying and they didn't say anything or make fun of me," Milo said in his tiny voice.

Giles made a soft shushing sound and began to hum and sing to Milo under his breath. At first, Riley couldn't place the tune. Then he remembered that Giles was a Beatles fan.

Of course, he'd pick "Beautiful Boy."

Wendy had told Riley that Giles would never move out of the Olympia because it was his home and because of its proximity to Strawberry Fields and the Imagine mosaic in Central Park.

Riley wanted so badly to help comfort Milo, but he didn't want to intrude on something so precious for them. There would be a day when Milo wouldn't be able to curl up next to Giles and share his fears. And Giles would miss these moments with all his heart.

They were precious to Riley, too. As a nanny, he'd seen all sorts of families. Some were healthy and happy. But he'd witnessed some of the worst parenting on the planet and lots of parents just doing the minimum. It was rare for Riley to observe a bond like the one Giles and Milo shared, and it was even rarer to see a parent get so much so right in those unguarded moments.

You could say what you wanted about Giles Ashby and it would probably be true. Because Fin was right: Giles Ashby was just rude sometimes. But you couldn't say he didn't love his son and that Milo wasn't the center of Giles's universe. Riley also suspected that Fin was onto something about cranky guys being sexy. He didn't want to dwell on that, though, and went to inform Giles and Milo that dinner was ready.

Chapter Twelve

"You did *fine* and fuck that guy."

Giles repeated Claire's judgment with every stroke as he attempted to put the Fairway episode behind him on the rowing machine. Dr. Vargas said that Giles had the power to cast unimportant altercations overboard and row away from them. Giles could let them get carried off by the current until they were distant and forgotten.

Joe and their fight in Fairway hadn't caused any great waves in Giles's existence, but he felt different. Like Milo, Giles had been shaken for hours. He regretted his words as if he'd struck someone. He hadn't cared about what any bystanders thought of him, but Giles had acted like a pampered asshole. He'd proven Joe right and hadn't given Riley many reasons to believe that the new Giles was all that much better than the old one.

Why did I have to ask about the caviar?

It was alright, but Giles didn't care enough about caviar to make a pretentious ass out of himself in public over it. Claire *loved* caviar and usually stole it off Giles's plate. He just hadn't realized that it cost almost as much per ounce as his pot. *That* he understood how to shop for. And if he had to choose, Giles wouldn't choose the caviar. But he might want some of the little pancakes to snack on after he smoked...

If Giles had a nickel for every *Shark Tank*-style pitch that had been lobbed at him while he was out minding his own business, he'd probably be worth twice as much and have twice as many problems. And it usually happened when Giles was already overwhelmed and frustrated. The unwanted attention and the expectations turned a visit to the doctor's office or a shopping trip into Giles's version of a shark tank and he felt like he was trapped and drowning.

But Riley hadn't gotten mad at Giles. If anything, he seemed annoyed at Joe for disrupting what had been a relatively steady moment for them. Giles was coping with the sensory overload and hadn't put his foot in his mouth. He was almost enjoying their outing because Riley seemed like he was in his element and there would be cake.

Riley had said that he was a good cook and could bake and further explained that he'd learned a lot from past clients and while visiting Fin in France. And Milo had been tickled as Riley recounted all the carrot cakes he'd baked to aid his cousin on her journey to becoming a champion cake eater. Thanks to that story, Milo now had another dream, along with being a renowned astrophysicist.

But none of that prepared Giles for how *good* the cake would be. He'd been impressed by the bakery-quality piping and the little frosting carrots and orange leaves on top. It was just big enough to serve Giles and Milo, but Riley had taken so much care that it seemed a shame to cut it in half and eat it. And somehow, Riley had turned a few humble ingredients into something that tasted like *heaven* with just a bowl, some spoons, the oven, and his warmth. Giles could taste it in every bite and wondered how a cake could taste like a person, but the cake was warm and sweet and comforting like Riley.

"Riley's the best, Dad!"

Milo had stated the obvious around a giant bite of cake, groaning as he chewed. He'd then proceeded to give a long list of reasons why their new nanny was the best nanny in the world. Giles thought they had a strong case and hummed along in agreement as they cleaned up after dinner and went through Milo's bedtime routine.

Everything was fine until Milo fell asleep and Giles found himself alone with his thoughts. They crackled and hummed like an old radio and Joe's *Your mother!* was a high-pitched whine amidst the day's static. Giles called Claire and planned to smoke after he did his time in the sauna, but he had to row away from Joe, first. Giles didn't want to dwell on how he'd acted like a rich asshole in front of Riley while he was smoking.

He'd probably get down about it when the rest of the day had been rather...nice.

Giles had offered to steer the cart because he didn't know how else to be useful and it seemed like a task he could handle. Grocery shopping was a lot like navigating the subway, but with cumbersome little trollies. Although, Fairway was a lot cleaner than the subway. Joe was not wrong about the state of the trains and the stations. New Yorkers deserved better and Giles made a point of telling the city's officials whenever he had their attention.

Mass transit and the world's great terminals and stations were Giles's most ironic passions. The chaos of a busy airport or the subway at rush hour were Giles's idea of Hell. But he was enthralled by the marriage of architecture and technology and the efficient transportation of large groups of people. Giles was lucky enough to have visited many of the world's transportation marvels and had studied Grand Central Station and

JFK extensively, but the mayor and New York's transit authority hadn't welcomed his input. And Giles couldn't fix corruption and institution-wide mismanagement.

There would always be Joes who would never care one way or the other about Giles, and that was fine. He didn't particularly care about the Joes of the world either. They had their own lives and problems and the boring exploits of a clueless millionaire were none of their concern.

There was only one Riley Patrick Fitzgerald, though. And for a moment, they had almost held hands after Giles took the cart. They walked side by side, pushing it together like couples he'd seen on TV and Giles was dazzled. He caught a brief glimpse of what life might be like if Riley was his. Their hands touched and Giles had a reason to be as close to Riley as he wanted.

It was overwhelming being in a grocery store. Giles had entered bodegas and coffee shops a handful of times over the years but had managed to avoid shopping in public for the most part. Even trips to his beloved Bloomingdale's were solitary and streamlined so he didn't have to interact with other shoppers and more than an employee or two. But Giles was willing to endure much worse than Fairway and the Joes of the world for an afternoon with Riley and his carrot cake.

He'd endure a thousand Joes to hear Riley laugh again.

Giles rolled forward and released the rower's handlebars, smiling as he rested his forearms on his knees. He was winded from a hard workout and had even more trouble catching his breath when he recalled how he'd made Riley laugh. And not just a little. Riley had been insensate for several moments and he had Wendy in tears when he recounted Giles's joke about the birds in the freezer. Giles caught Riley giggling about it throughout the evening and it was *almost* enough to make him forget about Joe.

Giles Ashby Needs A Nanny

Riley's laughter was pure joy and had warmed Giles like sunshine. The sound made the hairs on Giles's neck stand. He had the same reaction when Milo was an infant. Milo's deep baby belly chuckles would give Giles goosebumps and make *him* laugh and keep him smiling for the rest of the day.

Being with Riley was like having an angel walking by your side. He wasn't cynical or selfish like most of the people Giles encountered when he left 8B. Riley made everyone smile and feel safer and left a room feeling warmer. What would someone that bright and beautiful see in someone like Giles? Especially after the way he'd behaved at Fairway and the things he said to Joe. Giles wanted to be the man who deserved someone who laughed like Riley, not the guy who lost his cool over a *Your mother!* and put a man down for having a job that required a rake.

Giles noted that while he hadn't learned much about shopping or cooking, he had stumbled upon the code to making Riley smile and laugh. He only had pieces because they'd only spent a few fraught days together, but Giles was starting to pick up Riley's language. And shockingly enough, it appeared to be a simple matter of letting Riley in and being himself. Because Riley seemed to like Giles when he was being his authentic, broken self.

"You did *fine* and fuck that guy." Giles gave the rower a nod, then stood.

He decided he would skip the sauna and spend the twenty minutes under the hot water in the shower instead. The sauna was great for muscle recovery, but Giles didn't enjoy being trapped in a hot, steamy box and was already in a better mood as he pulled on a heavier hoodie and joggers. He went out to his corner of the terrace with a preroll and Giles listened to Riley's laughter as he fell back on the daybed and lit up.

Like Riley, Giles was born and bred a Brooklyn boy, and

the sight of the city and the park would always stir something within his soul. While he might not like the average New Yorker or want to communicate with them on an individual basis, Giles *loved* his city and its people as a whole. He'd stopped visiting Park Slope after his grandmother died, but he occasionally missed the old street he and Riley had grown up on and the sights they'd pass on their way to school.

Now, Giles had a little piece of Park Slope and his childhood back and he'd brought one of the warmest memories from his childhood to 8B by bringing Riley into their lives. Giles might have botched *part* of his outing with Riley, but there would be other chances and he'd found a code he could solve to make Riley smile and laugh whenever he wanted.

Giles pondered that while he smoked and was lighter and happier as the last of the tension melted and his limbs became looser. Joe was behind them and Giles was like a feather; he could have been carried off by the breeze. He meditated on ways to take down the walls and let Riley see the real him, reminding himself that it was alright to be a mess. If anything, Riley seemed to *like* Giles when he was being honest and broken.

In a way, that made perfect sense and Giles wondered why he couldn't have figured that out years ago. Riley was a fixer and a helper and he was compassionate and generous to a fault. He would have defended Giles against the city when they were in middle school and high school if Riley had known. The thought warmed Giles's heart even more as he peeled himself off the daybed and headed for the shower. Joe might have been mocking Riley when he called him Giles's bodyguard. But Giles would have been invincible if he'd had Riley by his side as a child and a teen.

It was too late for Giles to go back and admit to Riley that he'd been scared of the world and needed his help. He couldn't tell Riley how much he really liked him then. But Giles could show him now.

In theory. Giles still had to work up the nerve to talk to Riley, and he hadn't figured out how to keep his foot out of his mouth. But Giles would get there. He had time to solve the code now that Riley would be spending his days with them in 8B.

Chapter Thirteen

Their first full week had gone a lot smoother than expected after Giles's *What is the point of you?* outburst and his naked stroll to the kitchen. Neither felt the need to acknowledge the events of that first Friday afternoon, although Giles continued to find several inane reasons to apologize profusely each day. And he was weirdly attentive while Milo was at school, quietly hovering whenever he was free in case Riley needed a hand or had questions, despite Giles not knowing where anything was in the kitchen or the extensive pantry.

Giles did know his way around the laundry room and how to get a stain out of anything. He and Wendy often argued about the best way to clean, amusing Riley with their bickering and passive-aggressive cleaning battles. It was Giles's habit to vacuum the carpeted rooms after Wendy left, often grumbling that Milo preferred to see the lines in the carpet running in a different direction.

Of course, Wendy knew better. The astute housekeeper also knew that Giles needed a little pushback and good-natured teasing now and then. He tried to blame it on Milo, saying disorder made the little boy nervous, but they shared the same sensitivity. Riley thought it was rather sweet, the way Giles did his best to anticipate the things that might trigger Milo's anxiety.

He'd created a safe haven for them in 8B, yet Riley sensed that Giles didn't want either of them to be stuck in there. Giles admitted his greatest fear was that Milo would inherit his borderline agoraphobia and his disconnect with "outside people." He didn't like to do it, but Giles remained tethered to the outside world for his son. Instead of feeling sorry for the anxious, introverted man Riley was coming to know, he was proud of Giles for all the little ways he faced his own fears and helped Milo navigate life.

He was also impressed with how open and honest Giles was compared to the aloof, brooding snob Riley had always made him out to be. And Riley was learning just how fortunate he was to be included in Giles's morning coffee ritual.

"Can I ask you something?" Riley's head tilted as he studied the pieces of the French press drying on the counter.

"Sure..." Giles sounded a touch wary, though, and there was a hint of a furrow to his brow.

"Why do you have a housekeeper?" Riley laughed as he nodded at the rack by the sink. All traces of the French press and their breakfast would be gone before Wendy arrived and the apartment was already as neat as a pin. "Not that Wendy isn't one of my favorite people in the world," he clarified.

"I'm only good at cleaning the things I *want* to clean. I don't do bathrooms and I don't know how often Wendy does things like the bed linens," Giles explained. "And cleaning the kitchen is part of my morning ritual. I like knowing that I'll be starting with a clean press and fresh coffee beans tomorrow. I only get to drink one cup of coffee a day because of my anxiety so I take my time and make sure it's exactly the way I want it."

"That makes a lot of sense, then," Riley replied, raising his cup in salute.

It went without saying that Giles was very hands-on when Milo was home. He may have "retired" before thirty, but Riley was learning from observing Giles that having a lot of money could be a full-time job in itself. Lawyers, accountants, and various assistants came and went throughout the week and Giles kept an earpiece in so he could babble at them whenever Milo was away.

Business calls and visitors were limited to school hours as much as possible, though, and Giles was hiding in his office less and less throughout the day. Riley enjoyed the company and had learned a lot about Giles in the span of a week. The insight he had gained was both fascinating and clarifying, giving new context to many of Giles's past behaviors.

And many of his peculiarities weren't all that peculiar once Riley began to see the world from Giles's perspective. Like Giles's vacuuming after Wendy. It was a humorous feud, but the act and the white noise calmed Giles after having an extra body zipping around 8B. Wendy was a wonderful woman who loved the Ashbys as much as her own children. Riley could see that Giles loved Wendy and considered her family as well. But the woman had a loud, bubbly personality and the vacuuming helped Giles feel a little more balanced and centered after she left.

Riley often worried about how much his presence unsettled Giles and had called Claire for advice on making the transition as smooth as possible. But she insisted that Riley had taken a huge weight off Giles's shoulders and that he was thrilled with how well things were going. She said that Giles was capable of retreating to his computers or his rower if he needed space and that his regular presence in the kitchen when Riley was there spoke volumes.

There was absolutely nothing peculiar about Giles and Claire's relationship or their divorce either. After several phone calls and texts, Riley understood why the two had married and how they had been able to separate so peacefully. They were no longer married, but Giles and Claire were still family and she would always love and care for him. And it was so easy to see why Giles loved Claire and felt safe with her.

In many ways, Claire was the female version of Giles. She was tall and had dark hair and brown eyes like Giles and had been a math and computer nerd in high school as well. But Claire had blossomed with the success of their company and had made being a lady nerd a hot commodity in a male-dominated industry. Giles had wanted Claire to spread her wings and fly higher, but it hadn't been easy for her to leave her boys behind. She told Riley to call or text her at any hour for anything. Even if it seemed like a small thing because there was no telling how big it might be to Giles and Milo.

Her support was invaluable and Riley appreciated all the little tips and anecdotes Claire sent him throughout the day. He was organizing them into cheat sheets and lists for meals, crafts, safe outings, and gifts.

Claire

Take Giles to Strawberry Fields when the weather's nice and it's quiet. It's his favorite and he turns into a great big golden retriever if you take him for a walk.

. . .

Riley wasn't entirely sure where to put that tidbit or what she was implying. In the end, he added Strawberry Fields to his list of safe places and the Beatles and John Lennon were solid gift ideas.

He considered Giles and Riley regretted his joke about Claire moving to Japan to get away from him. From everything Claire had said, Giles had been a golden retriever of a boyfriend and husband. And Riley could see that Giles was devoted and patient with the people he cared about. He believed he was a mess and a burden, but Giles just operated differently and New York City was a lot on a good day, even for a person without severe anxiety. It was honestly a wonder Giles even left 8B from all Riley had seen.

"You know, it's supposed to be unseasonably warm today," Riley said, glancing at the windows. "I was thinking of taking my tablet and working in the park if it's not too busy. I want to get a head start on next week's menus and plan some fun spring projects. Feel like hanging out in Strawberry Fields?"

"You and me and Strawberry Fields?" Giles asked weakly and cleared his throat. "I mean, are you sure you want company?"

"I'd love some company," Riley said sincerely, then scrunched his nose at Giles. "If you feel like being outside today. We could always come back and hang out on the terrace if there are too many tourists," he added.

Giles nodded and followed Riley as he went to rinse his cup. "I'd like that," he said with a shy smile. "If we go early enough, there's a shawarma and falafel place I like to get takeout from. If it's not slammed. And if you like shawarma and falafel. And if you think you'd be hungry," he said quickly, making Riley laugh.

"You can always assume I'll be hungry and there isn't a lot I *won't* eat." He meant to give Giles's shoulder a playful punch, but patted his chest instead. Giles's eyes dropped to Riley's hand.

"Okay."

Instead of moving his hand to Giles's shoulder or taking it off his chest, Riley stared at it as well. Time felt like it stopped as Riley noted how soft Giles's sweater was and wondered if it was cashmere. He even pondered how much of Giles's fall and winter wardrobe consisted of cashmere separates and if it was simply for the luxury or if it was a sensory preference. Riley appreciated the firm warmth beneath the decadent softness and how incredible Giles smelled. They were so close, Riley could detect a hint of mint on Giles's breath and his scent was a heady blend of bergamot and bay rum. Riley wasn't sure if it was his cologne or some kind of pomade or gel, but he had the urge to bury his face in Giles's hair and sift his fingers through it. He was dying to know if Giles's hair was as soft as it looked.

I'm still touching him...

Giles didn't seem inclined to move either. He was staring at Riley's lips, probably waiting for an explanation, but Riley was stumped and startled by how badly he wanted to press his lips against Giles's. The urge to lean in and rise on his toes was so powerful, Riley was about to give in when they heard Milo practicing his spelling words as he came down the hall.

"We can go after I get back from taking Milo to school and get lunch on the way home, if you're free," Riley said in a quick rush, breaking the spell. He went to retrieve his backpack and the mini waffle maker he'd brought to surprise Milo. "We're having fruit tacos for breakfast!" He announced and Milo cheered as he dropped his backpack by his stool and climbed up.

"Can I make the batter?"

"Yes! You and Dad can work on the waffles while I make the fruit salad and scramble some eggs."

Riley was grateful for the interruption because he had been just seconds away from disaster. Even though Riley could have sworn that Giles wanted to kiss him too. He risked a glance at Giles, who was studying the waffle maker's manual.

Would it have been a disaster?

His instincts told him that it would have been nice, but Riley couldn't trust himself anymore. He'd believed that Taylor and at least two dozen other men had been wildly in love with him and Riley had been way off all those times.

And kissing Giles Ashby? What came next? Probably throwing himself at Giles shamelessly. He'd never imagined coming onto anyone he worked with or worked for and it was all the more inappropriate because Riley wanted to risk it all for *Giles*, of all people…

But the more Riley thought about it as he chopped the ingredients for their fruit salad and quickly scrambled eggs, the more he wanted to lock the doors and see what would happen when they had the place to themselves.

Riley remained tuned in through breakfast and the walk to school with Milo, but a fire had started in the corner of his mind and a little piece of him had begun to burn for Giles Ashby again.

It was a lot like revisiting their old neighborhood as Riley walked back to the Olympia. It was a friend crush at first. Riley had done everything he could to draw Giles out because he wanted so desperately to be friends. But Giles kept to himself, becoming surly and mysterious just as Riley's hormones went into overdrive and overloaded his brain. Back then, Riley had lived in the upstairs hall bathroom of his parents' house because he could see the basketball hoop in Ida Ashby's backyard from there. Giles looked like he belonged in a boyband and took off his T-shirt when the weather was nice.

Giles played on a slab of concrete the size of a postage

stamp, next to a clothesline, but that tiny backyard had been a fertile playground for Riley's imagination. In his head, Riley found a way to win his Mr. Darcy's heart. Some of his daydreams were of the less romantic and more physical variety, but reality had been a little too on the nose when Riley heard Giles call him an urchin. Riley's heart had been bruised and his unrequited crush became a hate crush.

Like most high school crushes, Riley's faded after he went to college and got his heart stomped on by guys who knew he actually existed. The curse started with Riley's first true date his sophomore year. But the crush on Giles would rear its head for a few days a year when Riley spotted him in Park Slope around the holidays only to go dormant until the next sighting.

Now the crush was back and with a vengeance, Riley suspected. And he was truly damned this time because Giles wasn't the miserable snob Riley had imagined. Giles was actually charming in his own cranky way and he was also incredibly hot.

"I should have listened to Fin and got out while I had the chance," Riley scolded himself as he rode the elevator back up to 8B. He was definitely in danger, but the trick was to maintain his professionalism and keep a grip on reality.

Giles made it difficult, though. He got Riley's coat for him when it was time for them to leave for the park. And Giles stared as they walked and talked, hanging on Riley's every word. They found a bench in the sun and enjoyed an hour of peace close to the Imagine mosaic. Riley was able to put together a competent menu and grocery list and planned a cool science-themed scavenger hunt through the park despite Giles wreaking havoc on his nerves.

Not that Giles had done anything out of the ordinary. In fact, he was delightfully relaxed and appeared to be nodding off at one point. Riley looked up from his iPad and Giles's legs were stretched and his ankles were crossed. A soft smile curved his lips and Giles's eyes were shut behind the thick-framed glasses he'd donned as a disguise. He was radiant and impossibly handsome as he basked in the sunlight and the lovestruck teenager within Riley had a little bit of a meltdown, being this close to his childhood crush.

Their peaceful morning was brought to an end when Giles was recognized by a man with an idea for a key-finding app. Giles informed the man that despite appearances he was not, in fact, a patent clerk and that AirTags and several similar devices already existed. But he and Riley still shared a pleasant stroll, following the loop along Terrace Drive, coming out close to the Olympia.

They beat the rush and were able to pick up lunch without any drama. Giles was actually rather charming and had Riley laughing at his banter with the young men behind the counter. They knew his regular order because he often called for takeout and stopped in if he ventured out in the afternoons.

"Everything's good here," Giles told Riley, then stepped closer as if he was going to share a secret. "But the service is hit or miss and you have to listen to these jokers run their mouths," he said.

"You keep coming back, though, Ashby," one of the young men said and winked at Giles. "And you always want *extra sauce*," he added suggestively, but Giles remained totally unaware. He asked about the young man's mother while Riley ordered.

Riley waited until they were outside and headed back to the Olympia to tell Giles. "I think we should come up with a code word so I can tell you when someone's flirting with you."

"No. Don't," Giles said with a quick shake of his head. "And nobody was flirting. I'd never be able to go back to my favorite lunch place if that happened."

"You always want *extra sauce?*"

"But I do..." Giles replied cluelessly. "I like dipping my fries in the tahini and I like the hot sauce on everything."

"*Extra sauce?*" Riley teased again, then waved at the doorman as they turned into the building.

Giles nodded at the doorman and gave Riley a flat look. "Are you sauce-shaming me, Riley?"

Once again, Riley found himself giggling at Giles's dry humor and enjoying another afternoon with his new/old crush. Unfortunately.

Chapter Fourteen

"It's Saturday!" Milo announced as he charged into the room. Giles's eyes snapped open and he grinned as Milo dove onto the bed.

Giles caught Milo and gave his ribs a tickle. The ecstatic giggle made Giles's smile spread even wider. "It's Saturday!" He gave Milo a bear hug, then reached for the remote on the bedside table. "You get to pick."

While Giles had settled into an enjoyable routine on his weekends alone, Saturdays with Milo were sacred. They stayed in their pajamas and watched cartoons in bed and Giles ordered a big, late breakfast. The most pressing thing on their agenda was their *Animal Crossing* responsibilities. Once they'd fished, planted, and shopped on their imaginary island, Giles and Milo vegged in bed or in the living room, watching movies, playing board games, and doing puzzles.

This Saturday was shaping up to be particularly epic. They had completed the latest build for their Lego Super Mario kingdom and watched the extended version of *The Lord of the Rings: The Return of the King*.

"What are you thinking about for dinner?" Giles asked as they admired their Lego masterpiece.

Milo's shoulder bounced. "Wanna get a pie?"

Ah, Nerdvana.

"You read my mind," Giles said, offering his fist for a bump. He glanced at the windows, confirming that the day was still sunny and mild. "Dr. Vargas will give me extra credit for leaving the apartment two days in a row if we go and get it," he said and received another fist bump.

According to Dr. Vargas, it was important for Giles to go outside at least once a week, but to also focus on the quality of his outings whenever he left the Olympia. He was encouraged to stick to "safe" errands in places Giles still felt comfortable. And Dr. Vargas said that no outing was worth long-term trauma and for Giles to minimize his exposure to situations that might be harmful.

Giles knew that he had been asking for trouble when he invited himself to go grocery shopping with Riley. He'd been so intent on showing that he'd changed and was so hungry for more of Riley's time, Giles had forgotten Dr. Vargas's rule about sticking to safe places. But their walk to Strawberry Fields and lunch had felt like a dream and most importantly, Giles had made Riley laugh again.

Perhaps it was sad and a little bit of a cliché, but Giles could still be lured out of 8B for a pizza. It was one of man's greatest achievements and the blessed angels who worked behind the counter and made the pizzas didn't give a damn about who was in the shop. Neither did the other patrons because they were there to grab a slice between meetings or dinner on their way home after a long day. Everyone was there for one noble purpose—pizza—and all that was required of Giles was to pay for his pie and keep it moving. It was the definition of civilization to Giles and one of the customs of being a human that he was still happy to participate in.

Giles was able to make peace with his anxiety when Dr. Vargas explained that the human brain wasn't designed to be a safe, happy retreat. It was designed to protect us from predators and keep us from running off cliffs like lemmings. Giles's brain and endocrine system remained in that hyper-vigilant mode, like a machine with a broken lever. Most people bottled up their anxiety and hid their panic attacks so they wouldn't be perceived as being dramatic or called babies.

Not Giles, unfortunately. His way of defending himself from perceived threats was to lash out and put his foot in his mouth. But he'd learned from his father at a very young age that you could get away with being an arrogant shit if you were rich and blamed it on someone else.

The emotional fallout took a toll on Giles, though. It didn't matter if it wasn't Giles's fault, it took hours for the adrenaline to wear off and the recriminations could last for days. That awful feeling in the pit of his stomach could turn into an ulcer if Giles was actually at fault. Each trip outside his door could be Giles's last because there was no telling when the camel's back would break. What would be the event that sent Giles into permanent exile from the outside world?

That was why Dr. Vargas told Giles to hold onto the safe places and the activities that brought him joy, that were worth venturing out for. For Giles, permanent exile seemed inevitable. He could feel it creeping up on him, but Giles was doing his best to hold it off for as long as he could for Milo. They only had so many years until Milo would be off on his own adventures. Giles wanted to see his son fly to infinity and beyond, and reach his dreams.

For now, they pulled on coats and hats and headed outside to get a pizza.

Giles Ashby Needs A Nanny

Giles was able to make it to the pizza shop and back without being recognized by avoiding eye contact and wearing his nerd glasses. They ate their slices out of the box like barbarians and laughed when their sodas made them burp. There was enough leftover pizza for breakfast or lunch on Sunday and Giles was ruminating about how well his weekend was shaping up as they loaded the dishwasher.

He should have known Milo was waiting to spring a trap.

"Dad, can I ask you a question?"

"Is it a good one? You've only got three left for the day," Giles replied, then gave Milo's ribs a poke. "What's up?"

"Does it mean you like someone if you can't stop staring at them and you smile a lot when they're around?"

Giles cleared his throat and did his best to keep his lips straight. "Why? Do you like someone?" He asked and put his fist out again, but Milo shook his head.

"No. You stare at Riley a lot and sometimes you look like you really want to kiss him."

"No, I don't!" Giles whimpered in horror. His hand clapped over his mouth.

"You do, too! Mom says it's fate because the only way you were ever going to find your perfect person was if they magically appeared in 8B. She was worried you were going to die alone, but we think Riley's perfect."

"*We?*" Giles crossed his arms over his chest and Milo nodded.

"I'm keeping Mom posted. We don't want Riley to slip through your fingers," he informed Giles. The trip to Strawberry Fields no longer seemed so random and Giles realized that he was getting played.

"Let me tell you something," Giles said, putting a hand on Milo's head. He took a moment to cherish the softness of his son's hair and the innocence in his eyes. "There's going to be a trial one day and I want you to remember that your mother was a *traitor*."

Milo blinked up at Giles, then burst into giggles. "Dad!" He protested when Giles scooped him up and tickled him as they headed back to Milo's room. "You should tell Riley you like him!" He squirmed and kicked until Giles set him down in the closet.

"Get your pajamas and hit the shower."

"Why won't you tell Riley?" Milo pressed his hands together. "Just one date!" He pleaded. "You'll see that you were meant to be and Riley can live with us in 8B."

"That's—!" Giles made another nervous sound because the thought made him giddy and his tummy flipped. He had managed to hold it together long enough to pick up shawarma, but an actual date? "There's no way. I would blow it so catastrophically, he'd never come back," Giles predicted.

"We think Riley likes you too."

"I don't know..." Giles squinted at the shelf behind Milo's shoulder. "Being nice to everyone is sort of Riley's thing. And I haven't given him a lot of reasons to like me."

"I can help!" Milo started hopping, but Giles shushed him and aimed him at the bathroom.

"Do not help." He gave Milo a gentle shove and pointed at the shower. "And don't say *anything* to Riley," he added firmly.

Giles waited until Milo was in the shower to text Claire and tell her how wrong she was to have enlisted *his own son* to spy on him and play matchmaker.

Giles Ashby Needs A Nanny

Her response was immediate:

Claire

I swear, I said nothing BUT I wasn't going to tell him he was wrong when he shared his suspicions. And we have concluded that this is too good of an opportunity for you to pass on. How else are you going to meet someone decent who's willing to put up with you?

Giles

I don't want anyone to put up with me.

He put his phone away and went to straighten up in Milo's room and turn down the top bunk.

It was the *anyone* part that Giles had a problem with when it came to dating. A lot of people assumed that Giles wanted to have a lot of sex with a lot of people because he was young, fit, attractive... But Giles had to *know* someone before he could feel any kind of desire. He'd tried hooking up in college, but Giles was too nervous. And he was too conscious of the idea that he was being touched—that his personal space was being violated—by a stranger to enjoy those encounters.

He might not have *known* Riley when they were teens, but Giles had a whole mental database of smiles and laughs and he had years of imaginary conversations to draw upon. He'd fantasized about their first kiss for so long and it had been Riley's body Giles had dreamt of exploring. Perhaps it was because Riley had been so familiar and such a comfortable fixture in Giles's early life, but it seemed safe and natural that he'd be the one.

Why would anyone fantasize about someone who scared them and made them feel like they were about to jump out of their skin? Yet, that's what having a crush on a stranger equated to in Giles's mind. And what was it that compelled a sane person to invite someone they knew absolutely nothing about to call them and take them to an unknown location for sex or romance? *That* part truly baffled Giles.

He was quick to see past a person's good looks because Giles was all too aware of how little that was worth and that a pretty face could mask a lot of ugly. Smiles, though... Giles could fall in love with a smile if it was sincere and if a person seemed to smile with their whole soul. And if they were the kind of person who generously shared their smiles with the world, Giles was a goner.

That was rare to come by, in Giles's limited experience, and nobody smiled like Riley. His smiles seemed to come from deep within, instead of starting on his face. The soft curling of his lips was an easy, natural reaction, like leaves swaying in a soft breeze. There was an occasional wry quirk or a cocky smirk, but Riley's smiles were rarely sarcastic and they were never smarmy. They were comforting, like Riley, and freely given to whoever needed one.

Riley's smiles had captivated and haunted Giles and they had set the bar. There had always been something magical about Riley. Giles didn't like the idea of Riley "putting up with him" or settling when he deserved as much joy as he put out into the world.

"Dad!" Milo raced into the room, freshly bathed and his hair slicked back. "If you and Riley dated he wouldn't have to leave and he could spend the weekends with us. He could move in and that would be so cool!"

"Slow down." Giles gave Milo's ear a flick before lifting him and heaving him onto the top bunk. Milo bounced and giggled as he crawled under the duvet. "We're still figuring out how to be friends."

"But you *like him!*"

"And that makes it even trickier," Giles explained and leaned against the rail, next to Milo's pillow. "It's hard to tell if people like you the same way, sometimes. I really like Riley, but I don't want to make him uncomfortable if he just wants to be regular friends. And we'd be in trouble if he didn't want to be our nanny anymore."

Milo became serious and hummed thoughtfully. "I think we can do this. Riley likes things that other people don't like. Like his snowman sweater. Nobody wanted it but he loves it and he makes a lot of people happy when he wears it," he explained sagely.

Giles hummed in agreement. "I am a lot like an ugly old sweater no one wants."

"No, you're not!" Milo reached over and hugged Giles's neck. "I think he really likes you, Dad. He stares at you a lot too and he looks like he wants to kiss you when you're talking to each other."

There was a rush of hope and Giles felt a little giddy, but he didn't want to encourage Milo or risk disappointing him. "It's complicated because we've known each other a long time and I'm his boss now. Do you want him to quit because I made him uncomfortable?" He raised his brows at Milo, hoping that was enough.

"He wouldn't qui—" He started, but Giles cut him off.

"You don't know that for sure and I'm taking it slow. I don't want to lose him. Do you?"

Milo shook his head quickly. "It's been really good here and you're a lot happier than you used to be."

That stunned Giles. He didn't think Milo had noticed or that it would matter that much to him. "When did you get to be so smart?" He asked, making Milo smile. Giles gave his hair a tussle, then kissed his forehead. "Don't worry about me. I'll always be happy because I've got you."

"I love you, Dad."

"Love you too, pal, and I can't wait to hug you in the morning."

He hummed Milo's song and handed over the remote for the projector, then turned down the lamp. He paused at the door to smile and blow Milo another kiss. But Giles's smile faded as he eased the door shut and went to turn off all the lights.

Giles couldn't imagine how Riley could still be single. He was as beautiful on the inside as he was on the outside. And Riley had so much love to give. He lavished it on everyone, even strangers. But Giles felt a punch of jealousy at the thought of another man sweeping Riley off his feet.

Because someone would. There was no doubt that a smarter and braver man would come along and give Riley the family he obviously craved and deserved if Giles didn't say or do something soon. Most people didn't get a chance to start over or rewrite the past with their first and biggest crush and Giles would never forgive himself if he didn't at least *try* this time.

Maybe Milo had gotten to him, but Giles imagined shooting his shot and what life with Riley would be like if he wasn't a coward. The rush of longing was almost as powerful as the certainty that winning Riley's heart would also be the best thing that he could do for himself *and* as a parent. Which only left one question: was Giles finally going to do something about it?

Chapter Fifteen

It was probably too soon to pat himself on the back, but Riley's second week with the Ashbys had gone even smoother than the first and he was feeling extremely optimistic about the little team he was forming with Giles and Milo.

On Thursday, Giles had called a family meeting to discuss hiring a new cook and asked for Wendy's and Riley's input as both would be working more directly with whomever he hired. But Riley promised that managing their meals was no trouble and saved him time in the evenings after work. And for Riley, feeding the Ashbys was a natural extension of the caregiving he'd been hired to perform.

Both Ashbys were easy to please as neither was a picky eater, and Milo was turning into quite the little chef. Giles was becoming more of a "kitchen person" as well. He liked to hover while Riley was puttering in the pantry and often offered to pitch in with manual jobs like peeling potatoes or carrots.

So, it wasn't a surprise when Giles peeked into the kitchen one afternoon after school to see what they were up to.

Giles Ashby Needs A Nanny

"We're making pies!" Milo informed Giles, hefting the box with the apple peeler onto the counter. "Riley says I'm in charge of the apples," he boasted.

Riley had already prepared the crusts and they were chilling while he worked on the filling for the pot pie and Milo got to cranking with the apples. He had a feeling Milo would enjoy using the peeler and everyone loved apple pie. It was also a fun, easy recipe for a child to follow, making it perfect for practicing basic skills.

"I know what that is." Giles pointed at the peeler. "My grandma Ida had one. She made a lot of pies and I liked to help if I could be in charge of the apple contraption," he told Milo.

Riley fought back a smile as he diced a carrot. "Is that so? Why don't you show Milo how to use it, then? The chicken's cooled off and I'm about to have it all over my hands."

"I can do that," Giles said distractedly, earning a nudge from Milo to get moving. He had been staring at Riley's hands and the knife as he worked. "Right. Apples. Dinner smells nice," he added, flashing a cautious smile at Riley.

That did strange things to Riley's tummy and he was blushing as he went to the stove for the spatchcocked chicken. He quickly removed the breast meat for the pie and picked and packed away the carcass for next week's soups and stocks. Giles and Milo had successfully anchored the peeler to the counter and were working through the bowl of apples. Both were munching on the long peels as they took turns winding the crank.

Milo and Giles were actively engaged and relaxed so it seemed like a good opportunity to bring up Mrs. Simpson and the history report. Riley had spent the last few weeks getting to know Milo's teachers and friends and had won over the principal and the front office. Everyone raved about Milo, but there was one anomaly that concerned Riley.

He cleared his throat as he dried his hands. "So, I was talking to Mrs. Simpson today and I'm a little worried about your history report. She said it's two weeks late. I'm happy to help if you're having a hard time." Riley kept his tone gentle and reassuring, but Milo's face still crumpled and he shrank in shame.

"I don't want to get in trouble but I can't do it," he said in a small, wavering whisper.

"You won't get in trouble!" Riley promised.

"No." The furrow in Giles's brow was a concerning 8. "You won't get in trouble, but why don't you want to do it and why didn't you say anything?"

Riley had been praised for his portrayal of Oliver Twist in their school's production of *Oliver!* But he could never have looked as pathetic as Milo. Not that there was any doubting the little boy's misery. His giant brown eyes puddled and his nose began to run. He tried hiding behind the big mixing bowl, but Giles lowered to a knee and pulled him into a hug.

"What happened? We'll fix it."

"It's really not that big of a deal," Riley reassured them, but Milo shook his head and became more upset.

"I did my report about Clyde W. Tombaugh and how he discovered Pluto in 1930. But, I didn't want to turn it in because Mrs. Simpson said she'd take a letter grade off if my report was about Pluto again. So, I told her my report was about Chernobyl and that I lost it."

"She said she'd take a letter grade off if it was about Pluto?" Giles confirmed, then looked up at Riley. He was furious.

Riley hummed seriously. "That's messed up, right? Let me look into this," he said to Giles and rested his elbows on the counter so he could see around the bowl. "Why did you tell her it was about Chernobyl, buddy?"

"I don't know! I heard a woman talking about a show on

the train once and it just popped into my head. Mrs. Simpson said that was a good topic so I tried to do a new report. But I didn't know how bad it was! A lot of people got hurt and the scientists got sick and died and I keep having bad dreams about it!" Milo threw himself at Giles and cried into his chest.

Giles scooped him up and shushed softly, dancing from side to side like he was holding an infant again. They were the best people Riley had ever laid eyes on. His heart was about to explode and he was on the verge of tears as Giles crooned and comforted Milo. "It's okay. You don't have to do a report on that. We'll get this worked out," Giles promised.

Milo's head popped up and his soggy brown eyes were huge. "Did you know that there are four nuclear reactors in New York?" He asked Giles, then looked at Riley. "Indian Point Energy Center is only forty-three-and-a-half miles away! What if it had an explosion like Chernobyl?"

"No wonder you're having nightmares," Giles whispered into Milo's hair as he cradled his head. "That's not going to happen here. I know lots of smart scientists who know all about clean energy and they'd tell me if there was anything to worry about."

"Really?" Milo leaned back and searched his father's face.

"Really." Giles gave him a firm nod. "I wouldn't let you live close to something like that if it was dangerous." He gave Milo's ribs a tickle.

Riley had to hold onto the counter. He was in deep, deep trouble as Milo giggled and looked at Giles like he was a superhero.

He pulled himself together and focused. "Your dad is absolutely right. I'll have a talk with Mrs. Simpson on Monday. She seems really nice and she likes you a lot. I'm sure this is a misunderstanding."

"I don't see how," Giles said tightly, still holding Milo on one hip like he was a toddler.

"I'll talk to her." Riley held up a hand, gesturing for Giles to hear him out. "There is absolutely nothing to be gained by shaming a child for being passionate about something. I doubt it was her intention to discourage Milo from learning more about a topic that is perfectly safe and appropriate for a child his age."

"I should think not," Giles said, setting Milo down and giving his hair a tender ruffle. "Why don't you go and blow your nose and wash your face? We'll wait until you get back to finish making the pie."

Milo nodded before zipping from the room, no longer concerned about his report or the possibility of a nuclear meltdown.

Riley came around the island and leaned next to Giles. "Don't worry about the report. I'll clear things up with Mrs. Simpson. You're really great with him," he said, giving Giles a gentle nudge.

"It's easy when we're here in 8B," Giles said, then chuckled as he rubbed his brow. "I know what it's like to freeze up and say something awful. I'm always making things worse. Like... Chernobyl. That's why I need someone like you or Claire."

"Hey." Riley turned and squared up to Giles. "You're gonna stop talking about yourself like there's something wrong with you. Got it?"

"Am I?" Giles raised a brow dubiously.

Riley humphed as he crossed his arms over his chest. "There's nothing wrong with being an introvert and an inside kind of guy, Giles. Somewhere along the way, you were made to believe you were weak or broken because of your anxiety and that's not true. Someone should have been looking out for you the way you look out for Milo and they should have told you that the world needs quiet inside people too." He poked Giles's chest to make sure he was getting it, ignoring how firm it was. "That's why you need someone like me."

Giles's gaze dropped to Riley's finger as it pressed against his pec. "I..." He swayed a little closer and licked his lips as if he was going to say something or possibly kiss Riley. And Riley leaned in and his chin tipped back as if he was desperate to hear whatever Giles had to say. Or possibly kiss him back. "Thank you," Giles breathed.

The soft, warm huffs tasted like apples. "You're welcome," Riley whispered, his eyelids lowering.

"I'm back!" Milo announced and screeched to a halt when he saw them.

Riley pushed off Giles's chest and smiled brightly as he whipped around, immediately wiping the moment from his consciousness. "Great! Let's get to making that pie!" He clapped his hands together the way his brain clapped, erasing the moment and refusing to acknowledge that he and Giles had almost kissed.

I imagined that or we were both having a weird moment because why would he ever want to kiss me?

"Where did I put the recipe?" Riley asked Milo and they began hunting among the spices and bowls.

He put them to work, monitoring their progress as they double and triple-checked measurements and studiously stirred. Riley was impressed. Giles remembered far more about baking pies than even he realized and was adorably distressed when Riley coated the counter with flour for rolling. They had a little spat because Giles kept rushing in to wipe it all up before Riley was ready. But the three of them had fun and Giles and Milo both devoured two helpings of pot pie and big bowls of freshly-baked apple pie with vanilla ice cream before Riley left for the evening.

So much had changed in just a few weeks. Riley's whole world felt different as he made his way back to Brooklyn. He took the same route he always took to get home from Midtown, but everything looked a little brighter and made more sense because he had finally found *his* family. Not the way Fin had found the Camerons, obviously. But Reid had found a long term situation that felt like a good fit for Riley and the Ashbys.

Riley had fallen in love with being a nanny because he wanted to help children and families until he was lucky enough to have a family of his own. Now, he had an opportunity to offer more than childcare with the Ashbys. Riley could be Milo's advocate while helping him navigate the city and middle school. And he could be Giles's backup and buffer.

The dreaded trip to the Hayden was just around the corner, but Riley was feeling incredibly optimistic about his new little team. The only hitch he could find so far was the inconvenient return of his crush, but Riley would find a way to ignore his feelings for Giles. He had before.

Chapter Sixteen

Giles hadn't offered a lot of input when they bought 8B and Claire and Julie began decorating. He was clueless when it came to interior design, but he was firmly against carpet in high-traffic areas. Especially areas like the foyer and the hall to his wing because people carried the street in with them on their shoes. He *liked* mopping the tile in the entryway and the hardwood until everything gleamed, spotless and free of any outside germs and grime.

And if there had been a carpet, he would have worn a path in it pacing as he waited for Riley and Milo to return from school with an update about the small meltdown that had occurred in his kitchen. Luckily, Milo had bounced back and had chattered happily all weekend about Jack, the field trip, and Riley.

Much of Giles's non-Milo musings revolved around Riley, but the history report ate up a lot of his hard drive as well. He was upset that he had missed that his son was having nightmares and he hadn't noticed any signs that Milo was under a lot of stress. He'd seemed so normal that Giles felt blindsided.

Or had he been too distracted with Riley to notice that Milo was in distress? Giles had called Julie four times over the weekend and on Monday. She had reassured him that Milo was fine and that Giles hadn't missed anything.

"Kids never want to talk about nightmares, especially if they think they gave them to themselves. And they're good at 'forgetting' about homework or bad grades as soon as they throw their backpacks on the floor."

Julie and Ken had two boys. Jack was Milo's age and Theo was two years younger. Theo—a handful from the moment he could crawl—had already tested his parents in his seven short years so Giles often deferred to Julie and Ken. And both had agreed that Milo would be fine and that Giles could leave the history report in Riley's capable hands.

That didn't stop Giles from asking Riley several questions when he turned up on Monday to walk Milo to school. And Giles dogged Riley's steps after he returned and went about his day, preparing for the week's meals and planning fun indoor activities for them. The weather was supposed to be particularly gross for the next few weeks and Giles was looking forward to the extra company and whatever Riley had devised. *After* he learned the outcome of Riley's meeting with Mrs. Simpson.

The front door opened and Milo burst into the apartment. "Dad!" He called and ran to Giles as soon as he spotted him.

"What happened? How did it go?" He dropped to a knee and caught Milo.

"I can turn in my report tomorrow and Mrs. Simpson says she won't count it late!"

"Really?" Giles looked up at Riley and he was grinning as he hung his layers on the hooks by the door.

"It was all a misunderstanding and she feels terrible. She apologized to Milo and promised that she was joking about having to read *another* report about Pluto and that he can write as many as he wants."

"She was joking?" Giles stood and told Milo to go put his things away and change into his play clothes. He made sure they were alone before shaking his head at Riley. "I don't think she appreciates what he's been through."

"I promise, she does. And Milo says *he* understands and forgives her. Sometimes, people say things they don't mean, *Giles*," Riley said pointedly. "And you never know what weird things are going to get caught in a kid's brain and how they're going to misconstrue them. Kids internalize things in ways we can't always predict and we don't know when something's bothering them until they pipe up and tell us. And it often takes kids a little longer when they're scared. They like to pack those things away and pretend everything's just fine."

A soft laugh slipped from Giles and he relaxed. "That's what Julie said. And I could write a book about all the things a child can internalize and all the ways they can booby trap their own brains..." He rubbed his chin as he mentally flipped through a hundred similar episodes from his childhood.

"That's not a terrible idea," Riley said. Giles snorted at the thought, but Riley swatted his arm. "I mean it. Look at how much you've already helped Milo. He isn't alone and trapped in his head like you were at his age. He has friends and his teachers love him at school and he has Jack. *Why?* Because he's got a dad who understands and cares. You didn't have that!"

"No." Giles chuckled wryly. "I didn't and Milo's in much better shape than I was." He paused, his head pulling back and lips curving into a sincere smile as his eyes touched Riley's. "He's *a lot* happier than I was and he's doing great!"

"That's what I'm saying!" Riley hugged his chest and beamed back at Giles. "Maybe cut the two of you some slack. The last few months have been *a lot* for both of you with Claire moving to Japan and a new nanny to adjust to. All of that can be confusing and really distracting," he added as he tipped toward Giles. He winked playfully, but it caused all the butterflies in Giles's stomach to take flight.

"It has been confusing and very distracting, but I don't mind," he admitted in a dazed mumble. "It gets too quiet around here." He caught a whiff of something sweet and leaned in to see if it was Riley's lips. They glistened and the smell of vanilla hovered in the air between them.

"Everyone assumes that introverts want to be left alone, but I find they just don't like being around a lot of people all at once," Riley replied softly, his nose twitching cautiously as he edged just a bit closer. He reminded Giles of a rabbit and he ached to gather Riley's face in his hands and kiss his pert little nose and taste his full, glossy red lips.

"I don't like a lot of people," Giles confirmed. He wanted to tell Riley that he liked *him* quite a bit, but Giles wasn't feeling that brave yet.

"That's okay. You've got me now and this is exactly how we're going to handle things next week!" Riley gave the front of Giles's sweater an excited tug.

Giles liked it and he liked the way Riley didn't let go. "Next week?" Giles asked, wondering what would happen if he went ahead and brushed his lips against Riley's. They were just a few inches away and Riley looked like he might want Giles to kiss him, as unfathomable as that seemed.

"The field trip next week, silly!"

A big smile stretched across Giles's lips and it spread to his toes and made him feel lighter. "Silly?" No one other than Claire had ever called him silly.

"You and Milo are going to have a great time at the planetarium because you're going to let me handle *everything* else. A little diplomacy goes a long way and if that fails, I'm an expert at the ultra polite 'fuck you,'" Riley explained.

"I think you're right," Giles said, becoming excited as well. The planetarium had become their special place. Giles and Milo could have a blast there as long as they were allowed to enjoy themselves in relative peace.

Riley would protect them in his own valiant way and that's where Giles would show him how the new Giles was better than the old Giles. He was always at his best with Milo. All the loud things in his head grew quiet and Milo became Giles's universe. That's when Giles *felt* like the best version of himself and when he was most comfortable with the rest of the world.

The more he thought about it, the more Giles became convinced that he could turn everything around and finally make things right with Riley at the planetarium. He'd start by repaying Riley for his chivalry, Giles decided.

With a kiss?

He made the mistake of looking at Riley's lips again.

"Ahem!"

They jumped apart and Milo smirked knowingly at them from across the kitchen.

"We were talking about the field trip!" Riley insisted, rushing around Giles. "How about a snack while we work on dinner? We're making lasagna!"

"Lasagna!" Milo did the robot, then moonwalked on the tile floor. "Me and Dad love lasagna! Right, Dad?"

"Yes, we do," he said as he went to help. The prospect of lasagna was almost as enticing as Riley's lips, and Giles promised himself he'd get another chance to kiss him again soon. If the old Giles didn't get in the way of the new Giles and everything went *really* well at the planetarium.

Chapter Seventeen

A trifold board decorated with a hand-illustrated galaxy stood proudly on the dining room table. The various criteria for defining planets and an impressive array of planetary facts were displayed and a small model of the solar system rotated hypnotically as Milo made his very compelling argument in defense of Pluto.

"While it is not big enough to exert its orbital dominance and clear the neighborhood surrounding its orbit, as is required by IAU standards, Pluto meets *all* the other criteria. Like the other planets, Pluto orbits a star, it has sufficient mass to be spherical, and it has an atmosphere. It has mountains and water like Earth. Pluto also has a moon, called Charon." Milo took a deep breath and shuffled his cards.

Giles moved to get up from his chair but Riley raised a hand, stilling him. "Give him a moment," Riley said out of the side of his mouth.

"Yes!" Milo whispered when he found the right card. "The IAU's criteria is extremely narrow and only 2% of its members were present for the vote to demote Pluto. Many experts believe that the criteria should be expanded to include *more* planets, including Pluto, Ceris, Eris, and Makemake. Also, the head of NASA still defines Pluto as a planet, disagreeing with the IAU's categorization of it as a dwarf planet. In conclusion, Pluto should be reinstated as a planet by the IAU and the wider scientific community," he said, then offered them a half-bow.

Giles and Riley jumped to their feet and cheered.

"Nailed it!" Giles declared, pumping his fist as if Milo had kicked a field goal.

Riley nodded as he golf-clapped. "Flawless and informative."

"I almost got lost at the end again, but I numbered the cards at the top the way Riley told me to," Milo said, earning a hum of approval from Giles.

"That was your strongest presentation yet. You'll be able to do this in your sleep by the time the fair gets here," he said. Milo was beaming as he gathered the various pieces of his project and packed them back into his wagon for transport to his room.

Milo gave his big presentation every Thursday evening after school and Riley noticed that Giles had memorized the entire thing. He nodded along and mouthed facts with Milo as he read from his cards. Riley wasn't worried about Milo's performance and there was no doubt the project would be a contender, but it was a tragedy that most people would never witness Giles's A+ parenting.

Giles had deceived himself and the world again. He wasn't nearly as much of a mess as he proclaimed. Riley was beginning to understand why Giles had such a low threshold for the chaos of the outside world. Most of his outbursts were due to his being overwhelmed, and he regretted them almost as soon as they happened. But Riley had also discovered that Giles was incredibly compassionate and thoughtful to those who inhabited his "inside word."

And the person Giles was often angriest with was himself. He assumed most mistakes were his fault. Once, Riley had spilled a bag of rice in the kitchen and Giles appeared out of nowhere with a handheld vacuum, apologizing as he sucked up every loose grain. Instead of scolding him for being rude to others, Riley often urged Giles to be kinder and more patient with himself. And Riley often had to stifle his desire to criticize strangers for their behavior around Giles whenever the three of them were out as a team.

It was ironically eye-opening to see the world from Giles's perspective. While he'd be the last person to ever complain about his lot in life, the combination of wealth, celebrity status, and severe anxiety was a recipe for Howard Hughes-like eccentricity and reclusiveness. Riley was frankly surprised that Giles hadn't barricaded himself in 8B after observing how people treated Giles on a handful of outings with him and Milo.

Reid had said that Giles was the one who needed a nanny and Riley had set out to be his buffer, but protector and defender? Of Giles Ashby? The tables had turned so much, they were spinning into the atmosphere. Joe at the Fairway Market had been just the first of many. Riley had wanted to fight a woman for cornering Giles in the library to pitch her fitness tracker. People tended to assume that an encounter with Giles was an open opportunity to sell their big idea. They wanted a life-changing moment, but they were tormenting Giles and making it harder for him to leave the Olympia.

Riley had come to realize that Giles wasn't all that eccentric after all. He didn't own a yacht or a private jet and those seemed like the first things a rich recluse would insist upon. Giles preferred to take the train or fly coach if he needed to travel. He said that nothing made you stand out like standing out and that he actually enjoyed the train and traveling when he could blend in and go unnoticed. Giles confided that he loved the architecture of stations and airports. And he enjoyed long layovers that allowed him to wander early in the morning or late at night when those often crowded spaces were quiet.

He inspired Riley to pause when he visited JFK and Grand Central Station and take in the design around him. Riley had been moved to tears by the airy geometry and modernism of JFK's Mid-Century architecture. And he wondered how he'd missed the breathtaking beauty of Grand Central Station. He'd only passed through it thousands of times over the course of his life.

Those confessions revealed a gentle, curious soul beneath Giles's cold, cranky exterior. He appreciated a quieter, more beautiful world that most extroverts and rush-hour travelers often missed. And he craved harmony. Giles explained that rowing in his office was an act of meditation and a way of exorcising his frustrations with himself. But rowing on the water was about harmony. Whether he was alone, with one other rower, or a crew. It was about the harmony of rower, boat, and oar as they cut through the water.

Riley imagined that rowing's lack of yelling and tackling was also appealing. And it was an exclusive sport that was too expensive for most teenagers to get into. The signs had always been there, but so many of Giles's introverted tendencies were easily obscured by the inherent elitism of his existence. Riley had simply assumed that Giles got into rowing so he could get into Princeton and because that's what rich kids did, not because he was inspired by the harmony and peace he found on the water.

It was also incredibly telling when Giles explained that he didn't take accelerated math and science classes because he cared about college or proving he was smarter than everyone else. The kids were simply quieter and kinder to each other because they were all nerds like him.

And Riley and Giles had far more in common than he would have guessed. Giles was secretly a very good dancer and Riley had yet to hear him sing out loud, but his soft hums were promising. Giles enjoyed musicals and plays and said he'd brave more of them if he had someone to go with him. Milo and Claire weren't theater fans and Riley felt like he was dying inside, he was so willing to offer himself as a date whenever Giles needed one.

Like Riley, Giles enjoyed the *act* of shopping. Giles wasn't all that interested in fashion labels, but his budget was considerably higher than Riley's and Bloomingdale's was one of his "safe" places. He'd stumbled upon the rich nerd hack of a basic, everyday uniform and often bought the same things. Giles's uniform consisted of a shirt or sweater in a solid, neutral color, black or dark gray flat-front trousers, and black boots or shoes. In Giles's mind, he couldn't go wrong as long as he stuck to those parameters and high-end designers.

Which led to a revelation that shook Riley to his core. Giles *loved* to get stoned and go shopping on his weekends alone. He would get baked as he drank his coffee, then walk or hire a car, depending on the weather. Giles got breakfast along the way and was allowed to browse in peace for an hour before Bloomingdale's opened.

It was the antithesis of Riley's core values as a dedicated thrift shopper, but he had to find a way to tag along just once. He was fascinated and desperate to see what Giles was like when he was high. Julie said Giles was just quieter and more relaxed, but that he would babble your ear off if you called or caught him after he smoked.

But Giles generally limited his pot use to bedtime and his solo trips to Bloomingdale's or the theater. Which frustrated

Riley to no end. How was he supposed to invite himself along for any of that without being incredibly inappropriate? And why did he have to care so much about how Giles spent his evenings and his weekends?

The more he learned, the more confused Riley became about their past and his feelings toward Giles. It was clear that Giles wasn't the jerk that Riley had made him out to be and they were already becoming close friends. But did Riley want more?

Did Giles want more?

Riley glanced at Giles. He was returning their chairs to the table and replacing the vase of roses.

"The roast should be ready to come out," Riley said, pulling his eyes away from Giles's agile hands as they rearranged the roses and checked their water. He had really nice hands and they often caused Riley's mind to wander.

Giles followed Riley into the kitchen and perched on the stool by the pantry. Riley had put it there for Milo. But Giles had gotten into the habit of loitering with a book or his tablet while Milo was at school. They enjoyed each other's company and Riley learned something new and fascinating about Giles every day.

But, good grief, Riley couldn't think straight when they were alone. He'd find himself staring at Giles's hands or his shoulders and then Riley would think about his other parts. It was psychically jarring, going from thinking of Giles Ashby as the most miserable man in Manhattan to wanting him more than air within the space of a few weeks. Yet there Riley was, lusting after Giles and ready to throw his dignity down the chute with the evening's trash.

He'd imagined going down on Giles while they were in the pantry, earlier in the afternoon.

They had 8B to themselves until Milo got out of school

because it was Thursday. Riley was in the pantry pondering their lunch options and asked Giles if he was in the mood for pasta. Giles had leaned in and braced his hand on the shelf to answer just as Riley turned, bringing them chest-to-chest. He was so close and he smelled so good.

Riley grabbed Giles's face and kissed him hard.

In Riley's head. He'd never have the nerve to actually do something like that.

But in the filthy recesses of Riley's mind, he attacked Giles's face like their tongues had been glued together. Then, he slid to his knees and ripped Giles's fly open. Riley swallowed every throbbing inch of Giles's cock, gagging and slurping with glorious abandon. He made Giles sob his name, and then, Riley made him see stars. He came deep in Riley's throat, hissing and swearing in shared ecstasy.

"Are you alright?" Giles asked, giving Riley a shake and waking him from the dirty daydream.

"Yeah. Just a little lightheaded. I shouldn't have skipped breakfast," he said, and Giles blinked back at Riley.

"I saw you slam a banana panini and a cup of yogurt with Milo before school."

"Right. But that was just *one* breakfast," Riley said, wagging a finger.

Giles laughed and rested his shoulder against the jamb. "Whatever you're in the mood for is fine. Or I can order something," he suggested, but Riley gave an offended snort as he pushed Giles out of the pantry.

"That'll take twice as long. I'll be hallucinating by the time it gets here."

He sent Giles away so he could focus on lunch and get a roast in the oven for dinner. The sun had come out, making it too beautiful to eat their pasta indoors so Giles invited Riley to dine on his corner of the rooftop balcony. There was a daybed and a heater and they sat cross-legged with their bowls, sharing the view of the park.

It would have been a perfectly lovely date if the circumstances had been a touch different. Riley couldn't help but count back to see how many meals they had shared since he arrived at 8B. He also couldn't help but notice that if those had been dates, this would have been Riley's longest relationship. And it had been the happiest Riley had ever been with anyone who wasn't Fin.

Which made the matter all the more confusing, as the council at Briarwood Terrace had foreseen. Riley wasn't falling for his employer like Fin had. Instead, he'd dredged up a complicated piece of his past and had to re-examine his own identity to make sense of his feelings for Giles.

Accepting that he had feelings for Giles was just the first step and Riley had no idea what came next.

Chapter Eighteen

Field Trip Eve had finally arrived, but instead of feeling anxious and eaten up with dread, Giles was at ease and enjoying the view of the city and the park at sunset. He leaned against a window in his office with a scotch, reflecting on how *distressed* he had been just a month earlier. He'd stumbled from one fraught social encounter to the next and the field trip felt like a cataclysmic social meltdown in the making. Giles was certain he'd embarrass Milo in his Sistine Chapel in front of all of his peers, scarring his son for life.

Thanks to Riley, Giles was beginning to believe that he wasn't a mess or all that broken. Or that it was okay to be a little broken and that Giles deserved the same patience and understanding he showed Milo. He also had more faith in himself and the three of them as a team.

The thought brought a smile to Giles's lips as he sipped. Riley was the one who had turned them into a team and Giles felt stronger when they were together. There were times when Giles stepped up without a shield or a crutch, and then there were times when Giles leaned on Riley for support. He also let

Riley take the lead when neighbors, teachers, and other parents were involved, and the results spoke for themselves.

People smiled at Giles now when he came and went at the Olympia and they didn't crowd him in the lobbies and on the elevator. Riley intercepted nosey parents and strangers when they were at the park or out walking with Milo. Giles's life was so much fuller in ways that weren't overwhelming for him.

But would Giles be asking for too much, when Riley was already giving them most of his waking hours? He had a feeling that Riley took his work home with him and that his workday started well before he turned up at the Olympia to walk Milo to school. Had Giles proven that he had changed enough to be worthy of Riley's heart? Had he shown that he deserved even more of Riley's time and patience?

Thoughts of Riley led to a strong desire to see what he and Milo were up to. Giles was being more cautious and giving them more time together because he couldn't help but stare at Riley's lips or stand a little too close. Milo was on to him and it was only a matter of time before he gave Giles away.

He came around the hall and Giles's brows jumped at the sound of bouncy pop music in the living room. It wasn't unusual to find Riley and Milo engaging in light aerobics with a dance or guitar game or simulated sports. Whatever Riley had chosen, it was sure to be entertaining and Giles was not let down when he found them giggling and shimmying in front of the TV.

"What's going on in here?" Giles asked, fighting to keep from smiling.

Riley waved over his shoulder, acknowledging Giles. "Couldn't go to the park because of the rain so we're learning a new dance," he said but was focused on the screen. So was Milo. Both were flushed with pink cheeks and wild hair. Riley had stripped off his cardigan, and his vintage Dr. Pepper T-shirt clung to his lean frame as he shook out his arms and got ready. The music started and their hips swayed slowly from side to side as Meghan Trainor sang about Gucci and Louis Vuitton.

"Now the gloves!" Riley said as they mimicked the dancers in the video and pretended to pull on long gloves.

It was just a portion of a song and the adorably sassy routine ended too quickly, but to Giles's delight, they quickly got into position before it started over. Milo's movements were jerkier and off-beat, but Giles certainly had to look as Riley hopped and swung his hips with the music. He had always been a good dancer and one of the stars of their high school's theater program, but Giles was captivated by Riley's...other talents.

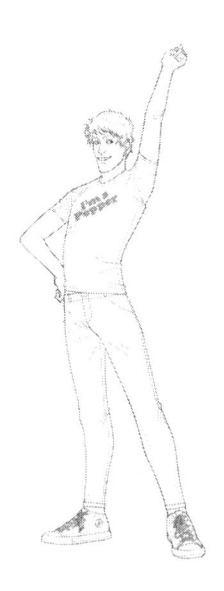

Riley's fist shot in the air as he wiggled his backside and it was almost obscene, the way his corduroys hugged his ass and made it look perfectly round and firm. God help Giles because he imagined that ass without any clothes and a weak groan slipped from him as he tugged at his collar.

"Don't listen to him. We've just about got it," Riley told Milo, then gasped and pointed the remote at the TV. "It's almost six! The pot pie's just about done and I've gotta get going!" He said, tossing the remote to Milo.

"Do you *have to*?" He asked, pouting as he crossed his arms over his chest.

"Yup. I'm teaching swimming lessons across town in an hour." Riley hurried from the room, disappearing around the wall.

There was a resigned sigh from Milo as he turned his attention to the menu on the TV. Giles's gaze slid to the cardigan draped over the back of the sectional. He took two steps to the left and checked to make sure Milo wasn't looking, then swiped the cardigan. Giles lifted it to his face and took a quick sniff, filling his sinuses with Riley's soft, clean scent.

A snorting giggle from Milo made Giles jump and he promptly replaced the cardigan. "I thought I smelled something strange, but this wasn't it. This smells fine," Giles declared, then ducked as if he was hunting for the mystery odor. "I swear I smelled something burning," he murmured.

"I saw what you were doing!" Milo whispered.

"Shhhh! You did not!" Giles whispered back and shot Milo a pleading look.

His son's eyes narrowed, wordlessly scolding Giles. "Tell him!" He mouthed.

"No." Giles pointed firmly when Riley returned.

"Give that about ten minutes to cool before you dig in. There's a mini carrot cake in there for dessert," Riley said to Giles as he put on his cardigan.

"You made another carrot cake?" Giles asked, not hiding his excitement.

"It's your favorite. And I had some extra time to kill until Milo got home because you had all those calls." Riley shrugged nonchalantly on his way to the door. He stopped to get his backpack off the hook and spun back to Milo. "Make sure you show your dad the outline for your next report! You crushed it and it's going to knock Mrs. Simpson's socks off," he predicted.

Milo nodded and smiled brightly, no longer pouting over Riley's departure and having a coward for a father. "I will. Can we have peanut butter and banana paninis for breakfast?"

"And blueberries," Riley announced. "Don't get into any trouble without me," he said with a jaunty wave of his mitten, then left them.

"I can't wait to see your outline," Giles said and hoped Milo would let him off the hook. He didn't.

"I think you should tell him!"

Giles flinched and recoiled. "I'm not sure yet. And I think Riley just puts up with me so he can hang out with you," he said as he escaped into the kitchen.

"That's not true! Mrs. Marcy from 2B said you were rude, but Riley told her you're secretly a softie and that you just don't like talking to people because you get nervous and you can be kind of awkward."

"Great." Giles planted his hands on his hips, not sure what to make of *that* or the masterpiece resting on the stove.

He didn't grow up eating pot pies, but Riley's had become one of his favorite dishes. Flaky, buttery crust snowflakes topped the pie, its heady aroma filling the kitchen. And a lovely little carrot cake on a mini cake stand stood proudly on the island. Once again, Giles's mind boggled that anyone would put so much care into something that small and just for them. Riley had even decorated the top with frosting snowflakes.

"You should tell him that he makes you swoon."

"What?" Giles's face pinched. "I do not swoon, and how do you even know what that means?"

"It's one of our February spelling words. You looked like you were swooning when we were dancing and when you were smelling his cardigan."

Giles groaned as he rubbed his temple. "I think the word you want is 'pining' and I'm not sure yet." He was getting a headache and his neck and shoulders were tightening. "Why don't you show me this outline? Or tell me about whatever you and Jack have going on this weekend. I'm sure you two are up to no good," he added with a smirk, knowing the worst those two junk food fiends would ever do is give themselves cavities. Neither Milo nor his cousin had a taste for rule-breaking, but they often conspired to pull off legendary snack heists.

The immediate brightening of Milo's eyes told Giles he'd steered them back to safer waters. "Riley gave me two bags of Takis! And he says he's going to make us some peanut butter cookies tomorrow!"

"Sounds like you'll have quite a haul."

Giles kept Milo talking about this weekend's inventory as he filled two bowls with pot pie and took them to the island. They also talked about the comic books he was taking to Jack's and Milo's book report. Dinner was delicious and they devoured the cake like animals.

Giles thought he was in the clear as he cleaned up their dishes and looked over the outline while Milo took his bath and got ready for bed. But Milo wasn't ready to let the matter rest as Giles tucked him in.

"You should ask Riley to be your Valentine. I asked if anyone had asked him out yet and Riley said he doesn't do Valentine's Day because he's cursed."

"I'm sure he's kidding and he doesn't want me to ask him,"

Giles said dismissively, then shushed Milo when he tried to argue.

"But what if he does!" Milo challenged. "What if you and Riley went on a date and then you got married? Could we have another baby?"

"Would you—?" Giles's voice broke and his throat tightened at the thought. The first few years of Milo's life were Giles's happiest. He missed carrying Milo around with him and knowing exactly where he was and that he was safe and warm. "You want a brother or a sister?"

A dreamy smile spread across Milo's face. "I wouldn't mind having a little brother like Jack, but I think it would be cool to have a sister. Theo's always in Jack's stuff and we don't have a lot of girls around here."

"That would be...amazing, but we need to slow down, alright? This is kind of like Pluto." Giles pulled Milo's face closer and kissed his forehead. "I have to come up with a plan and take it one step at a time."

"What's the first step?"

"I have to show Riley that I've changed. I wasn't this cool when we were kids," Giles said and bumped his forehead against Milo's, making him laugh. "But you can't say anything. Let's give Riley a little more time to get used to us and give me some time to figure out how dating works. I didn't have to figure any of that out with your mom. She took care of everything and made it easy for me."

"I can help!" Milo said before smothering a loud yawn. "And Riley would help too. He always wants to make things easy for us."

"You're probably right and I'll think about it," Giles said, bringing the conversation to an end. "It's your turn to read tonight," he reminded Milo and folded his arms on the bunk bed's rail so he could listen until Milo began to nod off.

Giles Ashby Needs A Nanny

But a different story was taking shape in the back of Giles's mind. He imagined rewriting the past at the planetarium and finally winning Riley's heart. They held hands as they walked in the park and picnicked in Strawberry Fields. There was a small wedding and Giles's heart felt like it could burst at the thought of his and Riley's child.

It all seemed like too much and bordering on impossible, but if everything went really well at the planetarium, Giles just might have a chance.

Chapter Nineteen

So far, things were going really, really well at the planetarium.

Riley had spent the week gently stalking Neil deGrasse Tyson's social media accounts and learned that the planetarium's celebrity director was attending a conference in London. Riley also rehearsed lines with Giles, in the event that someone did get past him.

But so far, Giles and Milo looked like they were having a great time. They sat together on the bus, huddled shoulder-to-shoulder over the itinerary while Riley chatted up the teachers and other parents. One of the moms flirted shamelessly with Giles as they were waiting to board, but Riley neutralized her by loudly admiring her wedding ring. He gasped and gushed as he held her hand up for everyone to see.

"Somebody really loves you!" He proclaimed, then slid her his most withering look. She practically evaporated from shame and was now hiding among the other moms.

Riley was absurdly proud of his three-man team as he walked a few paces behind Giles and Milo, charmed by their super nerd space banter and obliviousness. The other teachers and parents had gotten the message and were allowing them to enjoy the guided tour in peace.

It did require more intervention on Riley's part than he had been expecting, considering it was a field trip. Being a famous technology and media mogul, Giles was received by the other parents and planetarium visitors with a combination of awe, envy, and disdain, but Riley was able to intercept all their questions and comments. Eventually, Giles's presence was accepted and set aside and everyone was able to enjoy an extremely typical fourth-grade field trip.

So typical that Riley was reflecting on how little had changed in the two short decades since his first field trip to the Hayden. He glanced at Giles as they approached the Sphere and was going to ask if he remembered "the incident" when Riley spotted another incoming parent torpedo.

This time, it was a dad, and he was wearing cargo khakis, an AC/DC T-shirt, and a flannel. He barreled right up the ramp, squeezing against the rail in his haste to get to Giles. Riley slipped between Giles and Milo and offered the man an easy smile.

"You're heading in the wrong direction! The entrance is that way!" He said, cocking his chin at the line headed inside the Sphere for the next presentation.

"Just need to get past so I can talk to someone," the other man said, dismissing Riley.

"Oh?" Riley turned and looked at the stream of people behind them. "Did you get separated from your student?"

"No." The man frowned down at Riley as if he was being a nuisance. Which was the intent. He attempted to step around Riley again, but he weaved with him. "I just want to have a word with Giles Ashby," he ground out.

"Who?" Riley turned again and looked around Giles and Milo.

"Ashby. He's right—"

"Where?" Riley leaned, then rose on his toes and tried to see over Giles's head.

"That's him right—"

"Nope... I don't see him."

"What the fu—?" The man started and stopped when Giles's finger shot out in warning. Riley snatched that severely pointed digit and shushed Giles before swinging back around to address their foul-mouthed friend.

"I don't see the man you're looking for," Riley explained slowly and hitched his thumb over his shoulder at Giles. "That guy is just here to enjoy a field trip with his son like *everyone else*. In fact, it would be wildly inappropriate for a perfect stranger to butt in with a business pitch or a personal matter," he added, raising his brows and hoping the man got the hint.

He didn't. He shook his head and tried to squeeze past Riley again. "We met at a conference once and he said my webtoon app sounded promising." His voice had risen so Giles and everyone within a ten-yard radius could hear.

Riley got a little nervous when he saw Giles's fists clench and his nostrils flare. The other guy had it coming to him, honestly, but Riley knew Giles would be mortified and would blame himself for ruining the morning.

"I'm telling you, you're mistaken," Riley stated, keeping his tone even and enunciating clearly.

"Look." Mr. Oblivious straightened so he could loom over Riley. "I know that's Ashby and he *never* leaves the Olympia. I might not get another chance," he growled under his breath.

Riley's face pinched as if he'd smelled something equally as unpleasant as the naked desperation they were witnessing. "Pretty sure that proves it, then," he said with a wide gotcha!

smile. "Because *that man* has clearly left the Olympia and is minding his own business." A little girl peeked from around the man's legs, looking confused and concerned. Riley gasped loudly as he lowered and planted his hands on his knees so he could address her. "Hi there, princess! Is this *your daddy*?" He asked and she nodded quickly and looked up at her father. *That* finally got through to him and he turned a deep shade of red.

"Let's go," he muttered and took her hand.

They went back the way they came and Riley mentally wiped the sweat from his brow. "That man might be the densest thing in this museum," he said to himself, then found Giles smiling at him. "What?"

"How do you stay so cool and how do you always know exactly what to say?"

Riley laughed and shook his head as they made their way down the gentle ramp and headed under the Sphere. "Only half the time. The rest of the time, I lock up too and wish I'd said something better or what I was really thinking," he murmured, looking up and once again feeling like a speck, dazzled by the enormity of the universe.

"Wait a minute," Giles said. He caught Riley's elbow, halting him. Giles slid out of his coat and laid it on the floor in front of Riley's feet.

"What are you doing?" Riley laughed and looked around, bewildered and a little nervous as people began to crane their necks and lean in for a better look. "There isn't even a puddle."

Giles shrugged as if he wasn't blushing and a sheen of sweat hadn't glazed his brow. "You probably can't tell but a little girl cried here once. A very mean boy pushed another boy into her and he's waited a very long time to say he's sorry." He offered his arm and they were both shaking as Riley took it.

Milo was watching them raptly. He gave Giles's other

sleeve a tug. "A mean boy pushed Riley here once!" He said and Giles sighed heavily, his eyes clinging to Riley's.

"I remember and it was inexcusable," he said, his voice low and tender.

"Oh!" It was just a squeak and Riley had to grab hold of the rail. He felt dizzy and like the floor had dropped beneath his feet. "It was a long time ago and I've forgiven him."

"That's very kind of you."

"Sometimes people have bad days and say things they don't mean," Riley replied with a shaky laugh. He hoped he looked and sounded a lot cooler than he felt. On the inside, Riley was screaming, crying, kind of wanting to throw up... "Let's go. We're holding up the line."

Milo took Giles's other hand and was skipping as he led them into the Sphere. Absolutely nothing out of the ordinary occurred during the presentation. But Riley was aware of every outside inch of the left side of his body as he sat next to Giles in the dark. Every innocent bump and brush made him just a few degrees hotter. And Riley was sure Giles's knuckle traced his thigh on purpose at least twice.

What did that mean?

The question became a chorus that rang in Riley's head as they filed out of the planetarium and meandered around the rest of the museum. He nodded and intercepted questions like he wasn't cracking apart on the inside, but Riley *needed* to talk to Fin. And possibly scream. His lungs felt like they were going to explode by the time they returned to the school. Yet he managed to act like a competent nanny as he walked back to the Olympia with Giles and Milo, despite the heated, lingering glances.

Riley excused himself to run a quick errand, parting with Giles and Milo at the 72nd Street entrance. He had his phone out as soon as he was safely out of range.

Giles Ashby Needs A Nanny

"Please don't be busy!" Riley begged. He melted in relief when Fin answered.

"How was the field trip?" He asked urgently, making Riley smile. Only the very best of best friends would understand the stakes, as a nerd scorned and as a nanny.

"It couldn't have gone better!" Riley pressed his mittened hand against his chest, momentarily forgetting his existential crisis. "They were so cute, Fin, and they had *the best day*!"

"Thank goodness!"

"It was perfect and Giles didn't panic or blow up once!"

"That's great. He really has come a long way since he called you a clumsy jerk."

"A clumsy *little* jerk," Riley corrected. But a huge smile spread across his face and a giggle tickled his throat at the thought. He no longer felt the heavy bitterness, or ashamed for being too meek to stand up to Giles the Jerk.

Both of those little boys had grown up, apparently.

"He apologized and I forgave him."

Fin audibly swooned. "You're right. It sounds like the day couldn't have gone better."

"What if we almost kissed under the Sphere?"

Chapter Twenty

"How did it go?" Claire wasted no time greeting Giles after she answered the phone.

"Perfect!" Giles whispered and laughed softly as he shut his son's door. Milo had crashed right after the field trip for a nap, woke up for soup and a bath, then crawled up to his bunk with *The Hitchhiker's Guide to the Galaxy*. He hadn't lasted more than a few paragraphs.

The day had used up Milo's little social batteries and Giles needed to decompress and recharge over the weekend as well. Giles was feeling depleted from being around so many people and being civil, but the day had been a dream compared to previous experiences.

"And I take it there was no pushing this time and no one cried," she prodded, earning another laugh from Giles as he headed for his corner of the apartment. He decided he'd light a candle and smoke in the tub. He'd earned a little extra decadence with his evening's self-care ritual.

"No pushing or crying," he said, even though Riley looked like he'd been close to tears for a moment. "I apologized and he forgave me." He hadn't meant to sigh like a teenager as he lowered onto the sofa and opened the box with his smoking accoutrements.

"And then...?" She sounded impatient.

"We sat next to each other in the dark and I wondered what it would be like if I had the nerve to hold his hand."

"Giles." She let out a deeply frustrated groan. "Julie says the chemistry and attraction are *palpable*. She said that Riley looks at you like he wants to climb you and you really should let him."

"I... Palpable? You didn't tell her about the first trip to the planetarium or that he saw me naked, did you?"

She laughed maniacally. "Not yet because I know she'll take matters into her own hands, but she's so on to you two. Why didn't you ask him out?"

Giles frowned at the little plastic bottles of weed and selected a strong indica, then tapped a large bud onto his palm. "Baby steps. It took me twenty years to apologize." He broke up the bud and pressed the chunks into his grinder, checking for any large bits of stem before replacing the top and giving it several twists. "I felt like I was a kid again. I was so nervous sitting that close to him, and I kept staring at his face. It was so close and I wanted to kiss his cheek. Like, with my whole being, but I was also sweating and my hands were shaking so badly."

He'd dared himself to just touch the side of Riley's leg. Giles had ever so gently brushed his knuckle against Riley's thigh and nearly burst into nervous laughter. *Again. Again. Again.* He'd urged himself on in the dark, his mind clamoring like he was about to do something illicit.

And then there were the loud doubts. What if Riley wasn't into Giles like that? What if the tender, intimate moments they had shared were simply Riley being Riley? He was warm and affectionate with everyone, especially his friends. And it was his tenderness that made him such an exceptional caregiver.

Everyone received Riley's undivided attention when he was talking to them and he didn't shy away from fist bumps, hugs, and playful nudges. He had a way of sensing how much contact the other person was comfortable with and was happy to oblige if they needed more compassion and affection. What if Giles was reading too much into Riley's kindness and was hoping for something that wasn't there?

"At least you apologized and can finally let go of any guilt you've been carrying around about that," Claire said encouragingly. "If I know you, it's been eating you alive for years."

Giles snorted. "Only every sleepless night." He pinched a generous amount of the ground flower onto a sheet of rolling paper and smoothly curled it into a thick joint.

"What's your next move? You've shown him you've changed and you fixed the past."

"Hmmm..." Giles considered the joint. "My head's still too loud and my heart hasn't stopped pounding. We didn't talk about it—or anything—after we got home. He seemed really surprised and like he needed some time to think too."

"Fair enough," she said. "Good job with the field trip. Milo said he had fun with you today and I know how worried you were. I think you're amazing and the best dad ever."

"Thanks. I really miss you, but I feel like I've got a handle on this and I'm *happy* with where we are now."

"Me too. I love it here and I have zero regrets, but I don't think I can live this far from my guys and my sister for more than a year or two. I miss you all and I miss my city."

"You needed to do this and we're all going to be fine. And you'll be tripping over offers when you're ready to come back," he predicted, then sat up straight as *the best* idea hit him. "What if you got your own place in the Olympia? The co-op loves you and everyone misses you. They tell me every time I leave 8B and I think some of them still blame me."

She laughed, then groaned sympathetically. "I'm sure they don't, but I love this plan. Go unwind and we'll start scheming tomorrow."

"Can't wait. Have a good day over there."

"Will do and I love you."

"Love you too."

He hung up and tucked the joint behind his ear, locking the door on his way to the bathroom. Giles lit a candle, started the water, and turned down the lights. His thoughts revolved around Riley as he undressed. Giles imagined touching Riley's hand in the dark and feeling it in his, their fingers intertwined and their palms pressed together. The nakedness of it enthralled and terrified Giles. What could be more vulnerable or honest? More intimate? Riley would know everything if Giles had taken his hand. It could mean nothing else but love because why else would Giles long to feel Riley's hand in his? There could be no innocent explanation for something so tender and intimate *there,* in a room full of unaware stargazers.

Giles's thoughts were a lot less innocent, but no less tender as he lowered into the tub and reclined. Steam and smoke billowed around him as Giles puffed on the joint and let his hands wander. He closed his eyes and trailed his fingers along the inside of Riley's wrist and up his arm. Giles had stared at Riley's nimble fingers and that pale strip of skin countless times as he loitered in the kitchen. He'd dreamt of catching Riley's wrist and tracing the fine blue veins with his tongue and licking all the way up his arm.

Smoke plumed from his nostrils on a groan as Giles's hand slid down his body and around his already heavy erection. He ached to peel Riley's tight T-shirt off his lean body and taste and touch everything. His cock throbbed as he whisked away

Riley's corduroys and nibbled on the insides of his knees and thighs, making him squirm and giggle. Giles had no idea if Riley was ticklish, but in his fantasies, they laughed as they kissed and teased each other.

He pictured Riley's gentle smiles and heard his soft, amused hums as Giles reached lower and strummed his own hole. Need swelled as Giles feasted on Riley's ass, exploring with greedy fingers and his lips. Every sweep of his tongue tasted sweeter and Riley's cries grew louder as he begged Giles for more and to never stop. In the tub, Giles's fingers pushed into his ass and they became Riley's fingers and his tongue.

"Fuck!" Giles took a quick pull from the joint before letting it drop into the water with a faint hiss. His head fell back and Giles angled his hips so he could reach deeper and find his prostate. He stroked his shaft with his other hand as Riley rode him. He could see Riley smiling, his hand braced on the center of Giles's chest, over his heart. They fused, becoming one hot, writhing entity and pleasure exploded in Giles's core, rolling down his limbs and up his spine. A swirl of cum floated among the soft waves between Giles's thighs before dissolving.

He felt like he was dissolving as well and would slide down the drain if he used his toe to pull the plug. Giles was boneless, utterly spent, and relieved on a cellular level. Every nerve and every voice had gone still and silent. He was alone with the steam and at complete peace as Giles shut his eyes and lost himself in memories of Riley and his sweet, soft smiles.

Chapter Twenty-One

Despite its towering presence on the corner of 72nd and Central Park West, the Olympia only had nine floors. Its impressive height was due to the building's extravagant fourteen-foot ceilings and dramatic gables. The Gilded Age castle was far less intimidating now, but Riley gulped as he looked up at 8B's windows Monday morning.

He had gone to Reid's on Saturday and Fin had been there. So was Penn and a new guy named Cyrus. Riley decided that Cyrus could be trusted since Reid trusted him with children. He told the assembled nannies and Gavin about what had occurred at the planetarium. They all conceded that while the episode had been a success for the Ashbys, it presented Riley with a conundrum.

What did it all mean—Giles's remark about never forgetting Riley and the apology under the Sphere? Was it a romantic gesture or was Giles simply asking for forgiveness? He had been more open and attentive, but what if Riley was wrong and Giles just wanted to be friends? Giles was always saying things he didn't necessarily mean.

And then there was the curse. Riley had a history of gaslighting himself into believing a man was in love with him when there wasn't anything there. Wanting to make amends with the person working in your home was perfectly understandable and made a little more sense the more Riley thought about it.

The gesture with the coat on the floor and those "almost" kisses, though...

Almost wasn't the same as actually kissing and they had ample opportunities before Riley left Friday evening. Milo had turned on *Cosmos: A Space Odyssey* and passed out in the living room shortly after they returned, leaving Riley and Giles with an awkward hour-and-a-half to burn. They stared at each other over cups of decaf tea in the kitchen, neither wanting to comment on anything other than how well the day had gone. Giles did thank Riley several times for ensuring that everything went smoothly. He was profoundly relieved, but that hadn't resulted in a kiss either.

Milo woke up right as Riley was ladling their broccoli soup into serving bowls. The three of them discussed plans for their own trip to the planetarium and Milo's upcoming presentation at the school science fair before Riley left them for the weekend.

Not that Riley had truly left them. His thoughts never strayed far from the Olympia. He wondered what Giles and Milo were up to when Saturday was cold, wet, and dreary, or if they got to enjoy the sun when it peeked through the gloom for a few hours Sunday afternoon. The apartment was still lonely without Fin, but now Riley had someplace else he longed to be.

He realized that the stakes were so much higher. Giles would never be like the many men who had broken Riley's heart time and time again.

Riley had fooled himself into believing they were all Prince

Charming, but deep down, he knew none of them were "the one." Something in his gut told Riley that Giles might be the one, but...

Why him?

What would a man like Giles Ashby see in someone like Riley?

Riley had moments when he could suspend reality and imagine that Giles and Milo were his. They were all he could ever want and the thought of taking care of them for the rest of his life made Riley so ridiculously happy, he wanted to dance and sing. Then, he would remember how he'd fooled himself before; how much it had hurt when it was just an asshole Riley had only gone on a few dates with.

He could only stall for so long, though. Eventually, Riley had to face the great dilemma awaiting him. And Milo had to go to school. They had an hour until they needed to be on their way so Riley mustered his courage and hurried across the street.

"You, there! Wait for me!" A woman ordered as Riley exchanged a quick hello with the doorman.

Riley held his ground, not wanting to embarrass the Ashbys, but any courage he'd found before fizzled right up. The only thing that had stopped him from running was a lifetime of good manners as the last person any sane New Yorker wanted to encounter barreled toward him. At a quarter to seven, no less.

"God help me," he whispered.

It was Muriel Hormsby and her apricot poodle, Calista. The older woman was bundled in a fur coat and turban. Calista was also garbed in a matching fur coat. Fin had warned Riley that the eccentric harridan lived at the Olympia, but he assumed she only left the building for soirées or to accost billionaires in Central Park. He never thought he'd cross paths with her this early or after something as banal as Calista's morning constitutional.

He begged fate to let them part ways at the courtyard but Muriel and Calista followed him across the breezeway.

"Morning, Carl!" Riley attempted casually when the doorman greeted them.

"Morning, Riley! Mrs. Hormsby," Carl tugged on the brim of his hat, then walked with them. "They say we're getting a doozy of a storm this weekend! Hope you got someone to stay cozy with!" He laughed and elbowed Riley.

"Nope! But I've got lots of tea and reading to catch up on!" Riley informed him.

Muriel snorted at them and gestured for Carl to run ahead and get the button for the elevator. "Who are you?" She asked Riley, pushing her glasses up her nose and leaning in for a closer look.

"That's Riley!" Carl said and gave Riley's back an affectionate slap. "8B's new nanny!"

"You're Ashby's new nanny?" Muriel's eyes narrowed suspiciously at Riley.

There was a ding as the elevator doors opened, but Riley wished for *any* excuse to catch the next one. He wasn't Catholic but Riley crossed himself as he stepped inside.

"Have a nice day!" Carl waved and backed away, giving Riley an apologetic cringe and a thumbs-up.

"Get on with it," Muriel barked. "Push six and eight."

Riley nodded and pressed the buttons, causing the doors to close and the elevator to shrink as time ground to a halt.

"Who are you?" She demanded again, aiming her cane at Riley.

He blinked back at Muriel, wishing he still had Carl for backup. "I... I'm the Ashbys' nanny."

"Huh!" She squinted and her lips puckered with disapproval as she scanned him from head to toe. "Another one of Reid Marshall's, I'll bet."

That fixed Riley's backbone. It snapped straight and his chin tilted back. "I might be. What of it?"

"Just pay attention to where you are, *boy*." The end of the cane pressed against Riley's sternum, backing him into the corner of the elevator. "I was as surprised as everyone else when Ashby went with *that* agency. Everyone assumed he was as straight as that stick he keeps up his ass, but he's not desperate. A man like that can have damn near anyone he wants and this is the Olympia. He won't settle for some common...twink just because you've got a tight ass and a pretty face."

"What?" Riley asked in alarm and shook his head quickly. "Reid isn't running that kind of agency and I know Giles! We grew up—"

"Save it. You're nobody, but you're exactly the type Marshall would hire. I looked into him after that stunt his brother pulled with Walker Cameron. Reid Marshall's making quite a name for himself with his connections, especially Cameron and Gavin Selby. Even though Selby's burned all his bridges."

"A stunt?" Riley protested. "Fin would *never* and you leave Gavin out of this. His family treated him terribly."

That got a loud cackle from Muriel. Her fur turban swung back and she flailed a gaudily bejeweled glove. "*Poor* Gavin Selby! He's still rich and Briarwood Terrace is worth a fortune." She became stern and superior again as she turned her nose upward. "You, on the other hand... are a no-one and have no money. There isn't anything even remotely interesting about you, as far as I can tell. And you aren't famous. I'd know if you were."

She had Riley there. "All of that's true..." he said, nodding slowly. This time, all the right comebacks tickled his tongue, but the last thing Riley wanted to do was piss off Muriel Hormsby. Making an enemy of the loudest dragon in Manhattan would bring the wrong kind of attention to Reid's agency and there was no telling what would happen when word spread around the building. Gossip traveled fast in the Olympia. Everyone was going to know that Muriel Hormsby got into it with the Ashbys' nanny. He didn't want to dignify any of her accusations because then they'd be arguing about an affair. He composed himself and smiled at Muriel as if she was six years old instead of a woman in her late sixties who ought to have known better. "Which makes me wonder. Why are you so worried about me, ma'am?"

She reeled back and spluttered. "I'm not worried about *you*. I'm worried about that nephew of mine. Jonathon might have a chance with Ashby as long as one of Marshall's nannies doesn't get in the way again."

"I wouldn't dream of it!" Riley said with complete sincerity.

For once, he wanted to see Giles make a girl cry. He had no idea how Muriel imagined she could push her nephew at Giles since he never went out socially or entertained guests. Giles wasn't exactly putting out a single-and-ready-to-mingle vibe either. And while Riley might not know what Giles was into, he was fairly certain Jonathon wasn't it from everything he'd heard about the aspiring "influencer."

The elevator finally came to a stop on the sixth floor. Ending the interrogation. Muriel huffed indignantly, signaling that it was time to leave. Calista pranced out before her.

"I'm watching you and 8B. Don't try to get in my way," she warned, and Riley pressed the button for eight as fast and as hard as he could as soon as she'd cleared the elevator.

"Have a lovely day!" He waved as the doors closed, then muttered, "Money really can't buy manners. Although, she's probably spent most of it on turbans and those atrocious fur coats."

He arrived at his destination a few moments later and Riley told himself that Muriel was wrong as he took out his keys. He wasn't a no-one and he wasn't any of the other things she'd accused him of being. Giles might not want him, but someone would if Riley kept putting out the kind of love he hoped to receive.

"Soon would be nice," he said as he let himself into 8B and went to make breakfast.

"Good morning." Giles's smile was quick but cautious as he handed Riley his coffee, returning them to their awkward post-planetarium stalemate. Apparently, neither of them had made sense of Giles's poignant apology.

"It is! And a good morning to you!" Riley smiled back, dying on the inside as he raised his cup and sipped. *And a good morning to you?* Why did he have to say that like he was greeting Giles from across a cobbled street? The silence became awkward as they held onto their cups and saucers for dear life. "So... How was your weekend?"

"Great!" Giles replied immediately. "We were both feeling drained from Friday so we watched a lot of *Star Trek* and played chess on the terrace for a few hours on Sunday while it was nice."

"That sounds perfect," Riley said before Milo joined them.

He was fully recharged and ready to face the day after a quick breakfast. Giles got the door for them and blushed when his eyes touched Riley's.

"I'll see you when you get back."

He might as well have shot an arrow right into Riley's heart. He wasn't exactly sure what to make of that, as usual, but Giles sounded like he was looking forward to it. And there was something seeking and hopeful in the way his gaze held Riley's. "Alright."

Milo gave Riley's mitten a tug and he allowed himself to be dragged to the elevator, smiling at Giles over his shoulder.

"Did Dad tell you that we watched *Star Trek* and that I beat him at chess?" Milo did the robot, then held his hand up for a high five.

"He told me but he left out that very important detail. Awesome job!"

They hopped into the elevator at the same time and Milo proceeded to explain every episode from their marathon because Riley hadn't watched a lot of *Star Trek*. Unfortunately, Riley didn't retain much. He was rather distracted, replaying his moment at the door with Giles and imagining the possibilities.

Riley left Milo with his teacher in front of the school and must have floated back to the Olympia. *It had to mean something good,* he told himself. Which presented Riley with some interesting possibilities. What if he and Muriel Homsby had been wrong? What if Riley did matter? And what if Giles *did* want him? Was something about to happen?

He told himself to keep his hopes reasonable because this was Giles Ashby and the man couldn't help but tie himself into knots and it could take him decades to make a move, not days or weeks.

But, what if?

Chapter Twenty-Two

Fate had turned against Giles. He was hoping for just one moment alone with Riley. He was going to go for it and ask if Riley would like to stay for dinner one evening or come into Manhattan to spend some time together while Milo was away at Jack and Julie's. All he needed was a few moments but the morning went sideways almost as soon as Riley returned.

Wendy was worried about the forecast when she arrived and hurried through her chores, limiting Giles to bashful glances as he lingered in the kitchen with Riley. But things didn't take a serious turn until Riley got a message from the school system. There were early closures due to inclement weather and the heat was out in several of the buildings, including Milo's elementary school. Giles insisted that Wendy and Riley leave as soon as possible and grabbed his chance while she was giving Milo's room a quick vacuum and gathering their laundry.

"You should go," Giles said, checking over his shoulder to

make sure she was still occupied. Riley was running out to grab a few things so he could leave Giles and Milo with a lasagna and another carrot cake. "I can pick Milo up and we'll get a pizza on the way. He won't mind."

Riley waved it off. "I think it's just going to be wet and gross. The storm of the century isn't coming until this weekend. I'm headed over to Reid's with Fin so I might as well hang out until then," he said.

"Are you sure? I wouldn't want you to get caught in the storm."

"Nah. Walker will send for a car if it's that bad. It's game night and Fin is dungeon master so it's gonna get rowdy. We usually play on Friday nights but Fin and Walker have plans for Valentine's, obviously. Expect me to be a touch hungover tomorrow," Riley predicted in a whisper, but Giles frowned back at him. He *knew* that Riley played *Dungeons & Dragons* with his friends once a month and Giles understood the basic premise. He had just never attended a game night or seen how it was actually played.

"I don't really understand what that means, but I hope it all works out?" He attempted.

Riley's lips twitched as he nodded. "It'll be a debacle because Fin's campaigns always are," he said, winding his scarf around his neck. Giles was bewitched by the amused tilt of Riley's lips and the sparkle in his eyes.

Just do it. "I was wondering..." Giles glanced at Milo's hallway, then pulled in a steadying breath. "If you might be free in the evenings or the weekends. If so...I'd like to see you," he mumbled in a rush.

"I might be," Riley said coyly, tugging on his mittens. "You should call me or text me sometime."

"Okay." Giles grabbed the wall, unable to hide that all the

blood had rushed from his head and that he was seeing floaters. "I swear, I thought I was breathing."

Riley gave him a playful swat and his hand lingered on Giles's arm. "You did fine and I'm glad you asked. I'll see you in a bit."

"Thanks. See you in a bit." Giles bowed as he backed away, then jumped when Wendy raced past with an empty laundry basket.

"See you on Wednesday, sweetheart," she said to Riley and blew him a kiss.

"Don't forget that I'll have a mountain of clothes and toys for you," he said.

"You're an angel!" She shouted from Giles's wing.

Riley made a giddy sound, widening his eyes at Giles as he opened the door. "The Camerons are very excited!" He said as he left, leaving Giles absurdly tickled. Wendy's son and daughter-in-law were adopting a pair of siblings and the little boy and his sister were the perfect age for gently-used hand-me-downs from Milo, Jack, and the Cameron girls. Riley and Julie had been coordinating efforts and Wendy's new grandbabies would have full closets and overflowing toy boxes when they arrived next week.

Giles was delighted for Wendy and her family and he was rather pleased with himself. He didn't get another moment alone with Riley, but the rest of the afternoon was still pleasant. Riley picked Milo up from school and the three of them worked on a puzzle and listened to a mystery podcast. They assembled a lasagna together and another mini carrot cake was waiting on the counter when Riley left to meet Fin.

"Did you ask him out yet?" Milo asked as they sat at the counter and ate their cake halves.

"Sort of," Giles said and received an excited gasp.

"What did he say?"

"He said I could call him."

"I told you. He wants to be courted." Milo gave Giles a pleased humph.

Giles blinked back at him. "New spelling word?" He guessed and Milo nodded quickly.

"I was afraid we wouldn't get the list today because we got out early and I started to get upset, but Riley told me everything would be posted online. I checked when we got home and he was right."

Half-days and snow days could be stressful for Milo, especially if he didn't have enough warning. But Riley had calmed Milo down on the way home and Giles had the podcast and the puzzle ready because they were great brain soothers.

"How do I court him without having to go out a lot? I've never really been on a date and I don't know if I can handle that kind of pressure while people are watching me."

"I don't think Riley likes going out. He said his friends drag him all over the city and he's getting too old for that."

"He doesn't mean that, but it's good for you to see what it's like when someone has friends and healthy hobbies," Giles said and pointed his fork at Milo to make sure he was listening. He nodded solemnly, giving Giles his full attention. "It's not important if you're popular and everyone doesn't have to like you. But try to have friends so you have a good support system. I didn't have anyone until I met your mom and that was kind of lonely."

"I'm glad I have Jack. He was already my best friend because he's my cousin and we were babies together."

"You're lucky you have Jack and that your mom's family is really cool."

Milo had been curious about Giles's parents when he was much younger. But Milo had intuitively understood and accepted Giles's simple explanation that they were very unhealthy people and that they weren't good for him and Milo. There was always the hope that his father would grow a heart and his mother would start caring, but Giles didn't waste a lot of time worrying because they had Claire's family.

Julie had accepted "just Giles" unconditionally before Claire had told her who he really was. And Julie and Ken had supported Giles and Claire's unconventional marriage and divorce, despite not always understanding. All that had mattered was what was best for their family. Julie and Ken had never failed Giles and Milo. Their love and support were the backbone of his and Milo's existence and Giles was mostly blessed to have gained Julie as a sister when he married Claire. Because she definitely treated Giles like they were siblings and he often felt like an irritated older brother.

"Riley said he would teach me and Jack how to play *Dungeons & Dragons*! Maybe we can have game nights at Jack's. Some of the kids on his street are nice."

"That sounds like a great idea. Ken was into fantasy and he probably played so he'll be on board. I'll make sure you have all the dice and snacks you need," Giles said and let Milo ramble about *D&D* while they washed up and put the rest of the lasagna away.

Yet again, Giles was proud of his family for adapting so well to so many big changes. They were all stronger and healthier, especially Milo. He wouldn't change a single thing about his son; Giles just didn't want Milo to be as lonely or as misunderstood as he had been as a child. And Giles was proud of himself for stopping the cycle and giving Milo a much fuller and happier childhood.

It was not lost on Giles as he turned down the lights and tucked Milo in that he wouldn't have the luxury of feeling so competent and content if it hadn't been for Riley. He thought about texting—it was infinitely easier than calling—but Giles didn't want to bother Riley while he was with his friends. So Giles poured himself a drink and went to prepare himself a joint and a bath. It seemed like a good place to ponder how he'd court Riley without leaving 8B. And other things...

Chapter Twenty-Three

Riley had to fill Fin in on every detail as they made their way to Briarwood Terrace. They both agreed that it was safe to assume that Giles was interested in Riley. And Riley was no longer denying that he was falling hard for Giles. He was excited to tell Reid and Gavin but also prepared to deliver a very heartfelt apology. It looked like there was a good chance Riley was about to break the curse with his boss.

"Please don't kill me," Riley said, holding out a bottle of Cabernet Sauvignon when Reid met them at the door.

Reid squinted back at Riley, looking exasperated. "Is this about you and Ashby?"

"What have you heard?"

"I don't have to be an actual wizard. We all saw this coming and tried to tell you." Reid grabbed the bottle and gestured for them to get inside. "Gavin's on his way. Warm up while I get the glasses."

They gathered around the coffee table and Riley recounted what had transpired throughout the day, culminating in Giles's breathless question. Reid agreed that the curse was about to be broken and raised his glass to propose a toast, but paused when Gavin burst through the door.

"Sorry, I'm late. I missed the train, but you're never going to believe what I just learned." Gavin grimaced at Riley as he unwound his scarf.

"Whatever it was, I swear it was an accident," Riley said, holding up his hands.

"It wasn't you. It was your boss."

"Giles?" Riley asked, craning his neck to watch as Gavin went to prepare himself a cup of tea. Reid always kept the kettle ready on game night because Gavin wasn't much of a drinker. "Not that I'm surprised that it was Giles. He's always goofing up," Riley murmured, his senses tingling. In an ominous way.

"Giles Ashby was the one who got Riley and Fin fired," Gavin announced to the room as he lowered into an armchair with his teacup.

"Whoa!" Fin swiped his phone off the table and muted the game night playlist. "What are you talking about?"

Gavin hissed in warning before blowing on his tea. "You know how I like to get a cut and a shave if I'm close to 79th and Park Avenue. I was in the chair and minding my own business when Chad Dexter turns up. You remember Chad, Reid," he said with a curl of his lip and Reid's face pinched.

"Ugh. I remember. Got accepted to Fordham. What's he doing with himself and what does Chad Dexter have to do with Fin and Riley?"

"Dexter works for a gentleman named Wolford."

Fin and Riley's eyes were huge as they locked gazes across the coffee table. Fin recovered first. "The same Wolford who fired me last year?" He asked and Gavin hummed.

"Dexter was boasting about how he works for Wolford and

rubs elbows with the most influential people in the city in the course of his duties, including Ashby at the Olympia." Gavin raised his brows, signaling that the story was about to get very interesting. "Apparently, Dexter was at the Olympia several months ago getting some papers signed when our friend Ashby showed him a very interesting video of a performance from a fundraiser. Ashby wanted to know if Dexter could look into the fundraiser discreetly and find out if it had met its goal. It seems that Dexter hadn't heard of the fundraiser or *Hamilton*, but Dexter recognized Fin."

"Hold on!" Fin got up and pointed at Gavin. "You're telling me that Dexter has never heard of *Hamilton*? What planet is this alien from?" He asked, looking at Riley in disbelief.

"I can believe it. No decent human would work for a bigot like Wolford," Riley said with a shrug. "Can we focus on the fact that Giles might have outed us, please?" He scolded Fin, then turned back to Gavin. "What happened after the alien discovered *Hamilton*?" He prodded.

Gavin chuckled as he sipped. "Ashby confirmed that it was in fact Fin Marshall dressed as Eliza Schuyler in the video, and that the other performer was a Mr. Riley Fitzgerald. Dexter said he was appalled and that it was completely inappropriate for an employee of Mr. Wolford's to perform in drag. Especially if the employee is a nanny."

"Oh no." Riley set his wine down. He felt like he was going to be sick.

"Dexter was livid when Ashby informed him that both performers were gay and nannies," Gavin continued heavily. "He went straight to his employer and outed Fin, then placed a few calls and had Riley terminated."

"Son of a—!" Riley started but Gavin, Reid, and Fin all urged him to calm down.

"It all worked out and now Giles is stuck with you," Fin

joked with an apologetic wince.

That just made Riley angrier for some reason. "He outed us and got us fired! And then he hired me to fix his life for him!"

"You're getting paid *really* well to do it, though," Reid reminded Riley gently.

"That's not the point! And it never occurred to him to mention it or say he was sorry? He has to know that we got fired."

Gavin cleared his throat gently. "If we were talking about anyone other than Ashby, you'd have a point," he argued. "But I didn't get the sense that it was intentional on Ashby's part. Or that Dexter knew that Ashby isn't straight. This was before his divorce," he added, but Riley cocked his head and squinted back at Gavin.

"That's great for *him*. He still gets to choose if that part of his life is private. Fin and I don't!"

Reid stood and reached for Riley, attempting to calm him. "He can be an asshole, but I don't think he'd do something like that on purpose."

"He should know better, though!" Riley shook his head as he stepped around the table. He was so *angry* at Giles.

"What are you doing?" Fin asked and Riley realized he was at the door and pulling his coat on.

"I don't know. I need to think," he said as he yanked his mittens from his pockets.

"How about some company?" Fin was right behind Riley and reaching for his cardigan. Riley stopped him.

"I'll be fine. I just need a little time to clear my head."

Fin pulled him into a tight hug. "Check in if you're gonna be gone for more than an hour or I'm coming after you."

"I will."

"We're okay now," Fin whispered as he squeezed Riley.

"I know." Riley squeezed him back, then waved at everyone

as he left.

It started to rain and the wind picked up almost as soon as Riley stepped out of Briarwood Terrace so he flipped his hood over his beanie and ran into the subway to catch a train. He kept his head down and ignored the other passengers in the car, sinking into his disappointment and confusion.

They were okay now and Riley wouldn't change a thing, but he'd never been more scared or felt more financially desperate than when they were fired. Bills would have lapsed and he and Fin could have lost their apartment if Reid hadn't found them jobs as quickly as he had. And it had been such a callous and careless act on Giles's part that Riley couldn't make any sense of it. Unless Riley accepted that Giles truly didn't give a damn about them and thought that they were that far beneath him.

He hadn't made a conscious decision to get off at Central Park West or head up 72nd Street, but Riley found himself staring at the Olympia's opulent facade. His clothes and his Converse were soaking wet and his teeth were rattling as he shivered in the rain, but it took a violent crack of thunder to get him moving again.

"Evening, Riley! You're out late," one of the doormen noted as Riley jogged in out of the storm.

"Nanny emergency," Riley lied and rushed through the breezeway to the other lobby. He shushed and gestured for Carl to stay behind his desk when he found the elderly man nodding off. "I won't be long! Just forgot something," Riley said, then slipped into the open elevator. He smiled serenely at Carl and stabbed the button for the eighth floor. But Riley's face fell as soon as the doors shut and he began to tremble as a sob built in his chest. It didn't help that he was soggy, freezing, and furious when they opened again and he trudged out to face Giles.

His soaked mitten made a squishing sound, dampening Riley's fury as his fist beat against the door. He didn't want to ring the bell and wake Milo. The door swung open a few moments later and Giles was immediately concerned. Riley should have been concerned, too, because Giles's hair was slicked back and he was dressed in nothing but a silk robe.

"I was taking a bath. What happened?" He demanded. Giles attempted to pull him in by his elbow but Riley jerked his arm away.

"Don't touch me," Riley growled, mopping at his eyes with a soggy mitten and pointing it at Giles accusatively. "How could you?"

"What are you talking about?" Giles asked, approaching Riley with raised hands.

"You outed me and Fin to Chad Dexter and got us fired!"

Giles's eyes flared and his hands dropped to his sides. "Oh. That's why Fin went to work for Cameron..." He murmured distantly, then grimaced at Riley. "I didn't know that Dex—"

"Then, you shouldn't have said anything! Do you have any idea what it's like to lose a job in this city? Especially one you love?" Riley asked, his voice rising. "We didn't like who we worked for, but we loved the kids and we put everything into them. But they just fired us without a single explanation."

"Jesus! I am so sorry, Riley. I—"

"You what, Giles?" Riley demanded, then looked around the living room and the hall on the other side of the kitchen. "Milo's asleep?" He asked and Giles nodded so Riley continued. "You what, Giles? Forgot that most people can't hide in their fancy apartments and have to work for a living? Do you have any idea how scared I was? I had one month's rent in the bank and bills to pay when you decided to casually out me to some dickhead. And for what?" Riley asked, his arms flailing wildly.

"I'm sorry. I just..." Giles swore as he scrubbed his face with his hands, wafting his intoxicating scent at Riley.

But Riley's rage would not be doused by bay rum and bergamot or an intriguing glimpse of dark chest hair and firm, flat pecs. "You just...?" Riley prodded.

Giles's face turned pink. "I just wanted to know if the fundraiser had been a success. And I thought it was an incredible performance. Even if Fin was a little pitchy at times."

"What?" Riley blinked back at Giles, utterly dismayed. "Don't bring Fin's lack of range into this. What did you think was going to happen when you told a prick like Dexter that we were gay? Did you think he'd run to Wolford and tell him to give Fin an award? You got both of us fired!"

"I didn't mean to and I didn't know, Riley."

"No. You didn't care," Riley snapped back, daring Giles to deny it. "You would have been more careful about who you told about us if we had mattered to you. But all you cared about was how much money we'd raised." He'd scored a direct hit and Riley watched the wound spread. Giles looked almost as sick as Riley felt. "I'll see you tomorrow," he said and turned to storm back to the elevator, intending to leave Giles to wallow in his guilt.

"Wait!" Giles begged. He hurried after Riley carrying his heavy black overcoat. "Please. Take this." Giles's jaw twitched and his gaze hovered around Riley's chin as he swung the coat around. It landed on Riley's shoulders, shrouding him in heavy warmth and Giles's cologne. "I'm sorry and I promise, I'll fix this."

"There's nothing you can do to fix this," Riley grumbled weakly, but his anger was already fading as he became warmer. Giles tugged the coat tighter around Riley, bringing them closer until they were almost nose-to-nose. "You have no idea what it feels like to be small and helpless. You've never known what it's like to be so insignificant that your job—your *livelihood*—can just be taken away from you on a bigot's whim. You can opt out of all the awful *outside* things that make you uncomfortable and you can be queer when it suits you because most people assume you're straight. You didn't *need* a queer agency so you'd never have to face the fear and humiliation of losing a job again."

Riley tilted his chin back defiantly, but his knees almost buckled when Giles's head lowered in a solemn bow. Giles swore under his breath, the pot and scotch-scented huff grazing Riley's lips. "I... You're right. I'm sorry and I'll fix this."

It was getting too warm and Riley's heart was racing. He scrambled for a coherent thought and held on tight before he did something senseless and reckless, like stand on his tiptoes and mash their lips together. "You would have ruined both of our lives if it hadn't been for Reid." Riley held his breath and hoped that was enough because he was just about to let go.

Giles's brow furrowed into a severe 8 as he fumbled, his lips pursing and parting on aborted pleas. But he eventually relented, sighing as he nodded. "I understand that I've done something terrible and that I hurt you. I'm sorry and I'll find a way to make this right."

"Reid already took care of it. He saved me and Fin and we helped you put your life back together."

"Marshall's always looked out for everyone. He always knows best," Giles agreed. His weak smile was sincere, but his eyes shimmered as they clung to Riley's.

"Speaking of..." Riley retreated and gestured at the elevator behind him. "I need to check in with Reid and Fin. They're probably worried."

"Will you be alright? I'll call for a car if you'll wai—"

"No." Riley shook his head firmly. He was too confused and it was getting worse, the longer he lingered in Giles's amazing hypno-odor dream coat and stared at his lips. "I'll see you tomorrow."

"Okay." Giles offered Riley another solemn bow, then reached around him for the elevator call button. His chest bumped against Riley's shoulder and it was so tempting to lean into Giles. It would have felt a lot nicer to accept Giles's apology and the warm embrace that was sure to follow, but Riley was afraid of how small he'd feel when they had to face each other again in the morning.

The soft ding of the elevator came to Riley's rescue.

"Goodnight." He backed through the doors, holding his head high despite his quivering lip and runny nose.

"Goodnight, Riley." Giles waved as the chrome doors closed, leaving Riley alone with his pathetic, distorted reflection. He looked like he'd been dragged out of the Hudson and swaddled in a comforter. The coat's shoulders hung around Riley's elbows and the sleeves swallowed his arms. It came to his knees, making him look even shorter and scrawnier.

"Wonderful," Riley said and hoped no one noticed and mugged him for wearing a coat that cost as much as a car. "It's the curse that keeps on giving."

Chapter Twenty-Four

He didn't finish the joint he'd started because he didn't want to sleep and he didn't want his mind quiet. Giles paced all night, berating himself for his carelessness and searching for *any* way to undo what he had done. Then, just before the sun came up on Tuesday, it dawned on Giles that he *couldn't* undo what he'd done and that he wouldn't if he could.

How could Giles truly regret any action that had brought Riley to 8B? He deeply regretted the pain he'd caused Riley and Fin. But Giles needed Riley and he didn't want to give him back. He'd waited so long and the universe had finally returned Riley to Giles's orbit. Suddenly, all the work Giles had done to prove he'd changed had been demolished by a careless conversation from the past.

And Giles understood acutely how helpless Riley and Fin must have felt as the things he wanted the most—stability, peace, Riley—slipped through his fingers. He'd gone from visions of courting Riley to losing him in the space of an evening and Giles's world had been sapped of its warmth.

Riley returned the next morning looking shattered and Giles could tell by his red, puffy eyes and raw-looking nose that he'd spent the night crying. Giles apologized and Riley nodded and murmured that he'd get over it, but he didn't touch his coffee and wouldn't look at Giles. Riley did his best to be bubbly and bright for Milo, though. Watching him smile through the pain and make jokes with watery "allergy" eyes and a catch in his throat gutted Giles. Even Milo noticed the change and was worried.

"Something's wrong with Riley but he keeps telling me he's fine," Milo said to Giles after Riley had left for the evening. He'd roasted a chicken and Giles had a feeling it had been intended for a pot pie but that Riley had run out of energy or inspiration. Instead, a pan of roasted potatoes and a salad were waiting on the counter and there were no pies or mini carrot cakes.

"We'll make this right," Milo promised Giles over bowls of ice cream. "You're like Elsa in *Frozen*. She didn't mean to freeze everything and she got scared and ran away because nobody understood her. But she came back and fixed everything because she loved her sister."

"I don't have a sister," Giles replied, trying to understand how he was like Elsa and how she'd fix the mess he'd made.

"We have anxiety like Elsa and everyone thinks you're mean like her, but you're not. You're just awkward and panic when you don't know what to do so you stay in here instead of your ice castle."

"Keep going," Giles said as he rested his forearms on the counter, digging deeper into Milo's *Frozen* analogy for possible solutions. "How do I thaw the kingdom and save Anna? Am I saving Anna and is Riley Anna because that would suggest the presence of a Kristoff and that could make this even more complicated."

"No. You're Kristoff too because you're also the hero."

"Good. I was hoping I didn't have to kiss my sister."

"Riley isn't your sister," Milo said impatiently and moved his bowl to the side, getting serious. He rested a forearm on the counter even though he had to rise on his toes. "When you're scared and doing things you don't mean, you're like Elsa. But now you have Riley so you're more like Kristoff so you'll go back and save Anna because you love Riley."

"I see... So I don't have to unfreeze the town?"

"No. We're not worried about the town, we're just saving Riley."

"Good." Giles wasn't feeling up to saving a whole town. "How do I undo what I did and save Riley?"

"You have to stop the bad guy!" Milo said as he became excited. "If you stop the bad guy you can kiss Riley and save the day."

"I think I'm the bad guy this time. What about a snowman? We could build one and let him save the day."

They both glanced at the windows but as Riley had predicted, the snowstorm had been more of a rain and slush storm and had blown over. A bigger storm was predicted for the weekend and the city was preparing to hunker down.

"There has to be another bad guy. You couldn't have done something this bad by yourself," Milo said sagely and Giles's eyes grew wide.

"Now you're onto something..." Giles couldn't get Riley and Fin their old jobs back and he had a feeling that no one wanted that. But he could settle the score for Riley and Fin and give them a hell of a lot of satisfaction. "That's going to take a few days. What do I do in the meantime? I can't take seeing Riley like this."

"Me too," Milo whispered. His lips pulled tight as he

studied his bowl. "I think you have to start over and woo him again."

"Jesus." Giles scrubbed his face with his hands. "Why does there have to be wooing? I'll be so glad when this month is over." He thought the holidays had been a disaster but Valentine's Day was kicking his ass with spelling lists. "And I think the word you want is 'groveling.'"

Giles wouldn't have minded a little more wooing because he was starting to get the hang of that. But he got to groveling on Wednesday morning and hit the ground running. Riley was visibly stunned to find a Philodendron Gloriosum clipping with his coffee and his watery gasp gave Giles hope. Giles had tasked a young man with finding the rarest plant he could in an evening and had been dubious when he was handed a single giant leaf in a pot. But it did the trick and Riley showed signs of thawing.

Then every cookie cutter you could possibly imagine arrived in a big white box with a giant pink bow. Riley couldn't contain his delight and enlisted Milo to help him organize their new collection and pick their favorites.

Thursday morning's delivery was a tremendous hit as well. Giles had a team in to clear the small office off the kitchen and assemble a wall of AeroGardens and plenty of shelves. The tile floors, exposed brick walls, and floor-to-ceiling windows made it the perfect room for a mini conservatory, Giles suggested. He even mentioned that Riley could move some of his "babies" to 8B if he thought they might be happier there.

"I might do that," Riley said faintly. He was hugging an AeroGarden manual and looked like he was going to cry so Giles bowed and escaped before *he* started crying.

But Giles was ready again on Friday morning. Giles had come up with something that was sure to make Riley swoon. He was waiting in the kitchen when Riley returned from taking

Milo to school. Riley was hugging a crate of apples and one was wedged between his teeth.

"Let me help you," Giles said as he ran to get the door and the crate.

"Thanksh!" Riley replied and removed the apple once his hands were free. "Scored these from a friend in exchange for some dog sitting I did last weekend and they were waiting for me downstairs." He stuck the apple between his teeth again so he could take off his mittens and stuff them into the pockets of his coat. Giles watched as Riley dropped his backpack and stripped down to his Fiona Apple T-shirt. They both jumped when they realized Giles was staring.

"I'll take these to the kitchen." He turned and almost collided with Wendy.

"Sorry!" She said, dancing around him with the bucket of cleaning supplies. "What are you doing with all of those?" She asked Riley.

"Applesauce! I make amazing applesauce and who doesn't love applesauce? Especially little ones!" He said excitedly.

"You are such an angel." She blew Riley a kiss and hurried around the corner.

Riley rubbed his hands together, possibly to warm them. "It's the perfect day to do it! I have a feeling we won't see the sun and it's getting *cold!*" He sounded giddy.

"It is," Giles agreed. He set the crate on the counter and picked up the card he'd left for Riley. He'd taken great care with the name and phone number, and it had taken dozens of attempts before Giles had something that was elegant enough to look special. But not too pretentious. "I'd like you to have this," he said, pushing the card at Riley.

His head tilted as he read it. "Edward Gardiner?"

"This is the gentleman I contact when I want to see a show," Giles explained. "He can get any seat in any theater in the city with just a few days' notice. I've instructed him to take very good care of you and as many guests as you desire, whenever you wish and as often as you like, and to charge everything to my account."

"Holy shit," Riley whispered and grabbed hold of Giles's wrist to steady himself. "That's... You didn't have to do this!"

"Yes, I do. I can't rest knowing I've hurt you. I need you to forgive me." Giles's hand was shaking as he traced one of the buttons on Riley's cardigan. He wanted to cup his cheek or touch his lips, but the button was as far as Giles was willing to dare.

Riley nodded jerkily, but he couldn't bring his eyes to Giles's. "I know you didn't mean to get us fired and I know I have to forgive you—I have forgiven you—I just..." He gulped hard and wiped the corner of his eye. "You had to know what that guy was like. He wasn't a complete stranger to you."

Giles nodded. "I am aware of who he is and who he works for, and I always thought he seemed petty and unpleasant," he admitted. Giles could tell that he hadn't made things better by the way Riley squeezed his eyes shut and grunted like he'd taken a blow.

"So, you knew what he was like, but you went ahead and told him about me and Fin. Our welfare and happiness meant so little to you, that you didn't think about what would happen when he left here. I know you care *now* and that you hadn't meant to hurt me then. But I couldn't have mattered all that much to you, could I?"

"You did! You do," Giles corrected. "You've always— I wouldn't have asked if I didn't care. I just didn't *think* and I'm so sorry." He couldn't tell Riley that he'd been *obsessed* with the short video that had come across his Instagram feed.

Social media was an anxiety minefield for Giles and he didn't want access to more strangers or to give more strangers access to him. He only used the app because Claire had an account and often posted about her New York and Osaka adventures. He also peeked in on Riley from time to time and had followed the theater that was benefiting from the fundraiser. Giles figured he'd get updates about the show and possibly see any related videos and sure enough, they flooded his feed the days following the event. He didn't understand how such a short and utterly adorable video could have caused so much damage. "I did forget that my actions had consequences outside of 8B and that I hurt the people I care about the most when I forget how to be a human."

Riley pulled in a deep breath and offered Giles a fragile, watery smile. "I understand. Thank you."

Can I kiss you now? Please?

He couldn't be this close to Riley anymore and not feel the pull of his lips and the need to taste them. "I should let you get to your applesauce. Unless you could use a hand."

"In the mood to run the apple contraption?" Riley asked and swayed closer. Giles's eyes became heavy and his chin dipped, allowing him to taste Riley's breaths.

They heard Wendy just before she hustled into the kitchen with a load of dirty towels. "That's much better! Don't mind me," she said, but Riley had already spun away and run for the pantry.

She was right, though. That was much better. Giles was rather pleased with himself and cautiously relieved. He wasn't off the hook yet, but he'd gotten Riley to look at him, and most importantly, to *smile* at him.

Chapter Twenty-Five

You have to tell him to stop.

Riley was perched on the stool in the kitchen. Jars of applesauce were cooling on the counter while he stared at the card with Edward Gardiner's name on it. The last few days had been a cold blur and Riley had been numb. He'd gone into break-up mode, even though he and Giles had never been on an actual date. But it felt like he'd been dumped and a fantasy had been ruined until Giles gave Riley the most gorgeous Philodendron Gloriosum stem he had ever laid eyes on. He'd seen the rare plant in botanical gardens and in a few friends' collections, but Riley never thought he'd have one of his own.

Had Riley told Giles about his babies? He couldn't remember, but Giles had known and he continued to show Riley how closely he'd been paying attention with other little gifts and gestures throughout the week. Riley had promised Giles that he was forgiven and had apologized as well.

He knew how Giles could overreact, under-react, or just misunderstand something if he was distracted, overwhelmed, or confused. And Riley had scolded Giles for not giving Mrs. Simpson the benefit of the doubt during the Chernobyl incident. Why had it been so much harder to forgive Giles?

It had been frightening, and Giles should have known better than to tell Chad Dexter that Fin and Riley were gay, but Riley might have been a little harsh. He had a feeling it had more to do with his insecurities and his fear of the curse than being outed and getting fired. Neither Riley nor Fin wanted to work for bigots and they were much better off.

But he had been reminded of just how common and insignificant he was and how absurd it was to believe he truly had a chance with someone like Giles. They might flirt and they might even have a fling, but Giles was a genius and a multi-millionaire and he had been married to a genius and a multi-millionaire.

The incident with Chad Dexter had made it clear how unsuitable Riley was and how naive he'd been when he celebrated the end of the curse with Reid and Fin. Now, Riley didn't know what to think. Giles had gone to so much trouble and had been so thoughtful. If Riley accepted that the incident with Dexter had been unintentional and a simple lapse in judgment, then what did Giles's actions mean?

Riley took out his phone to message Fin when a text from Reid arrived, instructing him to call as soon as he had a few free minutes. Riley checked and he could hear Giles rowing in his suite and Wendy was folding laundry in the other room. He dialed Reid's number, and the phone only rang once.

"Hey. Everything okay?" Riley asked.

"Okay? Are you kidding? I don't know what you did, but *everything* is...so great!" Reid laughed.

Riley peeked around the kitchen wall, but there was still no sign of Wendy or Giles. "Me? What are you talking about?"

"First, Gavin starts yelling that I've got certified mail and it's *two* checks. One for the agency, to help with our PR and advertising. It's $250,000, Riley! From Frederick Wolford."

"What?" Riley croaked.

"And there was a matching check for Fin for Warm Things! Gavin called around and found out that Ashby pulled all of his accounts from Wolford's investment firm. Like, *all of them*. Hundreds of millions of dollars just yanked from Wolford's ledgers. Wolford's in a panic and he's mortified. Ashby released a statement saying he's taking his bisexual business elsewhere because he refuses to do business with a bigot like Wolford."

Riley couldn't feel his face and fell back against the wall when his legs started to shake. That was *a lot* of money for the agency and Fin's non-profit. Warm Things would be able to hire more people and recycle more clothes to donate to shelters and nursing homes. "What?"

"Gavin says Ashby's accountants are getting calls from every investment firm in Manhattan and it's a bloodbath at Wolford's. Dexter was fired, but Wolford's still hemorrhaging clients and money. Wolford's been in damage control and writing checks to make amends, but this is going to cost him *millions* by the time the dust settles."

"What?" he stammered. There really wasn't much else Riley could say or do at the moment. Although, throwing up seemed like a possibility as well.

"It's costing Ashby a fortune too, Gavin says."

That was enough to shake Riley. "*What? Why?*" He hurried around the counter and into the living room so he could see down Giles's hall. Riley could hear the faint whir of the rowing machine.

"The longer Ashby keeps that kind of money in the bank, the more money he loses. Gavin is sick about the penalties and the fees this has to be costing him, but Fin says that Ashby's been talking to Walker and he thinks the two of them are working something out."

"Wow."

"I know!" Reid added a humph. "I wouldn't be surprised if you get some mail or hear from an attorney soon," he warned and Riley shook his head quickly.

"I don't need anything else. This is already...so much!" He whispered as he drifted into the hallway and stretched his neck, listening. The rowing machine was still running. "How far is he rowing?" He wondered and glanced over his shoulder to make sure Wendy was still folding towels.

"Has he said anything about what happened or why he dumped Wolford?"

"No! I had no idea. He's been doing all these amazing things to say he's sorry but he didn't mention any of this."

"Hmmm."

Riley's eyes narrowed. "Why would you *Hmmm* at me?"

"Have you considered forgiving him? Because this looks a little like a man who's groveling."

"*I did* forgive him and I told him to stop," Riley said. He pulled his sleeve over his thumb and scratched his nose when it started to tickle and burn. "He did all of this for me?"

"Can I make an observation?"

Riley rolled his eyes. He knew what was coming. "We both know you're perfectly capable."

"*May* I make an observation?"

"You may."

"Start believing in yourself and let go of the past," Reid said.

"Those don't sound like observations."

"That's part one. You've got to let go of *all* your grudges against Giles and all the men who've hurt you. Two: you are the kindest and most patient person I've ever met and you're willing to give anyone a second chance. But you could never do that with Ashby when you were a kid and you're still having a hard time."

"He called me a clumsy little jerk and said I looked like a Dickensian urchin," Riley mumbled. His nose wrinkled at how silly he sounded. "He didn't have to be so hot and act like an asshole all the time either," he added. His lip pushed out as he sulked and kicked at the marble.

"He's always gotten under your skin and you've always been a little bit harder on him. Why is that?" Reid asked gently.

"I don't know. Can I get back to you?"

"Sure. Call me anytime you need to talk."

"Thanks. I'm going to see how Giles is doing."

"That's probably a good idea. Talk to you later," Reid said, then ended the call and left Riley alone with his conscience and a hell of a bombshell.

"Oh boy."

He had a feeling he owed Giles a way bigger apology. For starters.

Riley gathered his courage and tiptoed around the corner. The doors to Giles's office were open and Riley found him where he expected. Giles slid back and forth on the seat of the rowing machine as his arms pumped. His bare torso and toned arms glistened and sweat rolled down his face, neck, and chest.

"Riley?" Giles dropped the grips and swung his legs around. He hopped to his feet, then grabbed his forehead as he swayed. "Whoa. Too fast," he said to himself, then flashed Riley a strained smile. "Everything okay?" He huffed and planted his hands on his hips.

"Um." Riley pressed his lips together and focused really hard on Giles's face instead of his sleek black leggings. They were so tight and Giles's thighs looked so firm. Riley had a feeling the backside would look really nice too. "I heard about... what you did."

"The scholarship?" Giles asked and blushed as he swept a hand through his hair.

"The scholarship?" Riley asked loudly, shaking his head as he advanced on Giles.

Giles waved it off. "It's nothing. It's the least we could do and it's going to help a lot of kids like you."

"Like me?" Riley's voice had gone squeaky again and his vision began to blur.

"The Riley Fitzgerald Endowment for Queer Theater Nerds. That's not the official title, but I've raised close to a million with a generous contribution from Frederick Wolford," Giles explained in his low, dismissive rumble.

"No way!" Riley cried and ran to Giles. He jumped and was laughing as Giles caught him. "That's the most *amazing* thing ever!"

"I had to do something, Riley. I hurt you and I made you feel like you didn't matter but *you do*."

Riley noted that his legs were hooked around Giles's hips and was suddenly breathless. And Giles's hands were *hot* as they spread across his back. "This is the biggest thing anyone's ever done for me," Riley said shakily.

"We'd be lost without you. I'd be lost." One of Giles's hands slid upwards and the other hand gripped tighter, holding Riley closer.

"What about all your money? Gavin's worried."

Giles raised a shoulder and his eyes were heavy as they sank into Riley's. "I'm a little more liquid than usual, but this feels a lot better."

"It does?" Riley panted.

There was a loud cough as Wendy arrived with a stack of towels. "You two go right ahead. These are for the shower and the sauna, but I can leave one for ya," she said with a lewd wink.

Riley pushed off Giles's chest and cheered when he landed on his feet and spun. "I'm getting an endowment!" He boasted. "Well, not *me*, but a whole bunch of queer kids are going to go to college and *my name* is going to be on the paperwork!" He informed her.

"That's really great!" She threw an arm out and waved him in for a hug. "I'm not hot or half-naked, but I'm so proud of you!"

"You're beautiful and this is a lot less awkward," Riley whispered loudly as he hugged her. "And Giles did it."

"I did a terrible thing and had to make amends," Giles said. His voice had dropped to a low grumble and he was blushing.

Wendy made a knowing sound. "Why do I get the feeling you really stepped in it? I'm going to put these away and make myself scarce."

"You don't have to do that!" Riley called after her, then widened his eyes at Giles in disbelief. "I came to tell you I was sorry for being so hard on you. And to thank you for all the other things you've done," he said, earning a dismissive snort.

"It really was the least I could do," Giles said as his gaze dropped to the floor. He twisted his fingers before stomping a foot. "If there's anything else I can do, just tell me." His voice crumbled into a ragged plea. "You said there was nothing I could do to fix it, but I need to know that's not true."

"Giles, I..." Riley groaned when he recalled how hurt and angry he had been and all the things he had said. Reid's observations echoed in Riley's ear, making his conscience even heavier. "I hope you can forgive me. Turns out I've been carrying a chip on my shoulder about a lot of things since we were kids."

"I may have noticed," Giles confided in a whisper.

Riley's lips twisted. "Really? I didn't think you noticed me at all. Except when you called me a clumsy little jerk and a Dickensian urchin," he said, holding up a finger. Giles's jaw dropped in horror.

"Oh...*God*. You heard me call you an urchin?"

"A *Dickensian* urchin."

"I didn't mean it and I am so sorry! I was embarrassed and all I could think about was that you played Oliver Twist and everyone went on and on for weeks about it." Giles pressed his hands together, but Riley laughed and shushed him.

"I'm letting go of those old grudges. You don't have to liquidate anything else or start another endowment."

"Thank goodness, because my accountants have been *crying*."

"Oh, no." Riley grimaced sympathetically.

"It's actually been kind of fun." Giles said from behind his hand. "Our calls are usually really dry, but I'm getting my money's worth now."

That made Riley laugh. "You know, I called you a jerk that day at the planetarium too, and I was wrong. You can be really lovely when you let people in."

Giles's furrow was more of a bewildered 2 as he blinked back at Riley. "I see. Thank you."

"You're welcome." Riley tapped his brow and began his retreat, but Giles followed.

"Are you going home later?" He blurted.

"I was going to take off as soon as Julie picks Milo up for the weekend. Why?" Riley watched as Giles's furrow shifted through a range of intensities. He looked like he was growing frustrated so Riley thought he'd throw Giles a lifeline. "I'll probably cut through the park and stop by Rockefeller Center to see the ice skaters. If I'm lucky, I can catch a proposal or two before I take the train back to Brooklyn. You know how sappy everyone gets. But I won't dawdle for too long in case we get as much snow as they say we will."

"You don't have plans for later?" Giles asked.

Riley pulled a face. "The curse is at its most vicious on Valentine's Day so I'm thinking I'll treat myself to a bubble bath and a box of wine."

"The curse?"

"I think I've been dumped in every restaurant in this city. Valentine's dates are ten times worse and do not get me started on morning afters." Riley's hand cut through the air, forbidding further discussion and making Giles's lips twitch into a smile.

"It's probably safer if you stay in, then. And that storm is looking scarier the closer it gets. You don't have to wait for Julie. Take off early and let me fend for myself for dinner."

"We'll see." Riley gave him another salute as he turned on his heel. He'd stick around to help Milo pack and prepare something special for Giles for dinner. It *was* Valentine's Day, after all. Riley might be cursed, but he could still hope.

Chapter Twenty-Six

He was running out of time! Giles could tell by the heady aromas wafting from the kitchen that Riley had prepared something spectacular for dinner. He tried to peek and Riley had run him off, saying it was a surprise.

"For one?" Giles had protested.

Riley had laughed it off. "Milo won't be here and it would be weird if I invited myself to dinner tonight."

"... Right." Giles could have said so many *better* things. Starting with "Stay and..."

It was the *and* that stopped him.

He simply wanted Riley to stay.

How could he explain to Riley how much he'd missed him and that he was everything Giles had ever wanted? That Riley was even more beautiful in person than Giles had ever imagined and that it was magic being able to be this close to him again. That Riley had changed everything in just a handful of weeks and that Giles was completely and hopelessly in love with him.

He'd probably think you're obsessed and never come back.
He might stay if Giles could come up with a decent *and*.
...watch movies with me.
...listen to old records and dance until the storm passes.
...play some board games.
*...teach me to bake **your** favorite thing.*
...cuddle with me and maybe play with my hair.
...let me taste you.
...be mine.

Any of those would have been *amazing* and Giles wanted all of them all at once so he locked up. There was no reason Giles couldn't say any of them before Riley finished whatever he was whipping in the kitchen with the mixer or before he left in...

Giles glanced at the grandfather clock by the front door. "Fifteen minutes!"

Riley usually left at seven and Julie was due at any moment. There was a knock and Giles whimpered.

"Can you get that?" Riley called.

"Okay." Giles's hand slapped across his eyes and dragged down his face as he went to the door. He wasn't sure why Julie was knocking, though...

"Sorry. Hands full!" She announced and angled a tote bin through the door. "Leaving these clothes for Wendy's grandsons." She lowered it and pushed it against the wall so it was out of the way, then turned and whistled loudly around two fingers. "Let's get moving, Milo! Storm's heading for us and I want to be home before it starts snowing."

"He'll be right there," Riley said as he joined them. He'd taken off his apron and was pulling on his cardigan. "He decided he needed his green flannel pajamas and more snacks in case you guys get snowed in."

"We have plenty of snacks!" Julie yelled and ran down the hall to Milo's wing.

"You know how important it is for him to be prepared," Riley said with a wince. "Everything's ready in the kitchen so I'll go ahead and take off."

"Now?" Giles tried to recall *any* of the lovely *and* options he'd come up with, but...there was nothing.

Riley paused as he reached for his jacket. "Did you need something?"

"No! I mean—" Giles begged his brain to just *try*. "Teach me records and taste my hair!" He blurted and covered his mouth to hold back an anguished sob.

Riley started to say something, then stopped. Twice. "Are you alright?" He finally asked and Giles nodded.

"I meant, enjoy the ice skaters at Rockefeller Center."

"Ah." Riley pulled on his backpack and held onto the straps. "Are you sure because...?"

"I'm sure. Have a nice night and thank you for whatever you've done. It smells amazing."

"You're welcome. Have a nice night too," Riley said. He looked toward Milo's room, then made a swatting gesture. "I already gave him six hugs, but tell him I'll see him bright and early on Monday. And give Julie a hug for me."

"I will."

"See you on Monday."

"See you on Monday," Giles said with a weak wave. He watched Riley go and let out a disgruntled sigh. "See you on Monday," he repeated. It was better than *Teach me records and taste my hair,* at least.

"Where's Riley?" Julie asked as she hurried into the living room from the kitchen.

"He went home... After he swings by Rockefeller Center to see if anyone proposes," he said, checking his watch.

"Why did you let him leave?" She wailed, waving her fists at him.

"Because you're taking Milo?" He replied obviously.

That was the wrong answer, apparently. Julie reached for his throat. "*It's Valentine's Day!* I'm taking Milo for the weekend so you can have Riley to yourself!"

"Julie!" Giles looked around her to make sure Milo hadn't heard. "You have no idea what the last week has been like. I'm just glad Riley's talking to me and hasn't quit."

"Oh, I heard about it from Ken. He thinks you've gone off the deep end."

"Ken thought that when I sold the company and when we got the divorce," Giles argued.

Julie's eyes flicked upwards. "When you say it like that... You have had a rather erratic few years."

"I'm fine. Better than fine now that things between Riley and I are okay again."

"You'd be a lot better than okay if you'd put on your coat and go after him," she suggested.

He gave her a flat look, then glanced over her shoulder. "Milo! Pack faster!" He yelled. "I need you to get this woman out of my apartment," he added with a shake of his head at Julie. "I was thinking I'd make myself a drink and watch a movie," he said and headed to the kitchen to see what Riley had left for him. "You should get on the road before it starts to snow."

"I was just saying that so we could get out of your hair. It won't get bad until later tonight," she said with a wave. "Ken's got plenty of firewood stacked and ready to go and we're making s'mores!"

"I haven't had s'mores in forever," Giles noted as he pulled open the fridge, then frowned at a pastry-wrapped bundle resting on a parchment-lined baking sheet. Directions were written on the parchment. He carefully slid the pan out and set it on the counter.

"It's a little beef Wellington!" She gasped and bent to get a closer look. "It's adorable."

It was decorated with pastry hearts and had a shiny golden glaze.

"What am I supposed to do with it?" Giles whispered as if he was afraid he'd disturb it.

"Read the directions, you nerd!" She pointed at the pan, then went to the stove. "Here. It'll beep when it reaches 425°. You put the pan on the center rack, close the door, and set a timer for twenty-five minutes. When it goes off, take the pan out and let it rest for five minutes."

"Then what?" Giles asked warily, his gaze flicking between the pan and the oven.

"You eat it, you robot." She threw him a scolding look as she went to the refrigerator and opened the door. "And there's a gorgeous little salad and what looks like chocolate mousse. Why did you let him leave?" She asked and leaned to stare around the door at him expectantly. "He's *perfect*, Giles."

"Probably. Which makes me wonder why he'd waste his time on a broken robot," he countered.

A hard guffaw burst from Julie. "You're a catch, Giles Ashby! Minus your obvious personality flaws," she said out of the side of her mouth.

"But I have so many," he said, then grunted when she gave his arm a punch.

"I was joking. And I don't think Riley minds. Look at how much love he put into this mini Wellington. I don't think that's store-bought puff pastry," she mused. That seemed significant and she was impressed, so Giles made a note to compliment Riley on it later.

"That's the way Riley does everything."

"That's why he's so perfect for you." Julie threw her arms around Giles, bear-hugging him. He made a weary sound but smiled.

"He can do a lot better," Giles argued, earning a mutinous look.

"There isn't anyone better. I know this because you were married to my sister. It's my job to be critical and not like the men she picks and I think you're perfect. Even with your personality flaws."

"I've hurt him a lot. Since we were kids. He might be a little too aware of my flaws."

"Probably, but he still loves you."

"I don't know that he lo—" Giles was going to contradict her and stopped when she growled and pointed at the Wellington, then pointed at the oven when it beeped loudly. Giles grabbed the pan and ran, then raced to put it in the oven like he was on a cooking game show.

"Bravo! Now, set the timer." She clapped and cheered before becoming serious. "He knows what you're really like and he still loves you. He hasn't resigned and you exposed yourself to him," she said, waving at Giles. "It's clearly love."

"Damn it, Claire!" Giles pinched the bridge of his nose. "Milo? Let's go or you'll both be stuck here with me. And I'd rather have my eyelashes plucked out," he added under his breath.

"I'm ready!" Milo panted as he dragged his largest duffle bag into the kitchen. His backpack was stuffed as well.

"You're just going for the weekend," Giles said and went to get the duffle bag.

Julie gestured for Giles to hand it over. "I can manage," she insisted and slung it over her shoulder while Giles hugged and kissed Milo goodbye.

"Call and check in later," Giles said as he stood and gave

Milo's hair one last ruffle, then flicked his ear playfully. "Take off." He kissed Julie on the cheek and waved as they left.

"He loves me," he told himself and decided he'd give Riley a few hours to visit the rink and get home before calling.

Chapter Twenty-Seven

What if the hearts were too much?
Riley paced in front of the elevator for ten minutes, debating if he should run back and pull them off before Giles saw them. It had been a confusing week for everyone and they had just forgiven each other. What if Giles wasn't ready to "be Valentines" and felt pressured? He'd already done so much just to prove that he cared about Riley. It wasn't fair to make him feel cornered when Giles was practically pinned down with Riley in 8B.

"I can tell him I just did it because it was Valentine's Day, not because I wanted him to be my Valentine," he repeated.

He nodded and gave the button a stab. It wasn't as obvious as a card or flowers. You couldn't hand someone a card, then say "Just kidding!" if they got uncomfortable. But Riley could say it was only a silly design and that he'd simply done it because he had new heart cookie cutters.

Unless Giles wanted to be Riley's Valentine. In that case, Riley totally meant it.

The plan seemed foolproof and the least likely to spook

Giles because he could pretend he hadn't noticed or thought anything of it if he didn't want to be Riley's Valentine.

What if he doesn't think anything of it or assumes I just wanted to use my heart cookie cutters?

He swore at the elevator when it dinged and the doors opened. Riley considered going back but chickened out. He jumped in and hit the button for the lobby. It was a subtle move for a subtle guy. There was no need to rush and they'd had a very intense week.

And he'd literally thrown himself at Giles earlier while he was half-naked. Riley didn't know how to be more obvious than that. They'd had so many almost-kisses, that Riley couldn't help but wonder what kept stopping Giles.

The elevator slowed between the seventh and sixth floors and Riley cried out and began jabbing at the lobby button, hoping it would stop the doors from opening.

"Please, please, noooooo!" He begged, but they opened and *she* was there. "Mrs. Hormsby! Lovely to see you!" He said as he scooted into the corner so Calista could prance into the elevator. She did an elegant turn before parking her rear in the very center, her snout pointing regally at the ceiling.

"You again," Muriel said, and gestured for him to push the button. The doors closed and Riley whistled as he rocked back and forth on his toes.

"Headed home early, I see." She smirked and Riley pushed back his sleeve with his mitten to check his watch.

"It's 7:25. I usually leave around this time," he noted.

Her smirk grew wider as she looked down her nose at Riley. "Huh. Guess you're not worth worrying about after all."

"I did tell you," Riley murmured, giving his head an irritated shake.

She tapped her chin. "Unless he's expecting someone else..."

"I truly wouldn't know." Even though Riley did know.

"A man like that has options and it's particularly telling when he doesn't reach for what's right in front of him. Especially on a night like tonight when it's so...cheap and easy," she added with an amused snort. "He definitely doesn't want you."

Riley *couldn't* defend himself even if he wanted to. He would never embarrass Giles, Reid, or himself in such a manner. But she wasn't totally off, either. Caring about Riley and wanting to mend their relationship wasn't the same as *wanting* Riley. And lots of men had thought they wanted Riley only to quickly lose interest and ghost him. No wonder Giles had been afraid to kiss Riley. How could they avoid each other after Giles gave Riley the It's-not-you-I'm-the-asshole speech?

He suddenly regretted the hearts.

"I hope you have a...special evening," he said to Muriel through a hard, wide smile, bolting as soon as the doors opened.

He wasn't even in the mood to watch the skaters or see any proposals anymore. But Riley needed something to look forward to, some sign that there was still hope for him. It was a half-hour walk through the park and Riley was glad to find the footpaths deserted for once. He felt lonely and confused as he thought about all the couples around the city celebrating first dates and anniversaries.

Would it ever be his turn?

He thought he was close with Giles before and Riley had been heartbroken when he found out about Dexter. It was over before it had begun, and Riley had been made to feel small and worthless without the awful first date or a crushing morning after. It had been his worst break-up ever and it hadn't even been real. What if they went on an actual date or two and went all the way and the curse struck again? Riley didn't know if he'd ever get over it.

Valentine's Day at Rockefeller Center wasn't as busy as

years past due to the storm. Riley was able to jog right down the steps and found a good spot overlooking the rink. Despite his wonky mood and his encounter with Muriel, Riley smiled at a young straight couple as they skated past holding hands. The woman was unsteady and started to slip until her date looped an arm around her waist. It was perfect, the way he swiftly pecked at her cheek and she laughed and kissed him back.

He had obviously decided that she was a keeper, from the way he held onto her waist and kept her other hand pressed against his chest.

Riley noticed the tender gestures, the unintentional hints of familiarity and affection that spoke of *real* intimacy. Those spontaneous acts of caring and adoration couldn't be faked and were private, unspoken conversations that Riley had never experienced. He tried to recall Reid's observations but once again, Riley felt cheap and like he had been discarded too many times to be worth keeping. As Muriel had so kindly pointed out.

No one had ever cared to keep Riley long enough to develop that kind of intimate, physical language that loving couples shared. Apparently, there was something fundamentally *un*lovable about Riley that made it easy for men to discard and forget about him.

He looked down at the ugly sweater beneath his scarf and coat and instead of feeling warm and cheerful, he wondered why Giles would want to keep him when no one else had. But Riley told himself that Giles wouldn't have done all those amazing things if he didn't care an awful lot. He tried his best to believe as he scanned all the keepers on the ice.

Riley stopped and held his breath when he spotted a gay couple across the rink. One of the men got down on one knee and Riley did what he always did and made a wish, that one day it would be his turn. Until Riley realized that he *knew* the man holding up the black velvet ring box.

It was Taylor, and Riley's heart sank right to his feet as the other man cried and nodded. Riley assumed that it was the oncologist, and he was obviously everything that Riley *wasn't*. He was tall, muscular, handsome, well-dressed... Masculine.

Riley backed away from the rink, cold and so bitter it hurt. He was almost thirty and Riley was still a... Twink. The word made his insides twist. Twinks were cute on social media and hot in porn. And they were fun to fool around with and to "try" for a night. But a tall, fit oncologist with a perfect five o'clock shadow and immaculate hair looked so much better in engagement announcements and made you look like a power couple at posh parties. Men like Taylor proposed to men like *that* and that was the kind of man who got recklessly passionate kisses in the pantry. He was a keeper and Riley was a maybe who dressed like someone's gramps.

He was being so naive when he placed those hearts on the Wellington. *That* was why Giles hadn't kissed him. Why would Giles turn his life upside down for a twenty-eight-year-old man who still wore a backpack like a middle schooler and played with cookie cutters? Riley's fashion aesthetic was that of an elderly man from Flushing and he wondered why Giles hadn't made a move? Why would he?

"I'm such an idiot." Riley turned away from the rink and stuffed his hand in his pocket for his phone, intending to text Fin. It wasn't there and panic flared as Riley checked all his pockets. "Oh, no." His gaze swept upward and over the trees to the Olympia. Riley could see his phone in the pantry by the cookie cutters. He'd taken it out to double-check the Wellington recipe and set it down to look for the right heart cutter. For a moment, Riley considered leaving it until Monday, but he couldn't cut off his communication with his parents,

Reid, and Fin when a major snowstorm was headed toward the city.

Riley checked his watch for the time, then swore at the clumps of snow dancing in the lamplight. He wrapped his arms around himself as he ran, working through a plan as he raced back to the Olympia. He'd wasted too much time worrying about the stupid hearts when he was already pushing his luck with a stop at Rockefeller Center. Now, he'd have to impose upon Fin and Walker if he couldn't get a train or a cab back to Brooklyn.

There were no cabs around Rockefeller Center and Riley suspected he'd be hit with surge pricing if he tried to catch an Uber. If he had his phone. A train wouldn't save him very much time so he turned around and cut through the park again. Riley's face was numb and his mittens were soggy and frosted when he hurried past the lone doorman at the 72nd Street entrance.

"You should be on your way home!" Carl said when he got the door for Riley. "It's gonna be a real blizzard this time. I can tell!"

"I left my phone," Riley said, hanging his head in shame. "I've got friends just around the corner. I can stay with them if it's too late to get back to Brooklyn."

"Hurry." Carl shooed him along. "I'm about to take off and there won't be anyone down here in an hour except a few guards."

"I'll be fine. I'm just gonna sneak in, grab my phone, and sneak back out," Riley promised. "Get home before your wife starts to worry."

"Have a good night, Riley." Carl gave Riley's back a warm pat as he got into the elevator.

"I will."

The doors closed, punctuating the lie and leaving Riley

Giles Ashby Needs A Nanny

with his bedraggled reflection in the glossy chrome. He couldn't see his face; it was a pink, droopy blur like the rest of him. Fin and Walker would feel even sorrier for Riley and he wondered if he could be more pathetic as he took out his keys and trudged back to 8B.

He was about to find out.

Chapter Twenty-Eight

The city was hunkering down for the storm. Giles could see the signs of life grinding to a halt from his bedroom window and was soothed. Brave taxis and a few buses crawled through hazy intersections while the night grew silent and brighter as snow blanketed the roads and sidewalks. The harsh, hustling world outside the Olympia was still and peaceful and Giles wished he could wander the barren streets and Central Park.

"Maybe if I had some snowshoes..." Giles mused. He wasn't foolish enough to risk going out at night when the temperature was dropping, but a morning walk in the park after a blizzard might be fun.

Giles's gaze swung to the hallway when he heard a soft creak and steps in the front hall. He went around the bed and grabbed the bat from under the mattress before hurrying into the hallway and through to the foyer. There was a trail of puddles on the marble tile, confirming Giles's fears and making his stomach clench and sour. He raised the bat over his head when he heard a soft swear in the kitchen. Giles rushed past the wall and the counter, ready to swing if the intruder was bigger than him.

"What are you doing?" He demanded, stunning a dripping-wet Riley.

"I'm so sorry! I forgot my phone and I thought I could sneak in without bothering you!" He cried, attempting to shield himself with his phone and a mitten.

"Jesus! I'm sorry!" Giles held out a hand as he set the bat on the counter. "I didn't mean to scare you."

Riley shook his head quickly, then dragged one of his red-striped mittens under his nose. Snow still clung to the threads and Riley's eyelashes, but Giles could see that his nose wasn't red from the cold. At least, the cold wasn't the only reason Riley's nose was red and he was sniffling. "No! It was my fault! It was me!" Riley rasped, before taking a deep, shuddering gulp. "Of course, it was me." His lip trembled as he avoided looking at Giles.

"What's your fault?" Giles asked and gasped when he remembered he had stripped off his sweater and T-shirt. He wrapped an arm around himself, suddenly self-conscious.

Riley let out a heavy sigh. "This..." He glanced down at his phone and shrugged. "Everything, probably. It has to be me, right? I keep blaming it on the curse, but it's just me. Nobody wants *a boy* who's a middle-aged gramps."

"A gramps?" Giles swept a hand through his hair, lost and feeling a touch helpless when Riley's eyes puddled with tears. He swallowed a hiccup, bravely fighting a sob. "Oh, God! Please don't cry!" Giles carefully reached for Riley, unsure if he'd be helping or if he wanted all that cold, wet wool against his skin. He was already chilled from the draft in the hall and Riley was still shivering.

"I won't!" Riley shook his head, but he was failing miserably. He tried to hide his face with his mittens and Giles's heart broke as Riley's shoulders folded inward.

Giles groaned, pulling Riley into his arms. "Come here!"

"I... I..." Riley's chest heaved as he leaned into Giles. He remained small and shuddering and he didn't return Giles's embrace, but it was still miraculous being able to put his arms around Riley. His cheek rested against Giles's pec and the damp, scratchy wool was forgotten. A hot, defeated huff feathered against Giles's skin, deepening the ache in his chest.

"Shhhh... Whatever happened, it couldn't have been your fault." Giles was able to rock him and rub his back soothingly for a few moments before Riley's head popped up and he leaned back.

"It has to be," Riley stated, certain despite his wavering voice and sniffles. "I keep telling myself that someone's going to want me. But I just saw my ex—if I can even call him that—and the guy he dumped me for, and it's pretty obvious that he's... everything I'm not. And I'll never be as tall or handsome or as successful as that guy. I'm always going to be this scrawny... nothing," he added softly.

"That's not true." Giles couldn't keep the hard edge out of his voice or hide what he thought of this ex and all the other men who'd been so damn wrong about Riley. "You're perfect just the way you are. You've always been perfect," he said firmly. "I don't know what's wrong with them, aside from the fact that men are...*men*, but you've always been perfect."

"Then, why am I still alone if I'm perfect? Why doesn't anyone want to keep me?" Riley challenged, sounding a touch bitter and defiant.

"I do! I've always wanted yo—" Giles's eyes widened and his jaw hung slack when his brain finally caught up to his mouth and his heart.

"Me?" Riley looked stunned as he blinked back at Giles,

then shook his head slowly. "You never said... Why would you want me?"

"Want you?" Giles brushed the hair away from Riley's tear and snow-streaked cheek and cradled it. "I think I was in love with you before I really understood what that meant. And when I did, it scared me and I acted like an even bigger jerk. I don't know why, but I could *never* say or do the right thing around you. You know what I'm like. *Now*," he said, flashing Riley a pained grimace.

"I do know." He rested a mitten on the center of Giles's chest as he rose on his toes. Surprised, Giles froze and his heart stopped beating as Riley's lips brushed his. He couldn't breathe, but he didn't want to. Giles didn't want to pop the bubble or break the spell. "Do you...still?" The word was just a breath against Giles's lips, but it might as well have been a cymbal clash. Riley must have felt Giles jump and the way his heart started with a hard kick beneath that mitten.

"More than ever. So much it hurts sometimes," Giles admitted. He was stunned again when Riley's other arm hooked around Giles's neck, pulling him down and closer. Riley's tongue swept between Giles's lips and he couldn't help the hungry groan that escaped from him. He gathered Riley in his arms and Giles's head spun as he danced them closer to the counter for support.

Nothing had ever felt as good or as easy as Riley's lips and tongue tangling and swirling with Giles's. It was even more intoxicating than his fantasies and Giles wasn't thinking as he lifted Riley and set him on the counter.

"More!" Riley ordered, tearing off a mitten. His hand was so warm as it captured Giles's cheek for another desperate kiss. Giles growled in agreement as he lapped and sucked. He grabbed Riley by the hips and pulled him to the edge, locking them together.

They became frantic and their breaths turned into grunts, hisses, and whimpers as they ground against each other and their hands wandered. Riley's legs were wound tight around Giles's hips and they were both hard and shaking.

"Should we...slow down?" Giles asked. The more logical and careful parts of Giles's brain said *yes*, but his tongue dragged along Riley's jaw and curled around his earlobe.

Fingers twisted in Giles's hair and Riley's cold mitten had found its way into the back of his trousers. "Probably. But... Please don't."

"Okay."

And Giles didn't. He quickly peeled off Riley's other mitten and his chunky wool cardigan. Giles had to know what was beneath those cheerful knits and baggy layers. He needed to touch and taste as much as he could get his hands and lips on.

He whisked away Riley's T-shirt and paused for just a moment so he could squint at the cartoon unicorn tattooed on Riley's pec. There were also beautiful vines crawling along his ribs and around his back.

"Don't stop!" Riley urged, his hair wild and his lips glistening and swollen as he reached for Giles.

"Sorry." Giles murmured the words against Riley's clavicle before he licked it. He sucked on Riley's shoulder and Giles let go. His hands attacked buckles and laces, shoving at clothes as his tongue washed over Riley's skin. He tugged at one of Riley's nipples with his teeth and Giles enjoyed his agonized yelp. And he really liked the way Riley writhed and clawed at his back and his ass.

"Oh, God!" Riley panted, rolling his hips for more friction. "My backpack!" His hand swatted blindly on the counter. Giles reached and pulled it closer, then promptly got distracted by the corner of Riley's jaw. It was so sharp and there was just a trace of stubble. He licked it and nibbled on the other earlobe, making Riley shudder. Giles thrilled at the goosebumps beneath his lips and hands, knowing *he* was holding Riley and making him frantic.

Because Giles would not take a second for granted or assume that he'd ever have another chance like this. He was either dreaming or this was a touch of madness brought on by the storm.

Riley pressed a condom and a packet of lube into Giles's palm, setting *every* teenage fantasy ablaze. Nothing his hormone-addled brain had conjured had ever been as hot as this.

"Here?" Giles asked, but his pants were already around his ankles.

"Here. Hurry!" Riley whispered, then made it almost impossible for Giles to focus. His hot, clever hands had found Giles's cock. They wandered and stroked between them, shredding Giles's control.

"Riley!" He captured Riley's lips for a deep, demanding kiss. Giles sheathed and coated his cock, but he teased Riley with slick fingers and his tongue first. He drank Riley's strangled cries and swears, winding him up and preparing him. Riley was so tight and hot and so beautiful as he clung to Giles's shoulders and begged for more.

Giles eased into clenching heat and the heady rush of pleasure and excitement was almost too much. "Oh fuck, fuck, fuck…" He could feel pressure swelling in his sac and needed a moment. He rested his forehead on Riley's and they were both drowning, chests heaving and their gazes drunken and unfocused. "I *dreamt* about this, but it's so much better and you're even more beautiful than I imagined."

"Beautiful?" Riley blinked at Giles, clearing his vision. His brows pulled together as if he was seeing something different or new and Giles prayed Riley still wanted what he saw. What if it was too much or too weird? "I never... I had no idea." Riley whispered. His soft yet clever fingers traced and explored Giles's shoulders and back, one hand drifting lower to delicately cup an ass cheek. "If I had known..." Nails bit into Giles's flesh, igniting his need and cindering his control.

"It feels like I've spent half my life wishing I could find the *right* words to tell you how beautiful you are and that I've always wanted to be closer to you."

"I didn't know!" Riley's arms tightened around Giles's neck and his kiss was seeking and urgent. "I told myself you'd never want me, but I couldn't stop thinking about you."

"Riley, I..." He couldn't tell Riley he loved him or how much he needed him so Giles showed him with his lips and his body. Giles kissed him with as much devotion and tenderness as he could muster and slowly slid deeper into Riley's ass. "I... I need you," he managed, flexing his hips and lifting Riley off the counter with each driving thrust.

"Yes. Please. Need me," Riley babbled, his head bobbing limply as he held on.

He might not have meant it and could have been saying it because he was caught up in the moment, but his words went straight to Giles's heart. It grew warmer and larger and began to beat harder. He felt like laughing and he was so damn *happy* as he wrapped his arms around Riley and let go. His face burrowed into the corner of Riley's neck and he buried himself in slick, gripping heat. Giles was drowning in Riley and it was one of the most glorious moments *of his life.*

"Always. I'll always need you," he said and scared himself.

What if Riley changed his mind in the morning? How could Giles go back to pretending he wasn't madly in love or that he didn't know the intoxicating joy of losing himself in Riley like this? His anxiety began to spike, but Giles shoved the panic away. He bit and sucked on Riley's shoulder, grounding himself and searing the moment in his memory. It might be all he had later so Giles used his hands, his lips, and his body to *show* Riley everything he couldn't express with words.

Giles leaned back and cupped Riley's cheek, cherishing it. Riley's lips were swollen and glistened from their rough kisses and were just as sweet as Giles thought they'd be. His big blue eyes were drunk with lust, but they followed Giles's hand as it explored and caressed. His ragged moans and stifled swears took Giles even higher and made everything so much hotter. Goosebumps trailed under Giles's fingertips as he explored the tight planes of Riley's chest and stomach, committing every detail to memory. He found the faint trail of hair beneath Riley's navel and Giles vowed he'd taste everything he touched before the night was through.

"Yes!" Riley snatched Giles's hand, guiding it lower. Giles gripped Riley's cock and gave it a tentative stroke.

"Like this?" He asked and received a quick, jerky nod.

"I'm so close!" Riley choked out, then bit into his lip to hold back a scream.

"Let me hear you!" Giles begged, bucking harder as he tightened his grip around Riley.

"Oh, God!"

Giles groaned encouragingly. "That's it. Come for me, I need to taste you."

"Giles!" Riley's head fell back on a hoarse sob, his body twitching as cum spilled over Giles's fist. That was all it took to push Giles over the edge and his soul burst into a million bright, hot pieces.

"Riley!" He captured Riley's lips for a breathless, shaking kiss. "Riley, Riley, Riley..." Giles was ecstatic and babbling as he nibbled on Riley's lips and licked the cum from his fingers.

"So perfect and so beautiful," he huffed, rubbing his forehead against Riley's.

"I feel beautiful. Thank you," Riley whispered. He flung an arm around Giles's shoulders. "Can we stay like this for a while?" He sounded drowsy as his cheek nuzzled Giles's.

"How about...?" Giles scooped him up and hooked Riley's legs around his waist. "We move someplace more comfortable?"

"Oh!" Riley hung on and looked around them with wide eyes. "You're *really* strong!"

Giles gave him a dubious look. "You're not that much heavier than my rowing gear," he noted, then caught Riley's pained wince. "Sorry! Not that you aren't—"

"I'm a little scrawny," Riley stated, and his back and neck had stiffened.

"Shhhh... That's not what I meant and I don't think you're scrawny, Riley." Giles paused and set him down so he could catch Riley by the chin. "Look at me. You were my first and *only* crush and I've never gotten over you. I thought I could pretend and ignore my feelings, or that I'd get used to being close to you every day. But it just got worse and I can't stop thinking about you," he confided with an apologetic grimace.

"Is that so?" Riley asked and a small, calculating smile tugged at his lips when Giles nodded. "In that case, you'd better pick me back up and get me to a bed in a hurry."

Chapter Twenty-Nine

T*here's no way.*
Every bit of Riley's common sense promised that there was no way he and Giles had done *it*. Twice, even. His vision was blurry but his eyes widened as he recalled what had happened in the kitchen and in Giles's bed. He was still wrapped in Giles's arms and the rising sun was beginning to glow against the frosted windows, filling the room with soft peaches and pinks. It made the morning even more surreal and Riley recalled the hours of teasing and kissing. They flirted and wound each other up until Riley took matters—and Giles—into his own hands.

Riley was both ashamed and proud, and his cheeks grew hot as he basked in every lewd detail. It started with the slowest, sluttiest blowjob Riley had ever performed. Which resulted in Giles begging Riley to sit on his face with things just getting dirtier after that. Riley mounted Giles backward and rode him like a Hippity Hop. He was feeling a little tender and wouldn't be surprised if they were both bruised, but it had been the most magical night of Riley's life.

And it had happened with Giles.

Riley wasn't sure if he was more surprised that Giles was secretly an animal or by all the revelations he had shared. It didn't seem possible and Riley was sure he'd dreamt the entire encounter in the kitchen. He remembered what they were like as teenagers and couldn't imagine what Giles had seen in him. There was also the biting irony that Prince Charming had been right there all along, camouflaged among the many toads Riley had kissed over the years.

Don't get ahead of yourself again. This is when the curse usually strikes.

He took a deep breath, gathering his courage before he rolled over and faced Giles and reality. Riley promised himself that this time was different as he reached for the hand curled against his chest and raised it. He gave Giles's knuckle a playful nip before wiggling around so they were nose-to-nose.

"Morning!" Riley said brightly, but his hopes buckled when he noted the tightening of Giles's lips and that his furrow was at a heavy 5 or a possible 6. "What...?" Riley croaked.

He heard the heavy sigh and reared back as Giles's frown intensified. "We have to talk. I—"

"Oh, no, no, no!" Riley shook his head as he rolled out of the bed. Sirens blared in his psyche, warning that another hit was imminent. The curse had struck again and it had struck in 8B. Riley's body vibrated with panic and mortification as all the awful consequences exploded in his conscience.

"Riley, wait!"

"No!" Riley held up a hand. "Please don't say anything! I should have known better!" He whimpered as he looked around for his clothes, then swore over his shoulder at the bedroom door. His clothes and his dignity were in the kitchen. "I thought this time was different, but I am fucking cursed!" He stumbled over a pillow, tripping as he dashed for the door.

Giles Ashby Needs A Nanny

"Riley, please!" Giles called after him. "I'm sorry, I didn't mean—" There was a loud bang, but Riley didn't look back.

He ran down the hall and past the living room. Riley spotted his backpack and his boxers on the kitchen counter and was like a guided missile, zipping through the kitchen gathering clothes and sneakers. He dressed like he was fleeing a fire and slipped out of the front door just as Giles came crashing out of the bedroom in his robe.

"Riley, wait!"

"I have to go!"

Riley ran for the open elevator and hit the button for the lobby as soon as he had cleared the doors.

"Wait!" Giles pleaded, but the doors closed, cutting him off.

"What was I thinking?" Riley scolded as he tugged on his beanie. He stuffed each fist into a mitten before giving himself several punches to the forehead. Everything had happened so quickly, but he'd trusted Giles and the little voice in his head that told Riley that this time *had* to be different. He knew Giles so much better than all those other men. And Giles had been perfect and had said all the things Riley had ever hoped to hear. "Now what am I going to do?"

He watched the numbers as they flashed on the display and mopped at his cheeks before the elevator came to a stop. The doors opened and Riley peeked out to give the lobby a quick scan. It was empty. Too empty, and Riley's heart sank faster when he noted that Carl wasn't at his post.

"Oh, no!" Riley ran to the courtyard and gasped in horror at all the bright white snow. He rushed through to the other lobby and found it abandoned as well. The city was buried in snow. It was everywhere and the streets and sidewalks were empty and silent as he used his shoulder to heave one of the doors open. The sidewalks and the street hadn't been cleared and salted yet. He had a feeling the trains wouldn't be running, but he couldn't bear the thought of showing his face at The Killian House this early. It would be obvious he was fleeing another disastrous one-night stand and it wouldn't be hard to guess where it had taken place. Riley groaned and trudged toward the park. "I'll cut through and see if I can get a taxi," he muttered, hoping there'd be more signs of life closer to Rockefeller Center.

He kept his head down, ducking from the wind and snowflakes that whipped at his cheeks. He didn't want to know if anyone was witnessing his stumble of shame as he slogged into Central Park and headed for the bridal path.

No one needed to see Riley's eyes puddle with tears as he replayed every kiss and every touch. He heard all the impossibly romantic confessions and promises and recalled how *right* it all had felt. But it wasn't and Riley's heart hurt even worse this time because he allowed himself to believe it had all been real when he fell asleep in Giles's arms.

"What am I going to do?" He staggered to a stop and looked around. All the paths were buried in snow and his Converse and socks were already soaked through. He wasn't sure if there would be any taxis or if he even wanted to go home. Fin wouldn't be there to tell him everything would be alright. There was Reid and Gavin's, but Riley would have to tell them what had happened and he wasn't ready to admit that he'd fooled himself and that the curse had struck again. He stopped to take stock and realized there was only one safe option. "There's nowhere to go but The Killian House," he said, turning back toward the Olympia.

Riley hung his head and began to cry in earnest because he didn't want to barge into Fin's fairytale life with another disastrous morning after. Which made him feel like a terrible friend for not being as happy for Fin as he should have been and for being jealous.

He couldn't remember feeling more alone as he covered his face and sobbed into his mittens. Then, he had a whole new reason to panic when he realized he wasn't all alone in the park. Riley heard a shrill cackle and whipped around when there were hoots and answering jeers from the bridge. A pack of older teenagers was roaming the park.

"I see someone!" One of them yelled and Riley ran back the way he had come as soon as the first snowball zipped past his ear. The second one pelted him between the shoulder blades, almost knocking Riley off his feet and making him trip and slip in the loosely packed snow. He covered his head as he clumsily fled, feeling truly pathetic.

"*Hey!*" A voice boomed. "Knock it off!" It ordered before a snowball flew past Riley from the other direction. Riley swung around just as it hit one of the teenagers in the shoulder. He screamed as his friend was hit in the chest.

"Let's go!" One of the kids yelled, waving for the rest of them to follow as he took off for the bridge. Riley pushed out a relieved breath, turning to thank his rescuer.

Of course, it's Giles.

And he looked like Mr. Darcy striding through a dewy pasture at sunrise. He'd pulled on the perfect cable knit sweater, a black overcoat, and sexy yet sensible black boots. His dark waves fluttered with the wind and his breath surrounded him with dramatic puffs of steam.

How is that even fair?

"Are you alright?" Giles asked, glowering at the bridge. He cradled Riley's cheek and his frown was severe as he searched Riley's eyes. "You were crying. Did they hurt you or was it me again?"

"I'll be alright," Riley lied in a weak, quivering voice. "I just... I just..." He started but Riley didn't know how to slap a Band-Aid on this one. "I thought last night was magic and that the curse had finally been broken. But I was wrong and I had to get out of there before I got dumped again."

"Dumped?" Giles's expression morphed into shock and he laughed wryly as he shook his head. "No, I was mad at myself because I don't want to go back to the way it was before. I can't pretend and I don't know if I'll be able to sleep without you after last night."

"Oh!" Riley would have taken several snowballs to the face, he felt so foolish. "That's what you wanted to talk about."

Giles's nose wrinkled as he nodded. "I don't know what last night was, but I can't lose you."

"Oh..." Riley blinked up at Giles. "I was way off, then."

Giles's deep chuckle slid through Riley, warming him to his toes. "It happens to the best of us."

"I'm sorry I panicked and ran," Riley said, leaning into Giles and stretching toward his lips.

"I probably could have smiled and said good morning first. I know better," Giles murmured. His lips nudged Riley's and a hand splayed possessively across his lower back.

"Maybe we should start over."

"I'd like that. Let's go home and get you into something warm. Your feet have to be freezing."

"I don't know. Can't really feel them," Riley sighed and hummed dreamily as he pecked at Giles's lips.

"What?" Giles jerked back, then hooked his arm around Riley's, towing him along. "You need coffee and a hot bath."

Riley smothered a giggle. "I meant it in the really nice, floaty way, but I like the sound of that too. Will you be joining me?" He asked, causing Giles to stumble this time. His face grew red as he nodded and grumbled under his breath about them getting sick. Which was adorable. And incredibly sexy.

Riley was looking forward to being naked with Giles again until he asked himself what that meant. "Hold on." He gave Giles's arm a hard tug, halting them.

"I think it's starting to snow again," Giles noted, sounding a touch impatient, and squinted up at the sky.

"Maybe," Riley said dismissively and gave Giles a shake. "What are we going to do about Milo?"

That earned Riley another one of Giles's deeply furrowed frowns. "Milo?"

"You know, your tiny clone. He's about this tall and he's the raddest little man on the planet," Riley said, raising his hand to the middle of his chest to remind Giles.

Giles captured Riley's hand and nodded. "I know the guy. He's my best friend. He's been on to me for weeks and wants me to ask you out."

"No." Riley shook his head, then paused and recalled some rather odd hints and comments from Milo. "That adds up, now that you mention it." He snorted and waved his mittens. "It doesn't matter. Milo's just a kid and he doesn't know better. But we do."

"We do?"

"Yes!" Riley pulled on Giles's sleeve to get them moving again. Now that he was back on earth, his toes *were* getting painfully cold. "This is only fun for Milo if everything goes the way he's hoping. What if we decide we're better off as friends later?" He asked. It was far better than the worst-case scenario, but it was bad enough in Riley's mind. "How's he going to feel if this doesn't turn out the way he's hoping?"

They had come out of the park and the street was still silent and blanketed in pristine white, save for two sets of tracks from the Olympia. Riley took a moment to appreciate the rare sight of the city in hibernation. Dirty tracks would crisscross over their footprints and the snow would turn to gray slush soon, but it was pristine and peaceful as dawn crept over rooftops and skyscrapers. He checked to see if Giles was finding it as moving, only to catch him staring at Riley instead.

"What?" He asked and gave the side of his beanie a tug, suddenly self-conscious. He'd practically jumped into his clothes and was sobbing as he fled from the Olympia. Riley could only imagine how miserable he looked. "I probably *need* a bath and fresh clothes."

"You *need* to get in where it's warm, but aside from that, you're perfect. That's not it, though," Giles said, raising Riley's mitten and kissing it as they crossed the street. Somehow, Riley's fingers grew warmer inside his mitten. "You *never* forget about Milo and you always put him first. I love—" His eyes widened as watched out for the curb, then offered Riley his arm. He coughed awkwardly, risking a glance at Riley. "I love that about you."

"That's kind of my job, and I *love* Milo," Riley replied with a shrug.

"I know and that's why I trust you. I don't like hiding things from Milo but we should probably figure out where this is going before we get his hopes up."

Giles got the door and Riley was immediately grateful for the warm blast of air on his face. He recalled that there were *supposed* to be doormen and that someone could materialize at any moment. He released Giles's hand so he could speedwalk through the lobby. Riley didn't look back as he hurried through the courtyard and the doors on the other side.

"What are you doing?" Giles asked when he caught up with Riley at the elevator.

Riley gave him a loaded look and pulled Giles with him when the doors opened. His cheeks puffed out while he waited for the doors to close. He turned to Giles once the elevator was in motion. "We need to be careful because Milo *will* get his hopes up if we get caught and he finds out. And you'll have to think about what will happen when he tells someone. We can't ask him to lie and help us hide an affair," he warned.

"I don't want him to hide it and this isn't an affair," Giles argued. "But I don't want to get his hopes up until we're sure."

"I'll make you a deal," Riley said, smiling as he rose on his tiptoes and offered his lips. "We'll take this slow so that neither of us panics again. And we'll keep being honest with each other."

By slow, you mean...?" Giles groaned and pecked at Riley's lips.

The elevator dinged and they parted on frustrated sighs when the doors opened. Giles leaned out and checked before grabbing Riley's hand and running for 8B. He quickly dealt with the lock and lifted Riley as he swept them into the apartment, kicking the door shut behind him.

Riley gasped as he attacked Giles's lips. "The relationship part. We're gonna have a lot of sex, but I don't want to rush the rest of this. You and Milo are too important to me."

"That sounds..." Giles's voice had dropped to a deep rasp. "Great. But not until you've warmed up and had some coffee. And we come clean and tell Milo the truth if he catches us," he stipulated.

Giles's large hands cradled Riley's ass as he strode down the hall and through his foyer to his bedroom. They passed the bed and Riley was giddy as Giles carried him into the bathroom and set him on his feet. Riley could only nod in agreement as Giles went to the tub and turned on the water. He stripped off his coat and tossed it at the closet as he prowled toward Riley. Steam was already billowing from the tub, making the moment even more surreal, and Giles even more dewy and dashing.

"You're freezing," Giles complained, shaking Riley from his trance.

"Right!" Riley hopped on one foot and yanked at his laces. He refused to acknowledge his reflection in any of the mirrors, afraid to know how wilted and soggy he looked during what would most likely be a pivotal moment for him.

And he couldn't watch as Giles stripped off his sweater and his boots. Riley had no faith in his ability to remain composed.

This is really happening!

"You are going to join me, though?" He asked, then bit down on his lips and scolded himself for being so horny. Which only got worse as Giles gathered Riley in his arms. He eased Riley's sweater off and backed him toward the tub.

"After I've made the coffee, but I just want to hold you and let this all sink in. I've waited a long time for you."

"Good luck with that." Riley cut his eyes at Giles. "You can't say something that perfect and *not* get laid," he said, warning Giles as he got in the tub.

Chapter Thirty

Giles would never be able to look at his bathtub again without getting turned on. He grinned at it through the mirror as he brushed his teeth and recalled every sultry detail of his first bath with Riley.

They didn't want to deal with a condom in the tub so they kissed and writhed against each other in the water. It was the most astoundingly sensual moment of Giles's life, holding Riley and lazily fingering him. He watched Riley's chest heave and goosebumps spread across his skin and Giles was living his wettest dream. His cock was nestled between the cheeks of Riley's ass and his fingers were gripped in slick, tight heat. Riley's moans and pleas mingled with the steam and Giles could still hear their echoes as he dried his face.

They decided they didn't need condoms when they ran out on Saturday morning. Neither wanted to make a bodega run in the snowpocalypse and Riley shared that he was on PrEP and his recent labs were clear and negative. They spent the day in bed and the sex was...astoundingly filthy and life-altering. Giles had always enjoyed sex, but spilling himself deep in Riley's ass and then licking him clean had changed Giles's understanding of what an orgasm could be and what it should taste like. And the hours of touching, whispering, and giggling had been *bliss*.

Giles wasn't feeling very relaxed as he pulled on his robe. He was asking a lot of his morning coffee ritual. Riley was still sleeping, snuggled under the duvet with a dreamy smile curving his lips. It was easy to guess why he was smiling and nothing could stop Giles's heart from racing or calm the flutter in his stomach.

The last twenty-four hours had been magical. Even the part when Riley had fled from the apartment. Giles had done exactly the right thing for once because he recognized that Riley had panicked. Giles knew that what he had felt had been real and that Riley had felt it too. He also got to play the hero in the park and had an excuse to pamper Riley for the rest of the morning.

But their fantasy weekend was coming to an end. The city had dug itself out from under the snow and Julie would have Milo home by dinner time. It was decided that Riley would leave a little after lunch and they'd be careful when Milo and Wendy were home until they were ready to tell them.

Giles didn't have any doubts and he was ready, but he understood why Riley had concerns. He hadn't been treated well in the past, from what Giles had gathered, and Riley was afraid of letting Milo down. To Giles, that was an opportunity to quietly show Riley that he could be a thoughtful and attentive partner and that the curse was truly broken.

Except he didn't want to hide how wildly in love he was. And Giles didn't want Riley to return to Brooklyn in the evenings. They would only be able to spend the weekend together when Milo was at Jack's. That would make for some long nights, but Giles couldn't fault Riley for putting Milo first and establishing some boundaries until he felt safe.

Giles suspected his therapist would suggest something similar when they talked later in the week. He was looking forward to telling Dr. Vargas that he'd finally gone for it with Riley. Dr. Vargas had insisted that Giles was ready to put himself out there and make an honest attempt at dating.

Which meant that Giles had to be honest about why he'd never dated and why he'd "retired" before he was thirty. Riley needed to understand just how much Claire had been a crutch so the pattern wouldn't repeat itself. And Giles had to be truthful and warn Riley about the shrinking of his world.

Riley was just waking up when Giles arrived with their coffee. "Thank you," Riley said as he sipped and eyed Giles over his cup. "That's a strong three," he said, humming in concern.

"What's a strong three?" Giles asked and Riley waved his cup at him.

"The furrow. I can tell how serious something is or how mad you are by the degree of your brow furrow. What's wrong?"

Giles snorted. "Nothing. Everything's great. We said we were going to be honest and I was thinking about my therapist and what he's going to say and I have a feeling he'd tell me to be honest too," he said, clearly rambling.

It was Riley's turn to frown and Giles wondered if he needed a scale to predict Riley's moods. "I'm always in favor of honesty, but you're worrying me again."

"No. It's nothing bad..." Giles shifted restlessly on the edge of the bed. "It's about the company and Claire. We didn't sell because it was holding her back and she was ready to move on. Well. She was and I knew it was holding her back, but that was my escape hatch."

"Your escape hatch?" Riley's brow arched. Giles could see the pieces quickly adding up in Riley's mind and nodded.

"I didn't want to do it anymore. The meetings and the calls and the dinners... It was getting to be too much and there was the constant push to chase what's next. I've never responded well to being pushed, but Claire thrives on the pressure and she wanted to keep growing. While I..." He raised a shoulder.

"Wanted to get smaller?" Riley guessed.

Giles sighed, releasing the tightness in his chest at the memory of all those late nights and long calls. All the stress and all the shouting, even when everything was going their way. "There was so much peace in just letting it all go. We made this amazing thing together and turned it into something worth millions and millions of dollars and that was all the glory I needed. I was only riding it out for Claire, but it was such a relief when she started taking calls from other tech companies and looking over the horizon. You can't sit still or stop growing in that world or your company and your product withers on the vine and I've never been cut out for that."

"You set her free. And now you're afraid you'll withdraw even more," Riley realized.

"I'm not afraid. It just seems inevitable. But I do worry that you won't be content with this small, inside life," Giles explained. "I don't mind traveling now and then if I have to and I *live* for Milo's recitals and school projects, but I'd be happy if I never had to leave the Olympia again."

Riley humphed seriously as he studied his cup. "That isn't much of a news flash, as far as you never wanting to leave. And I'm not surprised that you didn't have the bandwidth for that kind of life. Now that I know you," he amended with a grimace. "From the outside, it looked like you did it for the money and because you could. I thought you were just being rich and eccentric."

"No. Just rich and dysfunctional," Giles murmured and took a sip of his coffee.

Riley gave him another one of his scolding looks. He was so good at them and secretly, they got Giles a little hot. "You're not dysfunctional," Riley stated, giving Giles a firm nod. "You have a disability, but that doesn't mean there's anything wrong with you or the way you live. And you have me now. I won't let you lose touch with the world and I'll protect this small inside life because you deserve to feel safe."

"Safe?" Giles mouthed, unable to find his voice.

"*Yes,*" Riley insisted. He took their cups and put them on the bedside table so he could hold Giles's hands. "The way you protect Milo and do whatever it takes to make this place as safe and soothing for him as you can. I can do that for you."

No one had ever offered to be Giles's defender before. Not even Claire. She'd acted as his shield so he didn't have to give speeches or meet with teachers, but she'd always warned that Giles would have to face the world on his own someday. She'd worried that she was enabling and stunting his ability to cope with his anxiety.

When in reality, there wasn't a pill Giles could take and no amount of therapy was ever going to extinguish all the fires in his brain. There was no magic cure for anxiety. Riley was the first person to accept that Giles would always have his anxiety and that he was fine exactly the way he was, that it was okay to choose a small, quiet inside life if that's where he felt safest.

"I always knew!" Giles tapped on the center of his chest. The words had rushed to his lips and his tongue was tied as he became overwhelmed with joy and gratitude. "I knew that if I could find a way to show you how I felt, that you'd understand that I wasn't...*awful,* and I knew I'd be safe with you. I just always knew, but I could never get close enough to you without messing up."

"I think I always knew too," Riley confided quietly. He had

to sniff and his voice wavered. "I used to imagine that you were my Mr. Darcy."

"Mr. Darcy?" Giles's eyes swept upward as he considered. "Is there a Mr. Wickham?"

"Um... There was a Mr. Wolford," Riley supplied sheepishly. "And Lady Muriel is determined to see you married to her nephew," he said, causing Giles's face to twist into a grimace.

"I think I've seen him, but I'd pass just because he's related to Muriel Hormsby."

"He can't help that," Riley said in his defense.

"No..." Giles agreed. "But I can choose not to attach myself to that dragon by marriage."

"I feel kind of sorry for that young man."

"Why? No one's forcing him to live with his aunt and take her money."

"I've heard he's got an expensive coke habit to support," Riley replied.

Giles was going to remember Muriel's nephew the next time Claire or his therapist mentioned dating. "I'm glad I stopped looking after I found you if that's what's out there," he said with a shudder.

Riley gasped at the clock. "Would you look at that? It's time for us to have sex again!"

"Is it?" Giles asked, then laughed when Riley grabbed the front of his robe and kissed him.

"It is. I am morally obligated to blow you every time you say something absurdly romantic and make my tummy flip."

"Are you? That's good to know," Giles murmured.

And, boy, was it good.

Chapter Thirty-One

It was probably for the best that Riley had to go home and spend the night in Brooklyn. He'd never had that much sex in less than forty-eight hours and his body was *aching* by the time he limped through his front door. He called Fin from the tub and told him everything while soaking in Epsom salt.

Both were happy to see that the curse had finally come to an end and had agreed that keeping things quiet for a while was the right call. And not just for the sake of Milo's hopes and Giles's anxiety. Riley didn't want the added pressure and scrutiny on him or Giles and he didn't want to get his own hopes up either.

He was certain he'd stumbled into a fairytale when he returned to the Olympia early Monday morning despite everything looking completely ordinary. Carl and the other doormen behaved just as they always did and everything was just as expected when Riley unlocked the door to 8B and carefully leaned over the threshold.

But Giles's eyes were hungry when Riley joined him in the

kitchen for coffee. They stared at each other over their cups as they sipped and mumbled the most inane things imaginable as they waited for Milo. Riley had no idea what they talked about as he prodded at his fruit salad and nibbled on a bagel, remarkably uninterested in eating anything except Giles.

He was able to follow along as Milo recapped his weekend with Jack building a snow space station and an astronaut snowman named Brrr! Aldrin. Riley chuckled about that all the way back to the Olympia after dropping Milo off. But all thoughts of blizzards and frozen astronauts fled as soon as Riley returned to 8B.

Unfortunately, Giles wasn't alone and they had to make more small talk while Wendy went about her perfectly normal Monday routine. Riley did his best to behave like it was the start of a typical week, working on the grocery list and sorting out their meals. He checked in with Milo's teachers online and made sure his day was running smoothly while Giles puttered around on his laptop at the kitchen counter.

"Finally!" Giles exclaimed as soon as the front door shut behind Wendy and Riley pulled him into the pantry for a wildly ravenous kiss. "Fuck! I missed you!" Giles dove into the corner of Riley's neck, licking and sucking anything he could get his mouth on.

They froze when the front door burst open. "Forgot my glasses!" Wendy called and Riley shoved Giles out of the pantry.

"No problem! See you on Wednesday!" Giles called back and waved as she snatched them off the dining room table.

Riley popped his head out of the pantry. "See you Wednesday!" He parroted.

"You boys stay out of trouble," she said with a playful wag of her finger.

"Mmmhmm!" Giles hummed loudly and continued to wave until the door closed behind her.

"That was close," Riley said, but he smirked at Giles as he slid out of his cardigan.

"Come here!" Giles growled, gathering Riley in his arms and rushing them from the kitchen. They tore at each other's clothes as they bumped into walls and Riley laughed when they fell onto Giles's bed.

"I don't know what's wrong with me. It's barely been twenty-four hours," Riley complained. He made a greedy, desperate sound as he pushed Giles onto his back. Riley was euphoric as he rubbed his face all over Giles's chest and nuzzled his armpit, inhaling deeply. He dragged his tongue along Giles's ribs and licked at the dark trail of hair beneath his navel, reveling in the tastes and textures of Giles's body.

Every inch of Giles was delectable, but Riley's mouth watered as he lapped at Giles's cock. He adored the taste of Giles's pre-cum and the way he moaned and swore when Riley tried to swallow every inch. And Riley *really* loved the taste of Giles's ass and the way he whimpered and his heels dug into the mattress.

But things were about to get so. Much. *Hotter.*

"Christ, Riley!" Giles clawed at the sheets as he writhed and rode Riley's tongue. "Could you—?" He choked out and Riley's eyes grew so big, they should have rolled right out of his head as Giles reached between his legs and plunged a finger into his hole.

"I've never been with a top who was into ass play!" Riley whispered excitedly. He licked and sucked on Giles's finger and groaned as he became harder and hungrier. He'd given numerous astounding blow jobs and ridden many men, but Riley had never had a chance to explore another man's ass.

Riley couldn't remember being more turned on as he spit on his fingers and eased one into Giles.

"Oh, fuck!" Giles threw an arm over his eyes and shook his head. "Not a top!" He panted breathlessly.

Riley stopped licking and his hand halted. "What?"

"I mean... I do, but I... Both?" Giles rasped, launching Riley into orbit.

"Oh. You're vers," he said coolly and calmly, but inside, Riley was cheering and sobbing as if he'd touched down on the moon. "I've never done that, but I've always wanted to try," he added smoothly.

"I liked when Claire used her strap-on, but I have toys if you aren't into that," Giles said in a drunken babble. His hand flopped over the side of the mattress and he pointed under the bed.

"Into that?" Riley laughed in disbelief. He was done being cool. "I am *so into that!*" He said and swore as he worked two fingers into Giles and curled them around his prostate.

There was another strained whimper from Giles and Riley thrilled at the heady rush of arousal and adrenaline. Riley wasn't naive and understood that he was considered a bit of a twink due to his lean frame and average height. It didn't help that Riley could go a week without shaving before seeing anything resembling stubble.

But Riley felt oddly *dominant* as he rose onto his knees and asked Giles for the lube. He coated his cock and had to take several steadying breaths. He guided the head to Giles's hole and the room spun as he rocked his hips, gently gliding into slick, gripping heat. Oh, and Giles was so, so tight. Riley shivered at the intense pressure gripping his shaft with each thrust. Normally, pleasure radiated from his core and...released from his cock.

Now, Riley was enthralled as he watched it plunge in and

out of Giles's ass. So much heat and pleasure swelled in his groin and Riley could feel the pressure building with every slide of his shaft. And Giles was falling apart, swearing and begging Riley's name. Sweat streaked the hair on his chest and his thighs quivered as he undulated beneath Riley.

"You like that?" Riley asked huskily. "That feel good?"

Giles's nod was jerky and his eyes were dazed and unfocused. "Yes!"

There was the sun. Riley was hurtling toward it as pressure and heat throbbed in his sac. "Giles. I can't hold on much— You're so hot. So good." He wasn't capable of anything more coherent or eloquent. Riley's hand dragged down Giles's chest and stomach and around his cock.

"Yes! Please!" Giles grabbed Riley's wrist, urging him to stroke.

Riley wrapped both hands around Giles's length and tugged in time with his hips and was rewarded with a shredded sob. Cum pumped from Giles's cock as he arched off the bed, spilling over Riley's fist. Riley raised one of his hands and stuffed his fingers in his mouth so he could suck on them, then planted the other hand on the bed behind him. Riley's hips slapped hard against Giles's ass, filling the room with swift claps and ecstatic gasps.

"Riley!" Giles's eyes rolled as he screamed and this time, Riley went with him.

He came on a silent roar, deep and hard in Giles's passage. Riley was utterly spent as he pulled out and crashed onto the bed. Giles caught him and they were both shattered and breathless as they kissed and clung to each other.

Giles was first to recover and whispered soft thank yous as he nibbled on Riley's lips. "That was incredible."

"No. *You* were incredible. I had no idea you were vers. I thought you'd be..." He wrinkled his nose apologetically at

Giles. "More vanilla," he added in a soft whisper, making Giles laugh.

"I never leave my apartment and I live on the internet. There are files on my hard drives that will self-destruct when I die."

"Really?" Riley purred and slid an arm around Giles's neck. "I'm very interested in hearing about those and these toys that you keep under your bed. Brave of you to do so with Wendy being in here as often as she is."

A hard snort huffed from Giles, tickling Riley's lips. "They're in a box with a lock and a label specifically warning Wendy not to even *think* about it."

Riley was useless for the next half hour. He had never laughed so hard in his life.

Chapter Thirty-Two

"You have an awesome weekend and don't forget to call me so we can say goodnight." Giles squeezed Milo tight and kissed his forehead.

"I love you and I'll miss you!" Milo gave Giles's neck one last squeeze, and they turned to check the lobby's windows when they heard a honk. A doorman hurried to get the door as Julie's Range Rover pulled up to the curb.

"I love you and I'll miss you too," Giles chuckled and ruffled his hair before releasing Milo into Julie's care for the weekend. He waved as they drove off, then whistled happily to himself as he strolled past the courtyard to the other lobby.

He would miss Milo because he always did whenever they were apart. But Giles was about to jump out of his skin, he was so excited about spending the night with Riley again. And it had absolutely nothing to do with sex.

Giles longed to fall asleep with Riley in his arms and to wake up with their limbs tangled. They'd had a lot of sex over the last two weeks, but they didn't have *time*. Hours were scarce, even on Tuesdays and Thursdays when Wendy wasn't there, because Riley's to-do list was always long and he stayed tuned into Milo's day at school to ensure everything was running smoothly.

Not that Giles didn't appreciate how much was involved in running that particular nine-year-old's day. He was extremely grateful, in fact. Giles just wished he didn't have to compartmentalize the two things he loved the most. He understood why it was necessary and Giles was making the most of this very private, quiet period in their relationship, but he yearned for the time when they didn't have to steal kisses and watch the clock.

And Giles craved the harmony he instinctively knew was waiting for the three of them as a family. It was already there when Milo dashed into the kitchen to join them for a quick breakfast before school and when they practiced his presentation every Thursday evening.

Perhaps that was why he gnashed his teeth when Carl whispered a warning as he got the door for Giles. "She's been waiting for you, sir."

Giles girded himself as the very antithesis of harmony, Muriel Hormsby, paced in front of the elevator, swathed in leopard print from head to toe. He knew who she was by reputation and that she lived in the building, but Giles had managed to avoid her up until then.

"There you are, Ashby!" She grabbed a bored-looking young man with long blond hair by the sleeve of his fur coat, dragging him with her. "I have left messages but I know for a fact those assistants of yours aren't giving them to you." She hauled the young man in front of Giles.

Giles reared back and shook his head. "They wouldn't because they're not permitted to discuss my personal affairs and I *never* involve them in private matters."

"Yes, but I—" She started, then stopped when Giles cocked his head.

"Do I know you?"

"Good heavens, Ashby. I'm Muriel Hormsby. My husband, the late Samuel—"

"I'm afraid I don't know him either." Giles raised his brows at her, waiting for her to explain why he should care. She drew an affronted breath and clutched at her wrap.

"That's hardly the point! This is Jonathon," she said, pushing the young man at Giles.

Giles threw his hands up in frustration. "Who are you people and what is it that you think I can do for you?" He asked loudly, his voice echoing off the marble. There was a muffled snicker from Carl and a woman by the mailboxes choked.

Muriel's eyelids fluttered as she stared at Giles in shock. "You can marry Jonathon."

"Absolutely not," Giles stated and reached around her for the call button. "Is there anything else?"

"No... And I... I have never been treated so shamefully." Muriel shook her head, looking stunned and offended. "It's that nanny, isn't it? I could tell as soon as I laid eyes on him. He's looking after a lot more than that child." She clicked her teeth, striking Giles's temper.

"First of all, you're going to watch what you say about Riley. Because, *him*, I know. I've known him since we were kids and it's none of your business what he is to me now."

There was a soft *whoop!* from Carl and Muriel's eyes flashed. "So it's true!" She said and snorted triumphantly. "I knew you'd take Jonathon or admit that you were taken."

"What?" Giles shook his head, stepping around her when the elevator opened. She started to follow with Jonathon in tow. "No! Don't even think about it," Giles said and pointed hard at her before jamming his finger into the eight button. "Not if he was the last person in Manhattan and my life depended upon it," he vowed, then offered Jonathon a pained look. "Sorry."

"Huh?" The young man squinted at Giles cluelessly.

The doors closed, ending Giles's suffering. "This is why I hate going outside." He groaned as he rubbed his temple. The soft ding reminded him that Riley was waiting, and Giles was happy to forget about Muriel and Jonathon until he recalled that he'd done it again. "This is why I needed Riley in the first place."

He said a quick prayer and let himself into the apartment, hoping he hadn't derailed their weekend before it even started.

"What's wrong?" Riley asked, tossing a towel on the counter as he came into the living room. Giles held up his hands.

"I might have done it again."

"What are you talking about?"

Giles turned and gestured at the door. "I ran into that Muriel Hormsby woman. And Jonathon."

Riley made a sympathetic sound. "Oh, dear. I did see this coming. How bad was it?"

"She definitely knows I won't be marrying her nephew. And I may have confirmed that there is something going on between us and threatened her just a little," Giles said and bit into a knuckle.

"You threatened Muriel Hormsby?"

"I told her not to talk about you and to mind her business."

"Well..." Riley raised a shoulder and was blushing as he stretched toward Giles's lips. "That wasn't too out of line. We'll ignore her and it'll probably blow over in a week."

"I wouldn't let them ride in the elevator with me either," Giles said, lowering his head so he could kiss Riley.

"I don't blame you." Riley pressed his lips to Giles's, erasing what was left of his worries. "Wait! I need to take the bread out of the oven!" He turned and raced around the sectional and the counter.

Giles went after him, pleased that their weekend was still on track. "It smells incredible." He eased in close so he could sniff over Riley's shoulder as he set a dutch oven on the stove. But Giles was intoxicated by the smell of Riley's hair and how much nicer it was being close to him.

"We have to let it cool but the lamb still needs about an hour," Riley said, glancing back at Giles. His lips were right there and it was *wonderful* being able to steal a quick kiss and linger and tease Riley in the kitchen without worrying about Wendy or Milo catching them.

"Good," Giles murmured, more interested in Riley's blue-striped cardigan. "Is this new?"

Riley chuckled as he picked up the loaf and tapped on the bottom. "No. I've had it for a while, but you know how things have a way of disappearing on the top shelf of a closet," he said absently.

Giles hummed even though he didn't know. He kept an inventory of his shelves and rotated everything according to season. "I really like it. I love all of your cardigans."

"You do not." Riley snorted dubiously.

"I do. And you have a way of making something perfectly cozy and innocent...slutty," Giles whispered in Riley's ear, making him giggle and squirm.

"I don't think a cardigan can be slutty."

"On you? So slutty. And when you take it off..." Giles growled appreciatively and rocked against Riley so he could feel what the conversation was doing to him. He reached around Riley and plucked at the buttons running down his chest. Hard heat swelled between them, a throbbing ache that grew stronger when Riley gasped and rubbed against Giles.

"Like this?" His hands trembled as he pulled the halves

wider and down his shoulders until the cardigan dropped and puddled on Giles's feet. Riley's chest rose and fell rapidly beneath his faded Ewok T-shirt.

"Mmmm..." Giles's lips trailed up the back of Riley's neck and into his hair. "You make me want to do the dirtiest things to you," he breathed.

"Right now? Can you do them right, right now?" Riley panted as he turned and pressed himself against Giles. His arms wound around Giles's neck and Riley was urgent as he danced them out of the kitchen and past the living room on his tiptoes.

"Right now?" Giles echoed. But it turned into a chuckle when Riley jumped and wrapped his legs around Giles's waist.

"Yes! Let's do the *dirtiest* thing you can imagine!"

"I don't know..."

Giles was about to tell Riley that his imagination could get pretty dirty when the door opened and Milo burst into the apartment.

"I forgot my pho—! Whoa." Milo froze, his eyes huge and his lips pursed.

"Oh, God!" Riley pushed against Giles's chest as he attempted to dismount. But their legs and feet got tangled when he landed, causing him to spill onto the foyer floor. "We weren't—" He started, then stopped and gave his head a shake before scrambling to his feet with Giles's help. "I don't want to lie to you. I'm so sorry, but some boundaries have been crossed," he explained delicately.

Giles grimaced and scrubbed the back of his neck. "Don't say it like that. It sounds like we did something wrong," he complained, even though they technically had because Giles was Riley's boss. But this wasn't about business or Riley's role as a nanny. This was about Giles's life and his heart. "I told

Riley I was in love with him during the storm and we've been hanging out a lot when you're not here."

"You're just going to tell him?" Riley asked in distress.

Giles's shoulders bounced. "I don't lie to Milo. He's my best friend and I might need his advice later," he said and Milo nodded, his grin bouncing between Giles and Riley and his eyes alight with anticipation.

"Are you gonna ask him to marry you?" He asked Giles.

"Whoa!" Riley waved his hands wildly. "It's only been a few weeks! You have to get to know someone really well before you... You know," he explained awkwardly. Milo looked at Giles.

"I already know," Giles whispered from behind his hand. "But Riley's right. We need a little more time and I need to find the right moment to ask him."

"Yes!" Milo ran to them and hugged their waists. "I gotta go. Aunt Julie is driving around the block. Can I tell her and Mom that you're together now?" He asked.

"Oh." Riley bit down on his lips and glanced at Giles.

The encounter with Muriel was still rather fresh in Giles's mind so he cleared his throat and grimaced at Milo. "How about, for now, we only tell the people we really trust, like Mom and Aunt Julie? You know how some people can go too far because they want to learn things about us that are private and personal?" He said carefully.

Milo's lips pulled into a hard line. "Like the paparazzi," he said heavily, making Giles and Riley laugh. Some of the kids at Milo's school had more famous parents.

"Something like that," Giles said. "Strangers are going to have a lot of questions and want to share their opinions, but they don't matter. You can tell Mom and Julie and Wendy because they know not to talk about us."

"I won't tell anyone else!" Milo said, then ran through the

kitchen to his wing, leaving Riley and Giles to recover. Riley muttered a swear as he clutched his forehead.

"Not even two weeks," he said with a groan.

Giles shushed softly as he gathered Riley in his arms. "As far as I'm concerned, everyone that matters knows now. We don't have to hide and I can tell you how much I love your cardigans and flirt with you whenever I want."

"You mean Milo and Muriel?" Riley asked. "She's going to be unbearable in the elevator."

"Do what I do and tell her to wait. But Milo's probably already messaged Claire and Wendy and Julie will know as soon as he jumps back in the car."

Milo sped through the kitchen and gave them another quick hug. "I gotta go! I'll see you on Sunday!"

He was gone a moment later.

"Why was I so worried about how he'd handle this?" Riley asked and waved at the door. "I *know* kids and Milo's smarter than both of us."

"I told you, he saw this coming weeks ago," Giles boasted.

Riley nodded. "I don't know why I thought we could get anything past him. But it's still a good idea to keep things as low-key as we can while we all get used to this. Especially with the science fair coming up. A bunch of strangers putting their noses in our business is only going to stress Milo out and be a distraction. I should probably call Reid and warn him."

"That's probably a good idea," Giles said, then held up a finger when his phone buzzed in his pocket. "That'll be Claire," he predicted.

"I'm going to put my head in the freezer and think about what I'm going to tell Reid."

"I don't think he'll be surprised." Giles was laughing as he answered. "Isn't it early there?" He asked Claire.

Giles Ashby Needs A Nanny

"I told Milo to message me at *any* time if you finally went for it and it sounds like you did."

"But you knew. I tell you everything," Giles said, making her laugh.

"It's official now and I don't have to pretend I don't know. And Milo says you're going to propose."

"For once, I'm pretty clear about what comes next. I'm just giving Riley a little more time to get used to the idea."

She sighed happily. "I'm so proud of how far you've come. And I really love Riley. He couldn't be more perfect for you, and Milo is over the moon, knowing you're happy and in good hands now."

"I really am," Giles said as he leaned and looked around the kitchen wall. He laughed because Riley had the freezer door open and was leaning in to cool himself. "And I don't think my life could get any better. Unless the Hayden decides to reinstate Pluto."

"Don't press your luck, Giles," she said, laughing softly.

"You're absolutely right," he said. "I don't think I'm entitled to any more miracles. I'm already the luckiest man in the city."

Chapter Thirty-Three

Oddly enough, very little had changed after Milo found out and the news trickled around the Olympia and Manhattan. The doormen and a few of the building's other residents smiled and congratulated Riley as he came and went, and his and Giles's names were whispered among the parents and teachers at school. But aside from those few instances, everything was fairly normal and Milo had been remarkably unfazed by the change in Giles and Riley's relationship.

If anything, Milo had taken it upon himself to incorporate Riley into his and Giles's evening and weekend routines. Riley was given a spot in the reading rotation of Milo's bedtime story and was in charge of the music and assigning tasks for big weekend breakfasts. Previously, Giles had had food delivered and they'd watched cartoons while they ate. But Milo was excited to cook with Riley and Giles in their pajamas. Afterward, they'd taken a long nap together on the sectional while Giles helped Claire with a software dilemma in his office.

They had a perfect Saturday and their Sunday was off to a

great start, but Riley left Giles and Milo to their space documentary while he checked in at Briarwood Terrace. He thought it was a good idea to give them a little time together and he wanted to see if there had been any fallout for Reid and the Marshall Agency.

"You've reached Reid and Gavin's. They're not in right now. How may I help you?" Penn asked when Riley rang the buzzer. His warm, relaxed drawl reminded Riley of an old radio broadcast with the intercom's crackle. It would have put a stupid grin on Riley's face if he wasn't already beaming.

"It's me. Where'd they go?" He asked.

"The basement," Penn replied ominously and there was a click as the door unlocked.

Penn was waiting to pull Riley into a hug when he came around the corner. "How's it going, brother?" He asked and clapped Riley on the back.

"Really great. How's your dad?"

"We upgraded his walker with a toolbox and basket and he's unstoppable now. I built a ramp for his shed yesterday and installed cameras so I can check on him whenever I can't get a hold of him on the phone," Penn said as they made their way to the kitchen.

"Nice!" Riley gave Penn a high five and went to peruse the pastries on the counter.

"How are things going with you and Giles?" Penn asked, cutting to the chase. Riley selected a bear claw, picking off an almond sliver and smirking at Penn.

"Really awesome. And I'm kind of a top now," he confided, then popped the sliver into his mouth. He winked so that Penn knew he was joking.

"I'm not surprised," Penn said and waved a hand at Riley airily. "You're a take-charge kind of guy and you've got excellent rhythm."

"Thanks! It turns out we're both vers and Giles is a lot more adventurous than I was expecting."

"Congratulations," Penn said sincerely. "You deserve someone amazing and I can tell that Giles and Milo make you really happy."

Riley's eyes watered and he lost his breath when he thought about how *happy* the last week had been for his new family. "I really love them," he said, his voice wavering and breaking. "Giles makes me feel beautiful and like I'm enough. And there's nothing I wouldn't do for him and Milo."

"Sounds like the three of you were meant for each other."

"I think so," Riley said with a soft laugh. "I was blind and I thought he was the most miserable person I'd ever met. And I didn't think he'd even noticed me, but it turns out he was waiting for *me* to see him."

"You finally caught up with each other and that's all that matters," Penn replied and raised his mug to Riley.

"What about you? You're going to be forty in a few years. Thought about settling down?" Riley widened his eyes at Penn but he just laughed.

"You know I'm more of a free spirit."

Penn preferred to keep his relationships casual. He claimed that it left him free to celebrate and explore whenever he felt a "primal spark" or a connection with someone. Reid said that the "primal spark" line was all an act and that Penn had made it up in college after getting his heart broken. It had happened before they were roommates so Reid didn't have a lot of details, unfortunately.

"Has Reid found you a new family yet?" Riley asked and Penn shook his head.

"I've got time and he's keeping me in reserve."

"That's probably a good call."

All of the nannies Reid had assembled were competent and

caring, but Penn was a human first aid kit and he could fix *anything* with his hands. If Bob Ross, Bob Vila, and Mr. Wizard had a love child, it would have been Pennsylvania Tucker. Riley took a moment and reflected on how different things would have been if Giles had called Reid just a week or two later or if Riley had his way. Penn or his sister would have been Milo's nanny instead of Riley.

They would have been a great fit for the Ashbys too. But Riley would still be off floating on his own, alone and feeling unwanted. It was one thing to tell yourself you were special and worthy of love, but it was an entirely different thing to actually believe it. Riley believed that now and he understood that there had never been anything wrong with him and there was never any curse. The universe was just keeping him in reserve for Giles and Milo.

Reid and Gavin returned as Riley was topping off his coffee, arguing about their trip to the basement. "I told you the punch bowl was down there," Reid said as he backed into the kitchen hugging a massive crystal vessel.

"It was more of a question as to why we would need it, than its location," Gavin replied, looking irritated as he returned to his window seat at the little table. "It *should* have been donated because why would we keep such a thing? We never use it."

"We're using it now," Reid said triumphantly and heaved it onto the counter. "And thanks for all the 'help.'" He gave Gavin a hard look, then smiled at Riley. "I've decided the theme for Gavin's birthday is Roaring Twenties since he's going to be 100. And I thought we could keep the bowl up here for when you want some cereal or soup!" He teased, but Riley nodded.

"Or you could brine a very fancy turkey. We love a kitchen multitasker!"

"Don't give him any ideas," Gavin grumbled and reclined with his paper.

Riley winced at Reid. "How bad has it been since Muriel Hormsby found out?"

"Bad?" Reid's neck craned and his lips pursed as he considered. "I'm interviewing two new nannies this week and we have a waitlist now."

"Thank goodness," Riley said, wiping his brow as he went to his seat. "The last thing I wanted was to cause you more trouble."

"You watch your mouth," Reid said gruffly. He went to his seat and lowered next to Riley, setting a hand on his shoulder. "I started this to help you and Fin and families like ours, but I'd shut the whole thing down without a second thought if it was a choice between this agency and your happiness."

Riley threw his arms around Reid, hugging him tightly. "You've always been *the best* big brother. Thank you for adopting me."

Reid hugged him back and chuckled softly. "Trust me, I got the better end of the deal. And I couldn't have handled Fin on my own."

There was a serious hum of agreement from Gavin. "You're the less chaotic of the two and I have always appreciated that."

They all laughed and the conversation turned to Gavin's birthday party. Riley thought it was a good time to warn the future birthday boy. "You might want to keep your head down and avoid the areas around Central Park."

Gavin gave Riley a disgruntled look. "That's not possible and why in the world would I? We live in Lenox Hill and I play in the park regularly," he said with a shake of his head.

"Suit yourself, but I think you're on Muriel Hormsby's list of suitors for Jonathon," Riley said with a shrug. "She knows you're secretly *rich* rich and that you're gay," he said, causing Reid and Penn to howl when Gavin's face twisted.

"No. Tell her I'm straight now and I'm moving to New Jersey."

The kitchen erupted into more laughter until Penn cleared his throat. "Has anyone considered checking on Jonathon to see if he needs rescuing?"

Riley's nose scrunched as he thought about the few times they'd crossed paths at the Olympia and around the Upper West Side. "I'd ask him to blink twice if he was being held against his will, but that would probably confuse him. And I get the sense that he might be playing a long game. Fin said that Walker told him that Jonathon's her only heir." He raised his brows suggestively and there were knowing hums around the table.

"He's staying in her good graces and keeping an eye on his inheritance," Reid speculated.

"He can just ride it out with Muriel instead of shackling himself to someone even worse for the rest of his life," Penn mused.

"In his mind, it's already his money," Gavin continued. "He just hasn't paid the estate tax yet. And if he can whittle that estate below...$7 million, he might not have to pay *any* on that inheritance," he said with an impressed snort.

Riley whistled as he sat back with his bear claw. "Secretly a mastermind. I cannot help but respect his ingenuity and root for him."

"Hear, hear." Reid raised his coffee and they all saluted Jonathon.

Riley elbowed Reid. "She's got a grudge against us now. She thinks it's our fault her nephew's failed to land a rich husband."

"That's gross and I don't care," Reid said simply. "I'm celebrating a personal win at the moment. It was my job to look out for you and Fin, and you're the happiest you've ever been and you both have beautiful families now. I couldn't ask for more. And I'm really happy for Ashby. He always seemed...lonely, and I had a feeling the two of you would click if you could give each other a chance."

Riley turned in his seat and gasped at Reid. "You were setting us up?" He accused, then looked around the table to see if anyone else was in on it. Gavin and Penn shook their heads rather quickly and smirked as they avoided Riley's glare. Reid held his hands up innocently.

"I always thought it was a shame that the two of you weren't friends. He seemed like he needed someone like you and you had that secret crush on him for like ten years. I knew you'd settle your differences and wind up friends, at least. Anything after that was just icing on the cake."

Penn shook his head. "I was totally hoping for a Valentine's Day fairytale," he said and Gavin hummed as he sipped his coffee.

"I wasn't sure he was good enough, but I had no choice but to respect him after the way he handled Wolford. The old gargoyle has been forced to retire, his reputation's worthless now. It does hurt my heart, the millions Ashby's lost to do it, though."

"I still don't know what to say," Riley admitted quietly.

Reid waved it off. "I have a feeling it was just money to Giles. He understands what you're worth and he made sure the whole world knows too."

"I guess," Riley whispered breathlessly, then narrowed his eyes at Reid and pointed. His finger swept around the table. "Watch your backs. I don't know how the three of you are still single, but your time will come," he said, and winced at Gavin. "I kind of understand why you are."

"Get out," Reid said, tossing his napkin at Riley as he got up.

Giles Ashby Needs A Nanny

Penn and Gavin grumbled in agreement and followed.

"Not cool," Penn complained and shook his head at Riley.

Riley laughed and ducked when Gavin swatted him with his paper. "I was just joking!" Riley said, giggling at their groans and eye rolls. "Or was I?"

Chapter Thirty-Four

The judges hadn't been impressed.
Yet.
Giles watched them closely as they made their way around the gymnasium. They had yet to be moved by dinosaurs or crystals, and the judge in the ugly mauve dress practically sneered at the little boy with the magnets.

None of them had a *working* solar system and Milo had twice as many sources cited than the girl with the hefty wind energy report. And it was obvious that Milo had spent a great deal more time preparing for his presentation than his peers.

They had every reason to feel confident, but Giles was a mess on the inside. Milo would be devastated if any of the judges laughed at him or told him that a cold little dwarf planet wasn't an exciting enough topic for the fair. And it would be crushing if Milo wasn't at least a finalist. Giles wasn't going to think about what would happen if Milo won and went on to compete in the national science fair. For the moment, he was terrified that all of Milo's dedication and determination wouldn't pay off and worried about the lesson his son might take from such a loss.

His hands remained light around Milo's shoulders, kneading reassuringly as the judges approached the table next to theirs. It was a compelling demonstration of the effects of an oil spill, but none of the judges looked intrigued or inspired. Giles felt terrible for the little boy as he stumbled through his report.

"Hey!" Riley whispered and waved, scooting along the narrow corridor between the rows of tables. He smiled at the other anxious parents before leaning in close. "I've been working my connections around the room and Wind Energy and Pluto were expected to be the favorites, but someone overheard one of the judges groan at Wind Energy. It would be a major upset if she doesn't get a ribbon," he informed them.

Milo's head whipped around and he was alarmed as he looked up at Giles.

"You have *nothing* to worry about!" Giles promised, lowering to a knee. "There are some great projects in this room, but this isn't just a project for you. You *know* Pluto. This is your passion and a cause you believe in. There's no question they can ask that you won't know the answer to and you could give this presentation in your sleep." He pulled Milo into a tight hug. "I'm so damn proud of you and I hope I can be half as cool as you one day."

Milo's chest expanded and he held his breath before laughing softly. "Thanks, Dad."

"Are you going to be okay?" Giles leaned back and searched his son's face.

"Yeah. I'm good now. I've got this," Milo said, erasing any of Giles's fears.

There was no way Milo could lose. Even if the judges were worthless and didn't know a future astronomy legend when they saw one. Milo would know that he could not have done a better job and that he had put his whole heart into it.

"Here they come!" Riley whispered out of the side of his mouth.

Giles kissed Milo's hair and wished him luck, then straightened. He and Riley stepped back and held their breaths as Milo made his way around the table to greet the judges. Ms. Mauve's eyes actually brightened behind her big round glasses and she leaned in to get a closer look at the rotating planets on the table.

"Oh, thank God!" Giles breathed. He didn't care who was looking, he shifted to his right and rested his shoulder against Riley's for support and so they could whisper to each other. "That has to be a good sign."

Riley nodded, intently focused on the judges as well. He was chewing on his thumb knuckle. "She's been unreadable all day."

The other two judges asked rather interesting questions and seemed impressed with Milo's thoughtful and well-informed responses. The lady in mauve complimented Milo on his sources and said his presentation was "highly informative."

Giles discreetly pumped a fist. Riley tugged excitedly at Giles's sleeve and they both were shaking when it was time to wave and thank the judges.

"I did it!" Milo said, rushing back around the table.

Giles leaned down and opened his arms to catch him. "You were incredible! You completely nailed it and they were so impressed!"

"You were so awesome!" Riley declared as he scooped Milo into a hug.

"Thanks! It was awesome, but I'm really glad it's over," Milo said, looking at Riley and then up at Giles. "I don't think I want to do that again."

"You don't?" Giles asked, frowning in confusion.

Milo shook his head. "I'm kind of tired now and I just want to go home," he said, making Riley and Giles laugh.

"What if you win and you have to compete against the district?" Giles asked, earning a shrug from Milo.

"I'll go and I'll do my best, but I would be okay if I didn't win. I just want to keep studying Pluto at home and at school."

"Oh." Giles's jaw dropped and he was too stunned to do anything but laugh. "That's... *Great.*" He gave Milo another hug and mouthed a "Thank goodness!" at Riley. He winked at Giles, then craned his neck to see over the other parents and around the row of trifold boards.

"I think you're going to be pleasantly disappointed, buddy," Riley said. "There're only a few projects left to be judged and I have a feeling you're the favorite. It would be a tremendous upset if you or Wind Energy didn't win and we saw how *that* went," he added under his breath and out of the side of his mouth. "But it shouldn't be much longer!"

"I wouldn't mind if Wind Energy won," Milo confided.

Wind Energy did not win and Milo was grinning from ear to ear when they placed the big blue ribbon on his board and presented him with a rather respectable trophy. Giles fought back tears as he gathered Milo in his arms for a celebratory hug. Nothing compared to the joy and pride he felt with Milo's arms wound around his neck and the whole room cheering for his little astrophysicist.

He probably wanted that win for Milo more than Milo wanted it for himself. But Giles felt *lucky.* It was an extraordinary thing to share in another person's victory and to be able to truly feel *all* the ups and downs along the way. Giles's own achievements often left him feeling numb and hollow, but he soared to greater emotional heights alongside Claire and Milo.

Now that Milo had his taste of science fair success, Giles

sensed that he had his fill of all the noise and people as well. The rest of the afternoon was for viewing projects and taking pictures. The kids would be collecting them the following morning and were free to leave whenever they were ready.

"Let's go!" Milo was impatient and no longer interested in the other boards and displays, putting his head down as he towed Giles and Riley through the crowded gymnasium.

"But I wanted to get more pictures of you in front of your *first place ribbon!*" Giles bragged when they reached the sidewalk in front of the school. He raised Milo's hand and waved it like he was a winning prizefighter.

Milo allowed Giles his moment but shrugged it off. "I don't think I'm cut out for the science fair circuit," he said simply. "I'm still going to fight for Pluto, but I'll do it through academic channels."

"I think that's a great plan," Riley said and held his hand out for Milo.

Everything felt so right in Giles's world as Milo took Riley's hand, linking the three of them. And after about a block, the traffic on the sidewalk thinned, leaving them with their own little patch of the city. The clouds had cleared and a contented glow radiated from them as they walked home. Giles wanted to pause the world and stay in that perfect, peaceful moment with Milo and Riley forever.

This is as good as your life could possibly get, he told himself. Giles made sure he cherished the way Milo's and Riley's hair fluttered in the breeze and the pinks of their cheeks. He noted Riley's striped mittens and the sly tilt of his lips as he shared a joke with Milo. Giles preserved their laughter and the feel of Milo's little hand in his.

He considered the Olympia as its iconic gables came into sight. Giles was no longer feeling like a recluse and a mess and his apartment felt like a true home again. His life was back on track and Giles had Riley to thank.

They were a team and Giles had one more person in his life whose joy and success meant more to him than his own. And Giles knew without a shadow of a doubt after more than twenty years of loving Riley from a distance that he'd only love him more with each passing day. He was also sure that one day he would propose to Riley and...

What am I waiting for, then?

"Hold on," Giles said, looking around for anything that would do.

"What's wrong?" Riley asked warily, but Giles held up a finger until he spotted a young woman wearing what looked like a yard of beads around her neck across the street.

"Give me just a minute," he said to Riley and Milo, then jogged between the parked cars to get to her. She gave Giles a hostile glance and attempted to step around him. "Just a moment please!" He said, holding up his hands and jogging backward to keep up. He scanned her fingers, noting several rings, and yanked his wallet out. "Any ring. Ask your price and I'll buy it from you."

That got her to stop. "What are you talking about?" She looked at her hands and then at Giles suspiciously.

"I need a ring," he whispered and swung his head toward Riley and Milo.

"Oh! No shit?" She said excitedly, turning Giles so his back was to them. "Take your pick!" Her hands splayed and her fingers danced as she waited.

"Hmmm..." Several were made of beads or curled wire but he pointed at a wire ring with a soft blue stone that reminded him of Riley's eyes. "I'll give you $1,000 for that one."

"Are you serious?"

Giles winced into his wallet. "It's all I have on me at the moment, I'm afraid..."

She yanked the ring off and shoved it at him. "You've got a deal."

He paid her and she waved at Riley and Milo before continuing down the sidewalk.

"Do you know her?" Milo asked when Giles ran back across the street.

"Nope," Giles said, confusing Milo and Riley even further. "I needed to ask her something, but I'm all set now." He took Riley's hand, freeing it from its mitten, and raised it to his lips.

"What are you doing?" Riley whispered, looking around nervously. "Someone's going to see you."

"I don't care. And they might as well get used to it."

Milo covered his mouth to hold back a giggle. "Are you gonna kiss Riley again?"

"I'd like to," Giles said, earning a startled look from Riley.

"I thought we agreed—"

"To keep this quiet until after the science fair and we're sure Milo's okay," Giles interrupted tenderly. "He knows and he's in love with you too. I don't care who else finds out now. This is exactly what I want and I don't need anyone's permission or approval."

Milo's fist shot into the air. "Yes! Say yes, Riley!"

Riley gave him a pointed look. "He hasn't asked me anything and that would be ridiculous!"

"Actually..." Giles got down on one knee.

"Yes!" Milo shouted, bouncing on his toes as Giles held up the ring while Riley looked utterly disoriented. His jaw hung slack with shock as his eyes pooled with tears.

"I don't understand," he whispered shakily at Giles.

"I love you and I'm the *happiest* I've ever been when I'm with you. Every day feels like a fresh start and an adventure.

Even when we never leave 8B," Giles said, sliding the ring onto Riley's finger. "Will you marry me, Riley Fitzgerald?"

"Marry you?" Riley asked softly, his eyes darting between Giles and Milo. "But, then you'd both be mine and I never thought I'd have…all of this!" He covered his mouth as he began to cry in earnest.

"Please say yes!" Milo begged, but Giles could already feel it coming as Riley nodded frantically. He was trembling as he gasped for breath. Giles rose just in time to catch Riley when he jumped.

"Yes!" Riley cried, throwing his arms around Giles's neck.

Giles laughed as he held him tight and grinned at Milo. "Happy now?" He asked and Milo gave him two big thumbs up.

"I can't wait to tell Mom and Aunt Julie. And we have to tell Wendy," he said as he took out his phone, forgetting Riley and Giles as he headed for the Olympia like a true little New Yorker. They shared amused grins and Riley held out a hand to Giles.

"Let's go home," he said, setting Giles's soul alight and making his heart race in the loveliest way.

"Let's go home," Giles said as he took his hand. They walked behind Milo as he texted everyone their good news and Giles caught Riley sneaking glances at him. "What?" Giles asked as they waited to cross the street.

Riley hugged Giles's arm and smiled up at him. "If I didn't know better, Mr. Ashby, I'd say you were happy," he said, and Giles hummed as he lowered his head and brushed his lips against Riley's.

"I am incandescently happy."

Epilogue

Six months later...

It was the perfect fall evening for a wedding. Central Park dazzled with blazing foliage as the setting sun painted the sky in shades of orange and dreamy purple. Seventeen of Riley's and Giles's closest friends and family had gathered on the Olympia's rooftop for a quiet, yet joyful celebration.

The grooms and Milo wore navy blue tuxedos with tasteful Asiatic lily boutonnieres, and no one would ever convince Riley that Giles and Milo weren't the most dashing gentlemen in Manhattan. Claire was Giles's best woman and Fin stood with Riley. Everyone cried, especially Riley's mother, who sobbed into Walker Cameron's shoulder through most of the ceremony. Riley's father made everyone laugh by holding onto his hand and lingering at the altar instead of handing him off to Giles.

But it was little Milo who stole the show. He walked his father down the aisle and unleashed the first wave of tears when he read his vows, promising to love, honor, and obey Riley, finishing with a tearful hug as Milo thanked him for loving his dad with his whole heart and making their family complete.

"I should have gone first," Giles complained as he wiped his eyes, making everyone laugh. He cleared his throat and Riley braced himself when Giles pulled in a shuddering breath and addressed their guests. "You probably don't know this, but Riley was my first crush. My *always* crush." There were sniffles and sighs, and Riley's mother swooned. Giles chuckled and his eyes were misty as they held Riley's. "You were always a ray of light and wrapped in a rainbow," he continued softly. "I never liked going outside because the world was so loud and hard and fast. But I liked seeing *you*. I'd wait so I could walk behind you every morning and as often as I could after school."

"Oh my God!" Riley whispered shakily. He reached over his shoulder and Fin was ready with a handkerchief. "I'm sorry. Go on," he mouthed and dabbed at his eyes. Riley needed to sob and blow his nose but he was trying to be elegant and somewhat dignified.

Giles sniffed hard and cleared his throat. "The next part might be worse," he warned Riley under his breath, causing more sighing and swooning. "You thought that I never noticed you, but there were days when you were the brightest thing I saw. And you were so warm and so kind to everyone. I wouldn't have believed that there were truly *good* people or that the outside world was worth suffering if I hadn't met you. Never in my wildest dreams did I expect to get a second chance with my always crush, but I promise to cherish and protect you for the rest of my life. And I will always love you for being the bright, beautiful boy who made it worth going outside when I really didn't want to and for saving me from the outside world when I couldn't handle it on my own."

He slid the simple wire ring on Riley's finger. They'd learned that the stone was blue lace agate, said to aid in communication and harmony. That settled the matter for Riley and he insisted that it was the only ring for him. He did consent to have the ring "refurbished" so it was more durable. Riley had missed his ring while it was with the jeweler and was glad to have it back on his hand where it belonged.

Riley smiled at Giles and their guests. "You see what he's really like?" He took Giles's hands in his and cherished his perpetual frown and his dark, brooding eyes. "I thought I knew you, but I was so wrong. You were not my opposite or my nemesis; you were my purpose and the universe has been pulling us together since we were kids. I spent years wondering where I belonged and if anyone would ever want me, but everything seemed to click into place when I turned up at 8B. I know why I'm here, but most importantly, I know *who* I am and what I'm worth now, thanks to you. And I have the family I've always wished for. You and Milo will always be my purpose, my greatest joy, and my heart." Riley placed an antique sapphire ring on Giles's finger. It was from Tiffany & Co. because Riley wanted something classically New York, like Giles.

They shared a brief kiss before Riley turned to Milo and lowered to a knee. He pulled a friendship bracelet out of his pocket and Milo's eyes lit up. "I love it!" He said as Riley tied it around his wrist. Riley had used blue, black, and gray threads and had woven them into a heart pattern and attached an infinity symbol charm.

"I was a little down when I first came to 8B because I really missed my best friend. Then, I met you and I immediately had a new best friend. I will always love you and I will always be here for you. No matter what. Forever."

"I love you too, Riley!" Milo threw his arms around Riley's neck and squeezed tight. Falling in love with Giles felt like a fairytale, but getting to be Milo's parent was an honor. They had their own instant, magical connection and it was sacred to Riley too.

"You're my world, little man." He kissed Milo's temple, then stood and faced Giles again.

Giles was struggling to hold himself together. Tears pooled in his eyes and he kept sniffling. "Please tell me this is almost over," he grumbled, giving everyone a much-needed moment of levity.

"We're almost there," Judge Carson chided with a chuckle. She was a family friend from Park Slope and had offered to officiate when she learned of Riley's engagement. "It has been a privilege to witness the union of *three* soulmates and it is with immense joy that I pronounce on behalf of the great State of New York you, Giles Ainsworth Ashby, and you, Riley Patrick Fitzgerald married. You may now kiss," she added and winked at Giles.

"Thank you!" He gasped and captured Riley's face for a quick, but still brain-scrambling kiss as everyone clapped and whistled. "I can't believe that this is real and that you're mine," Giles confided as they clung to each other for a moment.

"Forever, Giles Ashby," Riley vowed before they were swept into gleeful, tearful hugs.

A relaxed dinner party had been set up on the other side of the rooftop. Riley had prepared chicken pot pies because that was Giles and Milo's favorite dinner and it was perfect for a crisp fall evening. So was the two-tiered carrot cake.

Neither Giles nor Riley wanted a band, opting for a record player and classic jazz and blues to keep the evening intimate and relaxed. Riley pulled Giles to his feet for the first dance, making the evening all the more memorable for their guests.

Most weren't aware that Giles liked to dance and was rather good at it. They danced to "Across the Universe," and then "Fly Me to the Moon." Wendy and Milo joined them, along with Carl and his wife. Fin and Walker, Riley's parents, and Julie and Ken danced as well.

"I can't imagine a more perfect evening," Riley said, sighing contently as he wound his arms around Giles's neck.

"You and Reid did an incredible job."

"He's getting good at this and might need to make it a side gig if we keep this up," Riley whispered and risked a glance at Reid. He was reclining at the table with Claire, Gavin, and Penn. "But I meant the whole thing, not just the ceremony and dinner. Fairytales like this don't come true for scrawny theater nerds like me."

"You've always been my Prince Charming," Giles murmured into Riley's hair.

"It's a good thing they aren't expecting us to stay late," Riley said, already planning their exit. Claire and Milo were spending the weekend in Great Neck with Julie and Jack. Claire was staying in New York for three weeks so Riley and Giles could go on their honeymoon. They were going to Scotland and staying in a secluded country house. Riley couldn't wait to go on long walks and spend cozy nights with Giles in front of the fire. "And I'm so excited about Monday!" They were flying out of JFK just after midnight and had layovers planned for Copenhagen and Paris. They had added a few hours to their itinerary for wandering around the Charles de Gaulle airport while it was quiet.

"Me too," Giles said, raising Riley's hand to his lips and kissing his knuckles. "Milo and I have been thinking about a wedding gift for you, and Julie helped us come up with something we think will make you really happy."

"But I already have everything!" Riley protested.

"What about another child?" Giles suggested, and leaned back to watch Riley's reaction.

"Really?" It was barely a squeak. An incredible swell of joy and love rose within Riley and he clapped a hand over his mouth to hold back a delighted sob. "You want to have another —?" He couldn't even *think* of the word, he was about to dissolve into laughter and tears.

Giles nodded and smiled as he glanced at Milo. "I actually loved all the bottles and didn't mind changing diapers. I miss when Milo was a toddler. Julie says she'd love to be a surrogate for us, but we can adopt if you don't want to have a baby. Milo and I just know that we have room for one more here and he'd really like a little brother or a sister."

"Yes!" Riley grabbed Giles's face and kissed him hard. Everyone clapped because they must have overheard or been in on it. "We're having another child!" He declared as Giles held Riley tight and spun them. He kissed Giles and they were both breathless and smiling as their lips clung. "I'm so glad you called Reid and he sent me, despite all my whining and complaining about you."

Giles huffed dismissively. "You had every right to be concerned and I had my doubts too. But I'm so glad Reid prevailed because it turns out I *needed* this particular nanny."

The End

A Lullaby in 8B

Riley's Carrot Cake

- 2 cups all-purpose flour
- 2 teaspoons baking soda
- 2 teaspoons ground cinnamon
- 1/2 teaspoon nutmeg
- ¼ teaspoon salt
- 1 ½ cups white sugar
- 3 large eggs
- ¾ cup buttermilk
- ¾ cup vegetable oil
- 2 teaspoons vanilla extract
- 2 1/2 cups shredded carrots
- 12 ounces crushed pineapple
- 1 1/2 cup flaked coconut
- 1/2 cup chopped walnuts

For the cake:

- Preheat the oven to 350°. Grease and flour two 8 or 9-inch round pans.

- Drain most of the juice from the pineapple and reserve for frosting.

- Sift flour, baking soda, cinnamon, nutmeg, and salt together.

- In a separate bowl, mix sugar, eggs, buttermilk, oil, and vanilla. Gradually add flour mixture until just combined.

- Combine shredded carrots, pineapple, coconut, and walnuts in a separate bowl. Fold into cake batter just until combined. Pour batter into prepared pans.

- Bake in the preheated oven until a toothpick inserted into the center of the cake comes out clean, about 45 minutes. Allow cakes to cool before frosting.

For the frosting:

- 16 ounces of cream cheese, softened
- 1 cup of butter, softened
- 2 teaspoons vanilla
- few splashes of pineapple juice
- 6-8 cups of confectioners sugar

- Beat cream cheese, butter, vanilla, and pineapple juice together with an electric mixer until light and creamy.

- Gradually beat in confectioners sugar to desired sweetness and consistency.

Chapter Thirty-Five

"Little" Luna Louise Ashby was born at a whopping eight pounds, nine ounces and with the strongest set of lungs in Manhattan, screaming and waving her fist at the world as she was handed to her sobbing fathers. The first six months of her life had been just as thrilling as her birth and Riley liked to think that she got her flair for drama from him. She had his laugh as well and loved to be the center of attention. But she was also the sweetest little love bug and would immediately smile and coo when Giles or Milo walked into the room.

Riley had been the sperm donor and Claire was happy to provide her eggs so Milo and the baby would be genetic siblings. Julie had given birth to Luna just a few weeks after Riley and Giles's first anniversary. Life in 8B revolved around Luna and it was fair to say she was becoming rather spoiled, but it was obvious who her world revolved around. Giles could soothe her with just a kiss on her cheek and she hung on Milo's every word when he told her about his day and read to her.

The bond that Riley and Luna shared was just as intense

and precious. They were like two peas in a pod, but Riley could tell that Luna lived to see Giles laugh and smile. And she behaved as if her big brother was her favorite thing in the universe from the moment they first met at the hospital. Riley's parents swore that she was his clone and he suspected that was why she gravitated toward Giles and Milo. Like Riley, she lived to make their world brighter and warmer.

For Riley, one of the best things about having his own family was how much time he got to spend with Fin and his family. It was so easy to grab the diaper bag and their coats and head around the corner to The Killian House or meet them at the park for a picnic and an afternoon ramble. Fin and Walker often brought the girls up to 8B for movie nights and Milo loved when he could get out his telescope on a clear night. The rooftop of the Olympia was perfect for moon viewings and making s'mores with the Camerons.

But the *very* best thing in Riley's whole world was how consumed Giles was with him and their family. Giles kept to his routine while Milo was at school, but he carried Luna on his hip or in a sling just about every moment of the day. He wouldn't part with her, even if he was needed on a video call or had a meeting in 8B. It was his responsibility, according to Giles, to handle most of the "inside" parenting since Riley handled most of the harder "outside" tasks. And he was utterly besotted with Luna. Particularly when she was being a tiny tyrant.

Ironically, for someone who claimed to dislike children, Giles understood Luna's moods and the two shared their own unspoken language that never failed to amaze Riley. She'd have Riley spinning in circles, trying to appease her, and at the end of his wits only for Giles to stroll in and restore peace with a simple song change.

"She likes when you do the 'Made you look' dance. It's our favorite," Giles informed Riley on his way to the kitchen.

"It is?" Riley had had no idea and sure enough, Giles was right.

Riley spent the next half hour shaking his backside and messing up his hair while Giles and Luna giggled on the sectional.

"She wants us to take a nap with her," Giles said after she became fussy. "You can tell by the way she rubbed her nose with her whole hand. She mashes her fist into her right eye when she wants us to take her to her crib," he explained, then tugged Riley onto the sectional, and they snuggled and snoozed for a little over an hour.

The three of them often walked together to get Milo. Giles still disliked all the peopling and was vocal about how much he didn't like when strangers touched Luna. But he endured it all for her sake because he said she missed Milo so much while he was gone and that it was the highlight of her day. It was one of the many highlights of Riley's day too, the way Luna burst into excited squeals and bounced in Giles's arms when she saw Milo.

Giles and Milo used the walk home to update each other about any significant developments at school and with Luna. They discussed spelling words and any new foods that Luna may have tried and if she had crawled while Milo was away. He was very concerned that he would miss that milestone, but Giles promised she'd wait for him. Giles and Riley agreed that the first time Milo witnessed it would be the official first time and anything prior would just be "practice" and that there would be no need to tell him.

"She'll crawl for Milo. You'll see," Giles predicted. They were reclining on the sectional and watching Milo read to Luna on the floor. It was his night to read from *The Hitchhiker's*

Guide to the Galaxy. She was resting against Milo's side and tugging at her ear drowsily. "Not tonight, because she's obviously ready for a bath and bed. But she always wants to go with him and be by his side."

"I have a feeling you're right," Riley said, hugging Giles's middle. "Meet you back in our room in thirty?"

"Deal." Giles pressed a quick kiss to Riley's lips and went to scoop Luna off the floor. "Time to take my little Luna for her moon bath!"

She snuggled into the corner of his neck as he took her away and Riley sighed dreamily as he watched them go. "You ready to hit the shower, my little man?" He asked Milo.

The eleven-year-old nodded as he smothered a yawn, then stretched out on the rug. His toes pointed as his body twisted and Riley felt a pang of sadness. Milo had grown so much since Riley's first day with the Ashbys and it was bittersweet seeing him slowly turn into a teen. They still had a couple of years to go, but every day his cheeks became a little less round as he grew a little taller and Riley noticed less and less of the tiny, timid boy he met that first day.

Milo was still shy and struggled with his anxiety, but he was thriving in middle school and had a tight friend group that supported and protected him. Pluto was still his first love, but Milo was thinking bigger. Instead of the Hayden and reinstatement, Milo had his sights set on NASA. His new plan was to become the head of NASA's Astrophysics division because that was who controlled all the telescopes and the agency's science portfolio.

Almost twelve, their little boy wasn't so little anymore, and NASA and several prestigious schools and corporations were keeping an eye on Milo. There were already promising offers and he was taking high school and college classes. Riley often worried that Milo was rushing over too many milestones by racing through middle and high school. But then he'd remember how unhappy Giles had been in school. Giles had said that those had been some of the most stressful and traumatic years of his life and he'd only endured them so he could get into college. He was all for letting Milo decide what felt comfortable for him because he was the smartest person Giles knew.

There was no faulting Giles's judgment when it came to Milo. He understood his son better than anyone ever would and their worlds would always revolve around each other. They brought Riley and Luna into their peaceful orbit and Giles lived for his family. 8B was his world and Riley cherished their bedtime routine because that was when Giles's super dad powers were at their peak.

"Give me a hug!" Riley stood on the bottom rung of the ladder to reach Milo and they squeezed each other tight. "Love you." He kissed Milo's hair, sad that it was less curly than it used to be.

"I love you too, Riley," he said before muffling a yawn.

"Good night, my little man."

He went around to give Milo the remote and turned down the lamp, leaving the door cracked. Riley raced to the kitchen so he could watch what was left of bath time on his phone. The baby monitor's camera covered the entire nursery and Luna's moon bath was one of the highlights of Riley's day.

You couldn't imagine a more over-the-top nursery than Luna's. The tranquil moon theme and wrap-around windows made the space even dreamier with the lights turned down low. Riley propped his chin on his palm and wondered how much bigger his heart could get as he watched them. Giles had a raised tub installed by the changing station for bedtime baths and it was touching, watching him gently rinse the bubbles away from Luna's face and massage her little feet as she hummed and cooed drowsily.

Claire said that Giles had the same routine with Milo. He'd sing John Lennon's "Beautiful Boy" and she'd peek from the nursery door.

Now, Giles hummed and crooned his mesmerizing rendition of "Golden Slumbers" as he swaddled her in a towel and rocked her in the moonlight. He'd dressed her in decadently soft pajamas, and she was content and drifting off when Riley went to kiss her goodnight.

He slipped into the nursery and whispered, "See you soon," in Giles's ear before taking their sleepy princess. Riley cradled her in his arms as he danced them to the crib, whispering words of love and thanking her for lighting up their lives. Her intoxicating scent surrounded Riley, a soothing blend of Dreft and lavender. He'd always associate that smell with her and get a little emotional. Giles warned that the first few years would fly and that Riley would miss when she was small enough for them to hold and protect. He said that parenting got so much harder when you had to let them out of your sight and run amuck in the world.

As good as Riley was at caring for other people's children, it took having children of his own to appreciate how much he was trusting the world when Milo and Luna were out of his sight. He certainly understood how difficult that could be for an already anxious soul and why it might make someone like Giles feel even more vulnerable. Riley had so much more to lose, now that his life was so much bigger.

There were times when he wished he could keep them all safe inside 8B. And there were times when he wished he could freeze his family and keep them just the way they were forever. Then, he'd remember that Milo was going to work for NASA one day and Giles would find a way to give Luna the moon. Because that's the kind of father he was.

He would do anything to make their dreams come true, even if they were big and scared him. It was important to Giles for the kids to follow their passions and have adventures. They didn't have to be grand or even take them outside of 8B, as long as the kids were happy and felt safe to be their truest selves. Milo had already taken them on so many fun adventures and Riley couldn't wait to see where Luna would lead them.

"I love you to the moon and back, my sweet Luna." Riley kissed her temple, then carefully laid her in her crib.

Riley made it back to their room first and was glad Giles had lingered with Milo. He could use a little time to get ready...

Giles Ashby's
Perfect Playlist
Featuring the Beatles

Imagine

Across The Universe

Let It Be

I'm Only Sleeping

Blackbird

A Day In The Life

Lucy In The Sky With Diamonds

Nowhere Man

Strawberry Fields Forever

Here Comes The Sun

Golden Slumbers

Beautiful Boy

Chapter Thirty-Six

"I love you and I can't wait to hug you in the morning."

"I love you too, Dad." Milo was nodding off as he reached over the side of his bunk and hugged Giles's neck.

Giles kissed him, then eased away from the bed and quietly closed the door behind him. He hummed Milo's song as he passed through the kitchen, checking all the alarms and locks on his way. He was hoping to find Riley in bed with a book or stepping into the tub, but the lights were turned low and both the bedroom and the bathroom were vacant.

"Riley?"

"I'm out here," he called from the terrace.

The heater next to the daybed was running and Giles was delighted to find Riley curled up under the blanket. He was wearing Giles's robe and reclining with a glass of wine. A bottle and a glass were waiting for Giles and a joint was resting next to the ashtray.

"Are we celebrating?" Giles lowered onto the bed next to Riley and toed off his shoes. He peeked under one of the robe's lapels and felt like celebrating because Riley appeared to be naked.

"I am," Riley drawled, eyeing Giles over his glass as he sipped. "I'm married to the sexiest man in Manhattan."

That earned a dubious snort from Giles. "Are you forgetting that Denzel Washington and Hugh Jackman live here as well?"

Riley shrugged and rose on his knees. "They're both hot. But I don't want to have sex with them anymore."

"Thank goodness," Giles said dryly, but it turned into a strained chuckle as Riley threw a leg over his lap and straddled him. Riley reached for the joint and lit it for Giles. He wasn't a smoker but he had learned how to roll from watching Giles and would take a drag now and then in the evenings. "Thank you," Giles murmured around the joint when it was tucked between his lips. He took a deep hit and groaned in approval as Riley rolled his hips, rocking against Giles's hard-on.

"No. *Thank you.*" Riley raised his glass to Giles's lips so he could take a sip. He set the glass down, then cradled Giles's face and treated him to a slow, sultry kiss.

"Tell me what I did and I'll do it again," Giles begged and chased Riley's lips when they came up for air.

"You did what you've always done. You loved us with your whole heart and there's nothing you won't do for us."

"You're my world." Giles lapped at Riley's lips and whimpered when he broke the kiss.

Riley purred and slid down Giles's body. "I know. You show us every day. That's why you're so sexy. Don't forget to smoke," he scolded playfully, but Giles had forgotten about the joint. He took a quick pull, then had to hold in a cough as Riley attacked his belt and the fly of his trousers.

We're doing this out here?

Giles raised his head and looked around. They'd fooled

around a few times on the terrace, but it had been warmer and they'd had the apartment to themselves. The monitor's app was open on Riley's phone and both kids were sleeping soundly so Giles smoked a little more and reached for the wine.

He raised his hips when Riley tugged at the waist of his trousers and pulled them lower. Giles's cock was freed and smoke plumed from him on a gasp as Riley's tongue washed around the head. He licked greedily, savoring every inch before taking Giles deep in his throat and sucking hard.

"Riley!" Giles's fingers sifted through Riley's hair and his body faded until he was nothing but wet, sucking heat and throbbing pleasure. Slick fingers pushed into his ass and Giles's eyes rolled as warmth spilled down his legs. He was so high and so hard, and Riley's mouth was so soft as it wrapped around Giles's length. Riley's head bobbed slowly, making Giles feel lighter and lighter with every luscious slide of his lips. Need swelled in Giles's core and he craved more of Riley and ached to be closer. "Can we...?" He raised his head and blinked groggily. "I need—"

"I know what you need," Riley whispered. His tongue flicked at the end of Giles's cock, winding his nerves even tighter and making him even more desperate to fuse his body with Riley's.

Riley coated Giles's shaft with lube, then rose on his knees. The robe fell around his hips as he mounted Giles, taking him deep and setting a slow, grinding pace that was just as potent and enthralling as the pot and the wine humming in his veins.

"Magic," Giles panted against Riley's lips.

They were floating and were one as they kissed, rocked, writhed, and gasped on a daybed made of clouds. Time stopped and Giles was lost in Riley. He gorged himself on the sweet taste of Riley's lips and tongue and the tight, wet heat gripping Giles's cock. Riley's muffled moans and stifled sobs made the hairs on Giles's neck stand. His skin glowed wherever Riley touched him and Giles got so hot and so high, he burst into a galaxy of stars.

"Riley!" His arms locked tight around Riley and Giles bucked hard as cum pumped from his shaft.

"Oh—!" Riley arched and his head snapped back. His body jumped in Giles's arms and Riley was ethereal, wrapped in moonlight and covered in goosebumps. His chest heaved as he chanted Giles's name and it was the sweetest lullaby.

Giles gathered Riley in his arms and he had never known greater peace and joy. They kissed and giggled breathlessly until they were ready to gather all their things and head inside for a long, hot shower before falling into bed.

"Come here!" Riley got a little bossy and demanding when he was tired. But Giles thought it was adorable when Riley rubbed his eye with his fist and snuggled closer. It was so easy to see where Luna got it and that's why she hung the moon for Giles.

She was Riley's mini and Giles could shower her in all the love he wanted because that's what dads were supposed to do. It wasn't weird if he stared too long or showed strangers his pictures, which Giles had actually done in the park. He'd gushed to an older woman because she reminded him of his Grandma Ida. She said that Luna was the prettiest little girl she had ever seen and it had been almost as good as sharing the photos with his grandmother. Giles often missed her and hoped she was proud of him and the family he'd built with Claire, Julie, and Riley. She had been stoic and independent because she'd lived in Brooklyn her whole life, and Giles had inherited her snappy temper. But she had been his only family until he went to college and she had been devoted to Giles.

It was a terrible shame that she had passed before she could meet Luna. Grandma Ida would probably be tickled to learn that he had married "that little Fitzgerald boy" she'd always been on Giles to make friends with. She'd had a few years to dote on Milo and had insisted that he was perfect and would be just as extraordinary as his father. Giles knew his grandmother would be lovestruck by Luna's big blue eyes and her bright exuberance.

Giles would never comprehend how he could be so lucky. He only ventured outside 8B a few times a month and rarely went further than the school or Bloomingdale's, but Giles's inside life was full of love and laughter. And there was so much warmth and intimacy now that he had Riley.

Another New York day was coming to an end and Giles was profoundly grateful as he gathered Riley in his arms. The city or fate had brought him and Riley back together and this time, Giles had gotten everything exactly right.

A letter from K. Sterling

Dear Reader,

Thank you so much for your time and for reading *Giles Ashby Needs A Nanny*. I hope you had fun falling love with Riley and Giles! Before you go, I'd appreciate it if you'd consider leaving a review. Your review would really help me and help other readers find their way to us. And I promise, I read and appreciate every single one of them. Even the negative reviews. I want your honest feedback so I know how to steal your heart.

Please help me out by leaving a review!

Once again, thank you from the very bottom of my heart. I love you for sharing your time with us and hope we'll see you again soon.

Love and happy reading,
K.

About the Author

K. Sterling writes like a demon and is mother to Alex, Zoe, Stella, and numerous gay superheroes. She's also a history nerd, a *Lord of the Rings* fan, and a former counterintelligence agent. She has self-published dozens of M/M romance novels including the popular *Boys of Lake Cliff* series and *Beautiful Animal*. K. Sterling is known for fast-paced romantic thrillers and touching gay romcoms. There might be goosebumps and some gore but there's always true love and lots of laughter.

Coming Soon: The Handy Nanny

They call Pennsylvania Tucker the human Band-Aid because he can fix just about anything and make anyone feel better, but can Penn mend a broken heart? Reid Marshall thinks so and sends his master nanny on a very important and sensitive mission. A close friend is grieving and caring for his newborn niece after losing his twin sister.

Shy and quiet outside of the studio, Morris Mosby has been a myth in the music industry since he was sixteen. But his sister was the brains behind the "Mosby Machine" and Morris is tempted to walk away from his career and focus on his family. He's got to put his life back together and raise a baby without his best friend and half of his heart.

Not if Morris's parents and Penn have anything to say about it. The three of them team up to help Morris heal and rediscover his passion for music. Things heat up between Penn and Morris, but our handy nanny has some old wounds that need mending as well. Can two broken hearts heal each other or has Penn finally found a problem he can't fix?

Get The Handy Nanny now!

Manufactured by Amazon.ca
Bolton, ON